GENOMANCY

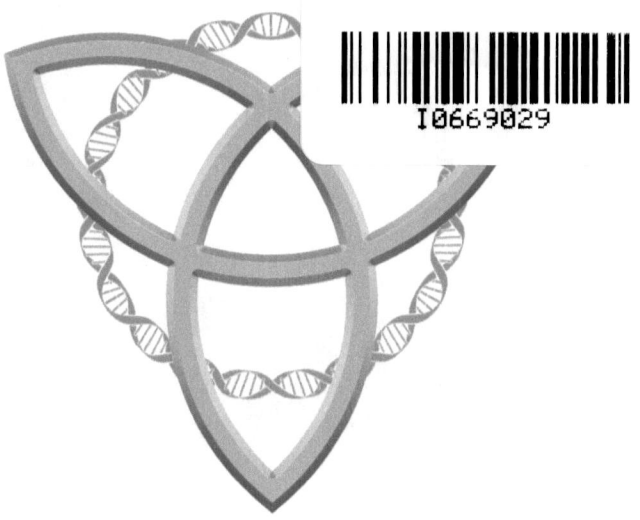

I0669029

XANDER VERSO

Ravenwise Publishing

ISBN: 979-8-9853997-8-3

Ravenwise  Publishing

For those who strive against all odds

Prologue

Never had such devastation raged across the lands, and the ancient city now lay very much in ruins. As twilight faded, illumination came from blinding streaks of plasma, along with raging fires left behind.

High atop the spire of the capital, Ixio observed the massacre, for there was little else to do.

"How goes evacuation?" he inquired.

"At this rate, they will overrun us all," replied his second-in-command. "Most defenses have been breached, and few remain to fight them off. If only we were bred for war."

"Our fate may not have been the same," Ixio considered, "but so too would our nature change. If this indeed must be our end, let us be proud of who we are. Go rally any that you can, for now we make our final stand."

Ixio then found himself alone, excluding a familiar presence lurking nearby.

"What could you possibly have left to say?" he wondered, breaking the heavy stillness.

From the shadows emerged a pale maiden, beneath whose ebon cowl and matching hair sat eyes of amethyst filled with sorrow.

By contrast of his argent mane, her dark appearance grew more pronounced as she approached, beseeching once again, "You don't have to confront him."

Ixio glared at her. "By what right does that concern you?"

"None of this was my design!" she cried. "I did everything I could, but his mind cannot be swayed."

"Then, why have you bothered coming?"

"I didn't want for you to die. Is that so hard to understand? Please, we can escape right now. Nobody would ever find us."

"Is that a life you want?" he asked.

"If it means we'd be together."

Ixio weighed the implications. "You would have me flee at such a dire moment?"

"What can still be done about this? Even if it were possible to buy more time, there's no stopping his obsession. He'll hunt them down beyond the grave."

"All the more reason I must try — to give them hope in some place far from here."

"And what of you?"

"Pray the next life will be kinder," Ixio responded.

Tearing silently, she knew his heart was resolute.

"You should return before you're missed," he added. "After so much death already, at least one of us might survive this day."

. . . Ixio descended through the tower, prepared to meet with destiny.

Seemingly unhindered, the sounds of raucous clamoring drew near, so he shifted focus to the trigonal pendant that hung around his neck.

Aether soon arose from depths unknown, then formed into a flowing sword and shield, which radiated indigo resembling his eyes of cobalt blue.

2

Ixio charged along the winding steps, cutting down a batch of Anakhari. Though greater in stature and ferocity, these invaders failed against the valor that opposed them, for his blade of light pierced through their armor, and his aegis blocked their shots.

Finally, he arrived in the central courtyard, where his brothers lay fallen by the legion. Dismayed, though undeterred, Ixio approached the enemy, burning with resolve.

"Ah, the champion steps forth," proclaimed Lord Xul, their Architect of Science. While not a military figure, his presence on the field commanded great respect. "Such noble fortitude you have, though wasted in futility."

"If that's how you regard our lives, then you really don't deserve our powers."

"As far as I have seen, the Zephyrans have not exactly shown their worth."

"And who are you to judge, given the depravity of your ways?"

"I am one who studies all," Xul boasted, flexing cold, metallic fingers that extended from a cybernetic forearm, "and knowledge is my specialty."

"In that case, prepare to learn a costly lesson," threatened Ixio.

"Stand down," Xul called out to his men, who readied themselves for retaliation. "This one is our greatest prospect."

"Allow me, then, to disappoint," said Ixio defiantly. He rushed in with his glowing sword, but Xul, to his surprise, blocked with one of orange. Not only differing in color, it bore a far more clinical dimension.

Their fierce exchange continued, neither backing down.

3

Ixio threw his shield, which maintained substance long enough to strike upon the wrist.

Xul's weapon dissipated from the shock, presenting opportunity.

Swinging for the kill, however, Ixio's blade was caught within a steely grip. Quick to improvise, he reached behind his back to draw a hidden dagger, then plunged it deep into the scaly abdomen.

With an aggravated bellow, Xul returned a violent kick, knocking Ixio to the ground. "Enough!" he shouted, the hilt of bone protruding from his torso.

For an additional response, he raised his metal arm, and the clawlike digits erupted in a flurry of connected wires, ensnaring Ixio in place.

Tightly bound, his options were quite limited, but he wasn't ready to concede.

Before the Architect could savor victory, a quake began to rumble from below.

"You're too late," said Ixio, recognizing that his people had been saved.

"In that case," growled Xul with rage, "your blood alone will have to do."

Straining against the serpentine constriction, Ixio grabbed his white stone pendant, and with abundant willpower, he channeled throughout his body streams of concentrated aether.

Xul hastened at the roiling energy, but he couldn't stop him fast enough, for as a final act of bold resistance, Ixio unleashed a passionate explosion.

Furiously rising to his feet, Xul found nothing but an iridescent shimmer from the object that survived. He staggered forward, attempting to retract his fingers, but there was too much damage, so he claimed it with his gray-skinned hand instead.

Xul beheld the bounty that came at such a cost, and in spite of all the havoc, a hungry madness filled his gaze, revealing so much more to come.

Thus he turned to leave, clutching his consolation prize.

"Salvage what you can," he barked, "then raze whatever stands." An afterthought occurred to him. "But first, someone find my daughter."

PART ONE

1

Waking with a violent start, Lucas Corvin reflected on his dream of epic sentiment. Of all its variations, this had been the most graphic one by far.

With his heart racing, a unique vibration arose upon his chest. He looked down at the white stone hanging from around his neck — the only tangible memory of his mother — noting from it a faint iridescence in the darkness.

Unable to return to sleep, he jumped right out of bed, then quietly dressed himself as usual before exiting his apartment.

Outside, the cold night would snap him even more awake, but the dreamland vision lingered in his mind.

So absorbed was he in fantasy, the surveillance drones patrolling overhead barely entered his peripheral awareness. Fortunately, Lucas knew their patterns well, and avoiding them proved second nature, aided by the inner voice that guided him along.

Compelled by a sudden urge, he donned his homemade Faraday hood, inveterately carried, then found a dingy alley away from their soaring watch.

Almost immediately, and not to his surprise, he chanced upon a Disciple thug standing beside a dumpster. Even through the metal-fabric mesh covering his eyes, Lucas recognized the unmistakable facial markings. Predictably, as well, a woman's cries of protest could be heard beneath him.

Spurred by resurgent memories long repressed, Lucas marched ahead, but the sight of approaching flint-gray uniforms halted him abruptly.

After concealing himself with haste, he waited for the pair to intervene, but his indignation mounted, as they simply left the scene. What else might be expected, though? They'd never challenge Eisencroft, even through his lowly goons.

Filled with nothing but disgust, Lucas rushed the target to serve his brand of justice. Not granting any mercy, he rained repeated blows against the vile threat to decency, his judgment quite decisive.

Panting from exertion, Lucas turned to help the girl . . . but found her running down the alley. He watched her call upon the officers, frozen at the sheer ingratitude, and before he could retreat, the Vanguard had him trapped.

"Don't you move!" one ordered, holding him at gunpoint. "Big mistake," he noted, glancing at the deed. "Do you have any idea what you did?"

Lucas glared into the smoky visor, angrily retorting, "Yeah — your *fucking job*."

In response, a punch to the gut then dropped him to his knees.

"That's a funny mask you've got, there," said the officer, taking a closer look at Lucas.

His partner hurried over. "Mask?" he wondered. "You don't think . . . What's the bounty up to?"

"More than a commendation, that's for sure."

"I'll say."

"In that case, do we bother trying to bring him in alive or just—"

Brimming with unbridled rage felt only once before, Lucas threw all caution to the wind and charged the so-called lawman.

Fueled by superhuman strength, he struck fiercely to the face, smashing the helmet with force enough to collapse the officer in a heap.

As the other drew his weapon, Lucas grabbed a hold, melting the alloy with his hand to both of their surprise.

Seizing his target by the throat, he unleashed the surging energy, warping space around him in a show of blinding light.

Once it finally subsided, naught was left but smoldering remains.

Staggering to his senses, Lucas hastily departed, but a vibrant numbness lingered through his body, mind, and soul.

Though beyond all comprehension, the strange occurrence bore a great familiarity, and not unlike the time before, he felt a strong connection to his pendant.

With the weight of tomorrow's venture becoming more apparent, he thought it best to head on home and get some needed rest.

Elsewhere in the city, down yet another alleyway, more nefarious business was afoot that night. A pair of Disciple enforcers met with their Vanguard contacts to discuss a pressing matter.

"The Baron is getting tired of this constant interference. I don't have to tell you what that means."

"No, you don't," one of the officers replied, the other standing back, "but you haven't given us much to work with — just some vague description and blurry footage. You couldn't even get his face."

"It's not our fault the guy wears a mask."

"Evidently one that blocks any tracking of his POD," the officer added.

"And what about your drones? They never seem to catch him, either."

"You really want them hanging around your operations? That's for your protection as much as ours. Do you have any idea how the public would react if they knew of this arrangement?"

"Speaking of which, your partner doesn't seem overly enthused," the enforcer noted, glancing at the sullen, dark-haired officer behind.

Acknowledging the claim, Corporal Victor Talos raised his head, replying with an umber glare.

"Don't worry about him," the first one reassured. "He knows the process well enough."

"In any case," continued the enforcer, "someone needs to get ahead of his next move, so we set up—"

A clanking interruption forced all four to start, and they identified a nosy boy spying from the shadows.

The second Disciple quickly drew his gun, but Victor rushed to seize it.

"What the hell do you think you're doing?!" snapped the noble officer.

"Covering our asses."

"How? You're only gonna draw more atten—"

A deafening shot pierced Victor's brief rebuke, filling him with horror.

"I told you," replied his colleague, "this is part of the—"

Victor spun around and shot him in the head.

He took out the Disciples next, who were not able to react in time.

Victor then approached the fallen child, but nothing could be done. After very nearly vomiting, he forced himself away.

With such a mess created, what options remained? Running wouldn't work, since eyes were everywhere. In any case, the city needed Victor, as did his Lenore.

Once decided on a plan, he carefully wiped the blaster, then placed it on the ground. Given his reputation, though, more would be required. He therefore found the other's gun and, with grim determination, aimed it at himself.

2

Hours later, Lucas awakened for the second time, now by the shining light of day. Still haunted by the previous excursion, he sat there to reflect on his momentous task ahead.

Already having deep misgivings, Lucas removed the treasured pendant from his neck — quite a rarity for him to do. Whatever role it played last night, he didn't need the added complication, so he stashed it in his wall, beside the books and other contraband.

After further preparations, he entered the kitchen and found his uncle sitting at the table.

"You sure look exhausted," noted Marlowe. "Trouble sleeping?"

"She was in my dream again," Lucas mentioned groggily. "No matter the setting, she always stays the same."

"How interesting," said his uncle, genuinely curious. "And you're sure she isn't someone from your past?"

Lucas shook his head. "I don't see how I could have possibly forgotten her, especially being as vivid as she was this time."

"And on the eve of such a day. Perhaps an omen?"

"I guess we'll find out soon enough."

"Hmm, I'm sure it will all make sense eventually," Marlowe said with confidence. As Lucas turned away, his uncle noticed a dark red stain against the silver hair. "That's not your blood, I hope?" he asked the vigilante.

"No," said Lucas, annoyed he missed a trace. "It's nothing to worry about — not with what you're planning. I mean, challenging The Order like this hasn't exactly worked out well for anyone, and given how everything's been going lately, now seems like the worst time you could choose. I won't be able to keep you alive if they make us face off on the Field."

Deciding not to pry, Marlowe smiled warmly and patted Lucas on the shoulder. "That's precisely why the time is right. People are looking for hope to guide them through the darkness, and now the impossible won't sound nearly as farfetched. The public *will* believe us if the truth can come to light."

"You might be overestimating their desperation," Lucas argued. "Many seem content with the world they know, as shit as it might be."

"When life has been a certain way this long, it's not so easy to imagine a better one. That's why they need someone else to show them what is possible and rouse them out of apathy."

"And you really think it'll be enough?"

"Trust me," his uncle promised.

Still unsure, Lucas nodded reluctantly.

"Maybe seeing it for yourself will help convince you," Marlowe offered.

"Is it ready now?"

"As ready as it'll ever be."

Lucas followed Marlowe to his bedroom.

"Be sure your NOVA POD is covered, just in case," warned his uncle.

"Always is." Lucas tapped the lens upon his temple.

"That's my boy." Marlowe then slid open the closet door, unveiling the fruits of all his labor.

"Wow!" His nephew stared in disbelief. "It's definitely not a Manna bar."

Marlowe chuckled. "Honestly, the stories don't do it justice, but not much can ever beat seeing something in person."

"I hope they'll agree," said Lucas.

"How could they not? Finally, they'll have a real symbol of what we've been missing on the ground — a reason to demand the change we need."

"That might be expecting too much from a population high on Zen," Lucas noted bitterly.

"If we can resonate with them at the core level, no drug will be strong enough to suppress that burning desire."

Lucas reflected with continued reservations. "Then we just force the city to land, join up with survivors, and live happily ever after?"

"One step at a time, but this is where it all begins. As to what might be waiting for us down there, I don't think the prospects are quite so bleak, considering how they exaggerate the Blight. I'd say overcoming that dogmatic fear is the greatest obstacle, and the rest will follow sure enough."

"Even so, the Beacon might just blast us from the sky," reminded Lucas.

"Which is why we can't give them any excuse," Marlowe stressed. "We have to do this as peaceably as possible."

"And these friends of yours . . . You really think they'll deliver?"

"We all want the same thing," Marlowe reassured, "and they understand that someone has to be the first to set our liberty in motion."

"You're asking them to take an awful risk."

"They know the bigger risk of doing nothing," Marlowe countered. "Besides, they haven't sold us out yet, so that has to count for something." He smiled optimistically.

"If you say so," conceded Lucas. "Shall we head on over, then?"

Marlowe suddenly became rather distant. "You know," he pondered, "I may have spent so much time working on the main attraction that I didn't give much thought to presentation."

Lucas took another glimpse. "I think it's quite presentable on its own."

"True," Marlowe acknowledged, "but we only get one chance at this, so we really have to make it count."

"Fair enough," said Lucas. "What did you have in mind?"

Marlowe glanced around their small apartment, "Well, we really don't have anything suitable. It might be worth a quick detour to the repo."

"Is there time?"

"Just barely, but you'd be faster on your own. We can meet at the Temple just before service begins. That should afford us a respectable enough audience."

"Anything specific I should look for?"

"I trust your judgment on the matter."

"All right," Lucas agreed. "I'll be there as fast as I can." He paused apprehensively before exiting the room. "So, this is really happening?"

"It is." Marlowe smiled again. "Today, my boy, we spark a revolution."

Lucas nodded cautiously. "Wouldn't that be something?" he considered. "Do be careful, though."

"Of course," Marlowe reassured. "I don't intend for this to be the end."

After Lucas then departed, his uncle took a breath, steadying his nerves for what he knew was coming next.

The halls of Empyrea General bustled with the usual course of patients and attendants, but away from prying eyes, it hid a most concerning secret.

Standing anxiously outside the morgue was Ross Avalon, MD, who awaited none other than one Gheriel Draconis, high commander of the Vanguard.

Two sentries barred all personnel from entry, so he could only guess at what sat lurking now inside.

Lacking any notable seniority, as evidenced by his youthful sandy hair, Ross had to trust his mentor's judgment that he could handle this alone.

Ross knew he had to focus, but a recent patient troubled him. As the sick wife of an officer — a decent man, no less — her kindness left a strong impression, especially from an Eisencroft. Since exhausting treatment options, all too commonly expected, Ross had difficulty coping. To make it worse, the officer had just been ambushed, narrowly surviving.

In his distracted self-reproach, Ross had barely registered the approaching dignitary: an imposing martial figure, whose ashen tunic bore all manner of insignia. His receding hairline foretold a man advanced in age, but he marched with no less vigor for it, and the guards indeed took notice.

"Dr. Avalon?" a stern voice called, its owner peering down his aquiline and stately nose.

"Yes, sir," Ross instinctively responded, his blue eyes wide and eager.

"Where's Kilvani?"

"The High Court needed him to testify, but he assured that my counsel would suffice."

"Follow me," Draconis ordered, briskly stepping through the doors.

The doctor nervously complied, wondering what could lie ahead to warrant such precaution.

Once inside, the high commander partially removed a tarp from three adjoining tables. "These two officers were murdered while on duty," he said. "The other appears to be a Disciple, found also at the scene. Naturally, this violation cannot stand."

"Of course, but what exactly happened?" Ross inquired, regarding the charred and mangled corpse.

"Your job is to determine that. If we're dealing with new types of weapons, they pose a grievous threat to our security. Any information you can gather will be of value to The Order."

"I'll do my best, Commander."

"And I trust you understand the need for full discretion. We certainly have no interest in causing panic, especially when keepers of the peace are under fire."

"Everything will stay between us."

Draconis turned to leave, sparing further comment.

"Sir, if I may ask," Ross added cautiously, "who was responsible for this?"

The high commander paused. "That remains a confidential matter," he replied. "Can you think of any reason why it might now be of relevance?"

"No, sir. I was just a little curious."

"Do be careful, Doctor . . . That can be infectious."

Draconis then departed, leaving Ross alone and slightly shaken.

With his overbearing presence gone, Ross examined the strange effects, unable to comprehend the means behind such injuries. Even electrical damage, like that from heavy Jolt abuse, never produced anything quite the same, at least that he had seen.

Whatever it was that he now gazed upon, the destructive power was quite clear. Nevertheless, the underlying force intrigued him, for it must have great potential.

As Draconis exited the morgue, he made his way throughout the halls to a certain patient's room. Without bothering to knock, he opened the door and entered.

"Corporal Talos," he addressed the man in bed, "I hope you're feeling better. My condolences to your wife."

"Thank you, sir," responded Victor, sitting up at once. "I'll be sure to pass it on."

"She hardly needed this on top of everything."

Victor quietly agreed.

"Regarding why you're here," continued the commander, "I trust you wouldn't mind a rather quick debriefing?"

"I'm honored that you came yourself, but you really didn't have to."

"When the Vanguard is attacked, I always take an interest."

"I understand," said Victor, tensing even more. "I didn't mean to imply otherwise."

Draconis walked around the room reflectively. "As per your account, one of the suspects drew his weapon first, and you responded in kind."

"That's right, Commander."

"Though, regrettably, too late to save your partner."

Victor humbly bowed his head. "Regrettably," he echoed.

"Still, quite fast on the draw — to take out both who had the jump on you . . . and only suffer a flesh wound."

"Thank you, sir." Victor stirred uneasily. "I'd have to credit my training."

Draconis inspected the medical report beside the bed. "Based on the shot's proximity," he ascertained, "there must have been a scuffle."

Victor gulped. "They really took us by surprise."

"I would imagine so," Draconis pondered. "It's not like the Disciples to so aggressively engage us. They usually prefer to flee."

"I'm not sure it occurred to them."

"What a shame," lamented the commander. "We might have avoided needless death, including the civilian. How unfortunate to be struck by crossfire in such a remote location. And worse, forensics indicate the shot came from your partner's gun."

"I was afraid that might have been the case."

"Naturally, I thought it best to not disclose such information that might sully his good name. No doubt you would agree?"

"Of course," Victor granted, hiding his contempt.

The commander stood reflecting for a moment longer, making Victor even more uncomfortable. "Curious, though," Draconis noted, "that he would have been so careless taking point."

Victor struggled for an answer. "Sometimes, we forget what's out there."

Draconis nodded thoughtfully. "Indeed, it serves a lesson for us all: no matter how safe you think you are, one misstep could cost you everything." He looked at Victor pointedly. "I hope you learned that well."

Victor sat there silently, not sure what to say.

On his way out, Draconis paused to share a final word of caution. "Remember what's at stake out there, and may you always choose the path of duty. There is no place for those who stray."

By contrast, the pristine halls of Capstone Industries maintained a pace of calm and order, for scientists and engineers kept mostly in their labs throughout the day.

One exception, though, was Carrie Hardwin, who raced to the high director's office to apprise him of her breakthrough.

Inside, opposite the guarded double door, Ceros Rinehart corporately perused reports across his desk, pausing at the interrupting visitor.

"Send her in," he curtly granted through his POD, mechanically adjusting the jacket of his charcoal suit.

Carrie impatiently entered to deliver the news, casting formalities aside in addressing his dead-eyed stare. "About those tissue samples you had me analyze," she panted lightly, "where exactly did they originate?"

"As I told you earlier, Miss Hardwin, those details are highly classified," Rinehart sternly answered.

"All right," said Carrie, respectful as could be. "Well, as it turns out, I detected traces from the DNA consistent with other certain readings."

"And what might those be?"

22

"You know how I was investigating the dark spectrum for possible sources of renewable energy? Well, just today—"

"I thought I told you to drop that line of research," he grumbled with annoyance.

"Technically, you only said it was 'not to interfere with more important matters'," she reminded him, "which is why I pursued it only in my spare time."

Although running out of patience, Rinehart needed answers, so he chose to overlook the insubordination. "What about it?" he inquired.

"I came across environmental measurements that couldn't be explained. Until today, I hadn't seen them anywhere before, but those samples' DNA had something similar imprinted." She seemed to gain from him at least a passing interest. "This residual signature, whatever it may be, shares harmonic frequencies with the field I discovered. Now, I can't say how it happened, but the evidence is clear: there's a biological impact from these ambient scalar waves."

The director shifted with a hint of curiosity, but that was just about the only change in his dispassionate demeanor. "A rather strange phenomenon," he noted. "You have no further data as it relates to your assignment?"

"Not yet," she confirmed, somewhat irked by his reaction, "but I think the bigger point is—"

"Submit the findings in your weekly report," he said without much care.

"I'm afraid this just can't wait," she stressed, not so easily deterred.

Confronted with her brash enthusiasm, Rinehart gave his full attention. "Go on, then," he begrudgingly responded.

"What I found appears to be, for all intents and purposes, the framework of our universe."

"Is that right?" Across his ever-stony face then flashed a telling twitch.

"It's more than just a unifying force; it's essentially the underlying code for reality itself. Though subtle, its effects on human DNA are undeniable."

Carrie saw the widening of Rinehart's hooded eyes, which inspired confidence that he appreciated the magnitude at hand.

"It isn't just a fringe idea!" she exclaimed. "If we can harness this kind of energy—"

"The scope of your task was clear," Rinehart interjected, "and you have far exceeded it."

She stared in sheer befuddlement. "I thought you'd understand."

"I understand that you are well beyond your purview — and meddling with elements about which we know nothing."

The excitement quickly faded, and Carrie's mood was now reflected less in the auburn of her hair and more in the cold slate of her eyes. "That's why I would suggest researching it," she stated bitterly.

"Out of the question, especially for you." He might as well inform her now. "As it just so happens, one of your colleagues felt compelled enough to voice her qualms to the Court."

"On what grounds?!"

"I would have preferred to resolve the matter quietly," said Rinehart, "as I don't consider violations of confidentiality acceptable under any circumstances, even concerning alleged heresy. Nevertheless, what's done is done, and a preliminary hearing has been scheduled for tomorrow."

"I don't believe this," Carrie uttered, rife with indignation.

"Given your father's influence, I expect this to be merely a formality, provided you henceforth focus *only* on your duties. Is that clear enough, Miss Hardwin?"

Of course it wasn't, but what choice did she have? "Fine," she snapped, and with her curt concession, she stormed out of the room.

Rinehart shot his gaze toward a sculpted marble owl, which sat within a bookcase by the wall. He rubbed his chin reflectively, calculating how to best proceed. Much as he'd prefer containment, the others had to be involved, for the implications were simply too disruptive.

Carrying a platter for display, Lucas hurried over to the Temple Paramount. Much to his dismay, however, he arrived to find a sea of spectators gathered at the steps, and far ahead was Marlowe, already speaking, with none around to shield or support him.

Not even within earshot, Lucas watched the moment of reveal they were supposed to both have shared.

Some let out a gasp, while others gawked in silence, but regardless of their emotions felt, they all were captivated by the red orb held aloft.

Pushing forward hastily, he once more checked the time — still early by the schedule they had recently agreed upon.

An uproar then exploded, as many were confused and angry.

Marlowe didn't flinch, though, and he continued with resolve, knowing just how much depended on this outcome.

After shoving through the masses, Lucas finally got close enough to hear his uncle's words.

"I'm sure you recognize it from the tales of our childhood, but this bounty born of nature is more than simple nourishment, for I hold here in my hand a symbol of our birthright, the world we long ago abandoned. Remember who we are. Remember where we came from. That's where we belong. Our destiny lies not above the clouds but among the lakes and meadows. See what life can yet be grown, even in a place like this, and imagine what is possible in our true home down below."

They longingly envisioned such a world, almost as if witnessing it firsthand.

An enthusiastic murmuring arose, giving Lucas hope, but before the sentiment could propagate, a strident voice erupted from the balcony. "Heresy!" it pompously declared. "Seize that man at once!"

Through massive doors emerged the Temple Guard, and they wasted no time restraining Marlowe in plain view of the crowd.

Soon appearing after them was Preston Foregrave, High Judicar of Xul, whose gaunt frame towered in a raven cassock atop the sacred steps, and with a vulture's countenance, he glowered at the agitator.

His focus turned then to the fallen fruit, which he took for swift inspection. Raising it past his sunken cheeks to eye level, he betrayed the slightest fear.

Finally at the front, Lucas could only stare in desperation as the last of his family was handed over to the Vanguard.

In response to the deep betrayal on his nephew's face, Marlowe smiled faintly. "I couldn't risk your safety," he explained. "Please understand."

"I'll find a way to save you!" shouted Lucas, but Marlowe shook his head.

"Worry about yourself," he reassured. "We haven't lost the fight just yet."

Once his uncle was removed from sight, Lucas turned in anger toward the visage looming over him.

The sallow pontiff caught his gaze, flashing back inclement scorn, and with dismissive self-importance, he returned inside, apple still in hand.

Powerlessly trapped between parishioners and lawmen, Lucas watched the judicar depart.

Such rank injustice truly hurt, even for the hardened cynic. Enraged, though not surprised, he prepared for what came next, knowing his ordeal had only just begun.

3

Once inside the courtroom, Lucas met that dour face again, as perched atop his bench, the judicar peered haughtily at the man whose fate now lay before him.

"You stand accused of heresy, sedition, and spreading rank disinformation," Foregrave sternly charged. "How, then, do you plead, Mr. Marlowe Ikewell?"

"Not guilty," replied his uncle, though with a trace of resignation in his voice.

"Have you any evidence to present in your defense?"

"I first would like to know the evidence against me," retorted Marlowe.

"You were apprehended *in flagrante* at the very steps of the holy Temple. Do you deny this?"

"No, but—"

"Aggravating factors shall be fully presented here today so as to leave little doubt of your culpability."

"I only spoke the truth," asserted Marlowe.

"Is that so?" the judicar inquired. "To provide a more authoritative stance, the High Court calls upon the expertise of Dr. John Kilvani."

An older, well-tanned man with slicked-back hair then climbed up to the stand.

"Dr. Kilvani," Foregrave spoke, "Your medical experience has long assisted the people of Empyrea. Now, the rather bold contention has been made that the Blight is nothing to be feared. What have you to say regarding such a notion?"

"Well," the man commenced, adjusting himself conceitedly, "it should come as no surprise that the science has long been put to rest. The effects of Blight-induced prion disease are quite clear, and even with innoculation, we really can't be sure what other dangers might exist, especially from radioactivity. As a healthcare practitioner, I can personally attest to some grisly cases of . . ."

Lucas tuned out from the monologue, which filled him with disgust. Though pathetically transparent, it proved nonetheless effective in terrifying the crowd.

After giving his performance, Kilvani went back to the gallery, then quietly consulted with a younger man beside him. Probably before too long, that sandy-haired protégé with sky-blue eyes would be their next official mouthpiece, bred to serve the clockwork.

"In light of directly hearing from a true and trusted source, do you still maintain your contradiction, Mr. Ikewell?"

"I do."

"Then, it remains to be determined whether your pernicious fallacies are driven by delusion or something more nefarious. To elucidate the full scope of your criminality, I call upon the prosecution's material witnesses: those you sought to enlist as co-conspirators in your blasphemy. Fortunately, these fine men and women were of higher character."

Lucas watched supposed friends and allies one by one disparage him. None betrayed the slightest hint of guilt, either knowing the cost of noncooperation, or truly ignorant of the lies they spewed. Though forsaken and betrayed, Marlowe stayed composed.

"Quite the compelling evidence," noted Foregrave once their testimonies ended. "Your guilt is looking strong."

"And when might I receive the chance to justify myself?"

"You seem to lack a fundamental understanding of our procedures, Mr. Ikewell. Nevertheless, we shall move on to character witnesses. I therefore call upon your nephew, Lucas Corvin, to testify before us."

"There's no need to involve him. I'm the one on trial here, and he has nothing—"

"The decision is not up to you," said Foregrave. "As a matter of public interest, Mr. Corvin *will* be questioned."

Lucas anxiously arose, managing to calm his nerves as he sat beside the bench.

"State your name," instructed Xul's high judicar.

"Lucas Corvin," he replied, careful not to falter.

"Marlowe Ikewell was, for many years, your designated guardian and only living relative?"

"That's correct," said Lucas.

"Surely, then, you must know each other well. Tell the High Court how you first came to his care."

In a torrent of unpleasant imagery, Lucas recalled his father bearing down, his mother rushing to defend him, then a storm of broken glass. One lurid color stained his memory more than any other, for it was the sea of red that made him snap, tackling the drunken savage to the floor to unleash all righteous hell.

Only when his muscles were expended did he stop, collapsing to the floor in anguish.

Flames then grew from their abandoned kitchen, spreading soon with ease, but just as Lucas had resigned himself to that inferno, a man burst through the door.

Relieved to see his uncle, Lucas fell unconscious on his shoulder, but not before he noticed Marlowe take the alabaster pendant from around his sister's neck.

"There was a fire," Lucas replied mechanically, avoiding his uncle's gaze.

"Yet somehow you survived?"

"Somehow," Lucas echoed. "I was too young to remember well."

"Regardless, knowing Mr. Ikewell intimately, how do you respond to the crimes he stands accused of, Mr. Corvin?"

"Marlowe Ikewell is the greatest man I've ever known," said Lucas honestly. "The evidence presented here today, damning as it seems, paints only a small picture of who he really is and what he hoped to achieve."

Lucas knew his words were pointless, as the outcome had been set, and he saw the same conclusion reflected by his uncle.

"And why should we believe you, considering your bias?" Foregrave asked the witness. "Would you not also seek to cover up involvement in his plot? Perhaps, given your proximity, we should expand the charges."

"I confess!" shouted Marlowe, bolting to his feet. "No further questioning is necessary."

The room erupted in commotion, drowning Lucas's objections.

Hammering his gavel, Foregrave called for silence.

Once order was restored, the judicar proceeded. "In that case, Mr. Ikewell," he piously proclaimed, "the verdict is decided. I therefore sentence you to exile, carried out forthwith."

Lucas felt a numbing sickness, and the final bang of so-called justice ran a shudder down his spine. Shaking in a trancelike state, he rose to follow out the door.

Marlowe's escort closely guarded him while many tagged along, so not until he got outside could Lucas catch a view.

Much to his despair, however, it was the sound that struck him first, for several booming shots rang out in plain sight of the Vanguard.

Lucas pushed on through, arriving at the steps, where motionless his uncle lay with no one else around.

The younger doctor from the trial fought his way to help, but officers denied his aid, forming an impenetrable barrier. Not only that, they were all content to simply watch the gunman flee.

Realizing that the task was now for him alone, Lucas charged ahead. His vision focused on a single point, and he cared for nothing else.

Aside he brushed a startled woman, whose auburn hair fell from its bow.

The tumult of the crowd became a distant muffle, and faces blurred to vacant orbs.

Bursting with energy as instinct overtook him, he raised his hands to blast a gust of wind. Though passersby were staggered, only one man hit the ground.

Lucas closed the gap between them, leaping with a primal roar to pin his mark.

No words at all were needed, for what was there to say? Crushing down upon his throat, Lucas lost himself to rage.

Onlookers gawked in horror as the fury burned throughout his eyes of cobalt. He couldn't tell whose scream was louder, but both were unrestrained.

By the time his rampage ended, nothing lingered but a skull of cinder. Exhausted, he collapsed, and only then did the Vanguard intervene, dragging him away.

Given the publicity and overwhelming threat he posed, a trial wasn't even feigned, so they made him disappear instead.

Incapacitated at the scene, Lucas didn't know his whereabouts, but the lab equipment present indicated some extraordinary prison.

His temple strongly ached from where the POD had been removed, and though strapped firmly to a table, he felt ironic liberation.

"Where am I?" Lucas asked the nearest officer, who watched him curiously.

"It's not my place to say," the dark-haired man replied.

"Just killing me would save a lot of trouble."

"That's not my call to make." The guard reflected briefly. "From what I hear, though, it would be more humane than what they're planning," he confessed.

"What makes me so special?"

"Do I really need to answer that? After what you did out there, I'd say you're more than just a little different."

"Fair enough," Lucas granted, "but you seem rather different yourself."

"Yeah? How so?" The comment appeared to strike a chord with him.

"Well, I hadn't met a Vanguard who'd give the time of day."

"Believe it or not, there's a few of us who aren't complete degenerates. And for what it's worth, I'm sorry about your uncle."

"Were you there?" asked Lucas.

The officer bowed his head. "I was. Blame me if you want, but there was nothing I could do."

"How often do you say that to yourself?"

"Interesting judgment from a killer and a demon."

Lucas mulled the branding, only half of which was true. Then again, perhaps he was more different than he'd ever comprehended. "Is that what you think I am?"

The officer gave a probing look. "Why don't you tell me?"

Lucas turned to stare off pensively. "If only I could."

"You're saying you don't know?"

"I can't explain what happened — or what it means about me. I won't deny a paranormal element, but I wouldn't call it evil, no matter how destructive it appeared."

"You mean melting someone's face off?"

Lucas glared at him. "I never hurt a man who didn't have it coming, and if you really care about your city, I'd be concerned what happens now. With no one left to clean these streets for real, things are about to get even worse."

"That was *you*?" the officer inferred, his voice filled with respect. "So, a demon with a halo?"

"Or an angel with a dagger," suggested Lucas, managing to smile.

"Talos, they're ready for processing," a colleague interjected. "Security says they can handle it from here."

Soon injected with a sedative by a lab-coat-wearing tech, Lucas had a final vision, much to his surprise, of a genuine apology within the soldier's umber eyes.

4

Several months had passed since Victor left the Vanguard. The graveyard shift at Capstone, though lacking in prestige, meant less overt corruption, so Victor made his peace.

What other options were there for a man in his position? Although able to retire on Lenore's ancestral fortune, the need to be of service burned within too strongly — and more so after losing her.

For all the whispered secrets hidden deep within these walls, surely one could justify his vigil. With Overseer Hardwin's daughter under investigation, her work, at least, must be truly promising.

Without much else to do, he strolled the empty halls.

Passing by an open lab, he overheard a single word, which froze him at the door. At the mention of her illness, he turned to listen carefully, desperate to know more.

"We need to synthesize another one," a voice inside relayed.

"Which family is it this time?" asked his colleague.

"Take a wild guess."

"Do you think it's from the inbreeding?"

"I hear that's not the only thing they're into, but I'm not gonna pry."

"Right, best be careful what you say. We don't need a visit from the boogeyman."

"Sevro's got better things to do — unless we leak the cure or something. Otherwise, a Disciple waiting down an alley would do the job just fine."

"So, can you handle this alone? I've gotta head out early."

"Sure thing."

"Thanks. I set up in Lab C. Just make sure you log out when you're done."

"Obviously. Give me a second, and I'll head right over."

The words left Victor sick and staggered, but instinctively, his legs then brought him to the lab in question.

Beyond the range of eyes or cameras, he entered quickly, having little care for self-preservation.

At the nearest active terminal, he found an open document, confirming the hidden truth.

Through racing thoughts and feelings, he knew he needed proof. Anything physical would be too risky, as they'd catch it at the door. What else could pass the scanners? Without recording options, disabled for this reason, his POD served little use. Then again, perhaps it might, though far less elegantly.

Opening a simple memo app, he copied down the data, transcribing every word and drawing every diagram.

After getting all he could, he promptly left the room. With others none the wiser, he walked back to his post.

Though he had secured the evidence discreetly, pretending not to know it was quite another matter.

Carrie once more left the Jolt house, but instead of inspiration or a boost in problem solving, she had sought this time what others often do: distraction from her worries. Forfeiting so much potential could not be taken lightly, for that striking application left a rather strong impression, regardless of the drug's intensity.

Abandoning her research had been difficult enough, but when she saw the same force channeled right in front of her, she gained a new appreciation. Though she couldn't prove it, the connection was clear to her.

How could such clear validation be ignored? Not only biologically compatible, it flowed without assistance. Did he actually control it, and what more could it do? If The Order deems that witchcraft, did she then discover magic?

So many implications rushed across her mind, and every one could help secure their future, but no one seemed to care.

The 'divine' technology powering the city might suffice for now, but such black-box systems could not be trusted, should they one day break beyond repair. This new kind of energy, whatever it may be, could match or even best Xul's offering, proving to be the key.

The high director had made his wishes clear, but Carrie still was motivated. Full of curiosity as usual, it also mixed with altruism — a feeling less familiar. Did either really warrant this audacious undertaking? To continue down the path of rank defiance, even her father's office might not save her, assuming he would care enough to try.

Perhaps, though, if the occult could be demystified, a newfound understanding might ensue. Freed from the shadows of obscurity, nature's laws would shine in harmony.

Even without the recognition she deserved, a legacy of progress would certainly be forged. Expecting, at the very least, for her efforts to endure, the choice ahead was clear. Damn the odds, she thus resolved, as nothing counts but action.

As Ross headed down the alley outside Empyrea General, he still thought back to that unreal sight outside the courthouse, for it was at that moment he solved the case assigned to him. Promptly terminated, the investigation left more questions than it answered, but he was not about to pry.

Of more recent concern, however, was the loss of yet another patient to the familiar malady that left its mark indelibly on his life, and her husband's unwavering devotion only compounded on the tragedy.

Before Ross could sink any deeper into reverie, a harsh voice pierced unexpectedly through the heavy silence.

"Long day, 'Doctor'?"

Ross turned to stare into the partially illuminated face of the very man who weighed so heavily on his conscience.

"Officer Talos?" Ross called out in disbelief. "What are you doing here?"

Victor stepped forward. "I could ask you the same question," he snapped.

"I'm afraid I don't understand," said Ross, bracing himself nervously as alcohol burned his nostrils.

"Then, let me make it clear," Victor slurred, brandishing a pistol.

"I-I did everything I could," stammered Ross.

"You're really gonna keep up the ruse, even now?"

Ross could only stare, confused. "I honestly have no idea—"

"You had the cure all along!" Victor shouted. "I knew the Baron wanted her gone, but I didn't think you'd be so eager to do his bidding. Hell, what was her life even worth to you?"

"What are you talking about?"

"I saw it for myself!"

"Saw what?"

Victor pushed the evidence wirelessly from his NOVA POD.

The doctor's eyes widened as he scanned the files.

"Do you still deny it?" Victor angrily demanded.

"Where did you find this?"

"The vault for all their dirty secrets: Capstone."

Ross collapsed against the wall, his disillusioned gaze hauntingly familiar. "My mother . . . You weren't the only one they lied to."

Rage gave way to pity, forcing Victor to lower the gun.

"I'm so sorry," said Ross with all sincerity, tears filling his eyes.

Reeling from the full systemic rot, all the former officer could manage was to stagger away into the darkness, leaving the doctor to his shared despair.

Deep into the night, Carrie labored over the finishing touches before her maiden test. Analysis on the Manna bar neared completion, so all that remained was the fabrication.

She could have started with something more elementary — and under normal circumstances, it would have been the wiser course — but as she only had so much time in the lab alone each day, every precious moment had to count. With her secret mission ever at risk of exposure, she would need something compelling to present in her defense, and she had never been closer to achieving it.

Finally, the waveform representation of her daily ration soon appeared. Ready to begin materialization, she fed the data through and eagerly awaited the results.

Before the process could conclude, however, she noticed a disturbance at the door. Her heart then sank at the sight of Director Rinehart, flanked by two security personnel.

"Miss Hardwin," he addressed her slowly, both angry and annoyed, "I thought we had reached an understanding."

"Director, I—" Carrie began, but as she scrambled to provide an explanation, her contraption signaled its completion.

Everyone turned to look.

"I did it!" she boasted, her spirits lifted instantly. "I told you I was on to something, and now I have the proof."

Rinehart stared intently at the unassuming foodstuff that now sat upon the tray. His eyes filled with a flash of horror, which Carrie optimistically misread. "So it would appear," he spoke through gritted teeth.

"Do you realize what this means?" she continued enthusiastically, unfazed by his demeanor.

Rinehart sharply glared at her. "Unfortunately for you, I do."

Expecting vindication, Carrie faltered at his tone. "Don't you see?" she asked him. "There's nothing abstract or demonic here. This proves it's just another force of nature, no different from electricity or magnetism. I can outline every step of the process for those who'd call it sorcery, then the judicar would have no reason to impugn it any further. Just think of everything we could do—"

"That's quite enough, Miss Hardwin," he sternly interjected. "I'm afraid you leave me now with only one solution: your services are terminated, and a formal hearing will ensue. The Court will determine what to do with you." He turned to his men. "Escort her out at once."

In utter shock from the wild emotional swings of the past minute, Carrie stammered incoherently, too distraught to do anything but allow herself to be dragged reluctantly from the room.

Rinehart walked over to her invention, taking note of the dedicated craftsmanship, especially for a prototype. He then reached into the housing and removed the synthesized Manna. Holding it up to eye level, he broke it in half, inhaling the familiar aroma. After a curious bite, his gaze fell back to the device responsible, and with a solemn shaking of his head, he quickly turned to leave.

Another guard stood waiting by the door.

"Remove every last trace of it," the high director ordered. "I have a most unpleasant call to make."

Over and over, Ross analyzed the data on his POD. It defied so much of what they'd taught him, but herein lay the scathing truth in all its raw simplicity. With so much evidence, there was little room for doubt.

So many lives could have been saved, had he only known it sooner. Nothing could bring them back, of course, but there were those now in his care still forced to suffer. Yet, despite the moral obligation, this could prove to be his own undoing, given their suppression of such knowledge.

Finally, the burden on his conscience became too great, and the risk had to be taken. While the past may have been decided, that was no excuse to wallow in regret and fear.

Throughout the day, Ross gathered the necessary supplies to avoid arousing suspicion, and with the limited means at his disposal, used his extensive medical understanding to formulate a suitable approximation of the treatments mentioned in the notes.

With a single dose prepared, he thought carefully about how best to administer the concoction. No side effects were mentioned, but for even the slightest chance of doing more harm than good, every precaution had to be taken.

The doctor therefore selected his most ailing patient for trial, keeping a close eye on her vital signs, even past the end of his shift and well into the night.

By no means could he have imagined the speed of remission witnessed. Unfortunately, Ross wasn't the only one to notice, and the steps taken to cover his tracks proved ultimately irrelevant in light of the miraculous treatment, sufficing to mark his guilt.

Unsure who made the call, he sat quietly waiting until the Vanguard arrived, offering little resistance as they hauled him away, for he now knew enough to recognize such futility.

5

The lower depths of Capstone sat still as ever, save for the rows of dormant prisoners in standing vats. Suddenly, one of the floating captives made an unexpected twitch.

Halfway back to waking consciousness, Lucas felt the sensors and electrodes, especially around his head. He kept his heartbeat calm, careful not to enter shock. Expanding his awareness, he found the boundary of the tank, and with a measured pulse of aether, breached the sturdy glass.

Rejoining with his body left him heavily off balance, but now was not the time to rest, so Lucas floundered to his feet, knowing that the noise would draw attention.

Sure enough, a door soon opened just as Lucas vanished behind cover.

Investigating the disturbance, the guard reached for his weapon, but before the news could be reported, Lucas rushed to tackle him. Aether flowed throughout his body, granting him erratic strength, and with one hand firmly on the gun, Lucas raised a shard of broken glass, striking at his target's neck.

Back upon his feet, once the guard was dead, Lucas checked the sidearm — melted, exactly as before.

Using the respite to catch a needed breath, he glanced back at the rows of vats. Though dozens more were trapped, he could do nothing for them now. "What a waste," he sighed, then continued on his way.

After changing into the guard's ill-fitting uniform, he quickly left the room.

Opting for the staircase, he made the climb to surface level.

Door then held ajar, he found an empty corridor, so he cautiously emerged, advancing on ahead.

Stopping at a corner, he heard the sounds of chatter. Although somewhat in the distance, they soon were overshadowed by a pair of boots approaching. With nowhere to retreat, Lucas hugged the wall, ready to attack.

Exploiting the briefest window of surprise, Lucas grabbed his target by the vest and spun him to the ground. About to knock the guard unconscious, Lucas froze instead, for the last thing he expected was a pair of umber eyes.

"Why the hell are you here?!" Lucas whispered.

"*Me*? You're the one supposed to be imprisoned."

A potent whiff of alcohol hit Lucas in the face. He let go of the soldier, and they both rose to their feet.

"I thought you were a Vanguard?" wondered Lucas.

"The corruption was a bit too much for me," said Victor, "but I can't seem to escape it anywhere." His attention turned toward the elevator, a vengeful longing in his eyes. "In any case, Rinehart will pay tonight."

"Is that really the best idea?"

"It's all that can be done."

"Maybe not," said Lucas. For whatever reason, the inner voice of doubt and gloom did not cry out to him. Instead, he felt a strange compassion for the clearly broken man. "I came back here with a plan, and it could use a guy like you."

"In all my years, I never made a dent against the system, and I'm not the first to try. What makes you think you'd win, when everyone has failed?"

"I've got myself an ally — an agent in their ranks. If you wanna make a difference, now's the time to fight."

Victor felt a stir of hope, but it was beneath a mountain of despair.

"Join me," Lucas told him, "and we'll set things right for good. While I can't ensure the outcome, I promise you a chance, at least."

The offer was appealing, but so was frontier justice. Could Victor be an executioner, now that another path presented? If they failed in such a grand ambition, his Lenore might never be avenged. He glanced from Lucas to the elevator, caught between two fleeting opportunities. In reality, however, it hardly was a choice.

. . . Lucas exited the building, marching on toward freedom. Thus, one of many hurdles had been cleared.

The spiral city called to him, a cold wind steeling his resolve. Would he still recognize the streets? Something told him yes.

With drones abounding overhead, he still had to be careful, but as he disappeared into the night, only one thought filled his mind: after such an agonizing wait, the revolution had begun.

6

By the time Carrie left the courthouse, the sun had already set. The sky was deathly still, given the unusual absence of surveillance drones. Though spared a harsher sentence, her career had been destroyed.

Lost and without purpose, she wandered through the streets, but as she came to realize, she did not do so alone. With mounting trepidation, she sped along much faster, and her pursuers quickly did the same.

Already quite unsettled, Carrie got another shock, as a voice then spoke abruptly through her NOVA POD. "Whatever you do, don't stop," it warned. "Those men are trying to kill you."

"Why?"

"I'll answer questions later, but for now, you'll have to trust me. Just follow my instructions, and I can help you stay alive."

"And who exactly are you?"

"A seeker of the truth," he said. "You're not the only one out there."

Despite the dire circumstances, she had to credit his abilities in bypassing her security.

Carrie sprinted down the alleys, turning as he ordered.

Eventually, she reached a dingy side street — relatively public, though far from granting safety.

Past her walked a Vanguard, but she knew better than to stop him.

Glancing over her shoulder, she spotted the pair of goons. Not only were they nearing her, a third now closely followed.

"You need to head into that building," the voice directed urgently.

By the neon lettering ahead, she recognized a seedy Jolt house. Though pausing with a brief aversion, she continued in reluctantly.

Inside, the familiar atmosphere barraged her senses. A cacophony of lights and music brought back not-so-distant memories. Never really interested in the merriment of crowds, she only sought that manic boost from several thousand volts, in spite of every headache and neuropathic twinge.

Suppressing her discomfort, she found an empty station.

"Be sure to keep your guard up; we're dealing with professionals."

"Professional what?" she asked.

"I think you know the answer."

She looked around the room. "So, what do I do now?"

"There's an exit in the corner. Once the coast is clear, you'll have to make a run for it."

Suddenly, a man joined her at the station. The scar across his cheek left little doubt of his identity.

Caught under his beady gaze, she loudly cleared her throat.

"Is everything okay?" the voice inquired.

She repeated her signal of distress.

"I see . . . In that case, please stand by."

Unsure what to do, she watched the calm assassin, who'd fixed his eyes on her. With malevolent indifference, he hardly even blinked.

"Sevro?" she tentatively guessed, filled with deep unease.

"I see you know my work," he admitted. "Your father must be quite the talker."

"Was he the one who sent you?" Carrie had to ask.

"Sorry to inform you, dear, but those calls are from a little higher up."

"Then, does he even know?" she pressed.

Mildly amused, Sevro leaned his head. "Would that make you feel better?"

Instinctively, she touched the teal silken ribbon in her hair, staring at the outlet just between them.

"How about one last hit?" he offered, noticing her tic. "I think that's fair enough, but don't try anything stupid."

Her guide gave no response, so without much else to do, she reached across the table, programming a final session.

Out popped two electrodes, which she slowly moved to grab, but instead of placing them on her temples, she fastened both together.

Before Sevro could react, she promptly cranked the dial, and sparks erupted all across his face. Not only that, the circuits quickly fried, cutting power to the building.

Cast in darkness, she seized her moment, rushing to the door. The other patrons' NOVA PODs just barely lit the way.

Outside once more, she suddenly ran into his accomplice, who eagerly awaited her.

He swiftly raised his gun, prepared to shoot her dead, but someone intervened, subduing him with ease.

"Are you injured?" asked her guardian, an apparent Vanguard officer.

"I'm fine," she answered, still not fully trusting.

"Never mind the uniform," he said. "It's only for appearances."

"Does this mean you're the one who hacked me?"

"I'll confess to that," a second voice announced nearby. He then removed his helmet, revealing striking silver hair.

"You're the 'demon' from the courthouse," she noted, remembering his eyes.

"I'm sure you know by now that nothing's as it seems, and if you come with us, I'll be happy to explain the truth about your research."

"I guess I don't have anywhere else to go," she realized, "so why the hell not?"

"Wonderful," said Lucas. "First, though, you'll wanna put this on."

He handed her a fine-mesh hood, expecting reluctance to comply. It therefore pleased him greatly when she readily understood.

"Clever," she noted, "but I can probably devise a more high-tech solution."

Lucas grinned. "I was hoping you'd say that."

The three sat around Victor's apartment, briefing Carrie fully on the state of affairs. Fortunately, she had already put her skills to work, scripting a temporary solution to their POD-tracking predicament.

"That certainly is a lot to process," she considered, "though I can't say it surprises me, especially after what I saw you do that day."

"You're far more open-minded than your profession would suggest," Lucas noted.

"It's a necessary virtue for a scientist," Carrie reasoned, "but I seem to be alone in recognizing that."

"And so they had to silence you, because they feared what you might learn. More than that, you sought to bring about a less imprisoned world."

"Through the source of 'magic' I discovered?"

"Others call it genomancy," Lucas clarified, "and I'd love to teach you more."

"Is that why you recruited me?"

"Saving your life was most important, but we could greatly use your talents."

"And what exactly is your goal?"

"Same as yours: expose the truth," he earnestly disclosed. "As long as they're suppressing knowledge, no one can be free. If you join us in our cause, we'll tear apart their lies, and you can help create a world without deception."

"That's really quite an offer," she said in disbelief.

"The odds are stacked against us," he admitted, "but we've got a fighting chance."

"Well, if it means defying The Order, you'd better count me in."

"Glad to have you on our side," Lucas welcomed.

An afterthought occurred to her. "Before we go much further, we'll need to hide our tracks. Even with my POD hack, there's still a chance to track us."

"Didn't you disable that?" asked Victor.

"I could only change the signal," she explained, "which their algorithms might uncover."

"How long would that take?"

"Hard to say, but without a permanent solution, we won't last long out there."

"Then, we'll have to take them out," concluded Victor.

"Pretty much."

"Is that something you could do?" asked Lucas.

"I'm not a doctor," she reminded. "I wouldn't take that risk."

"I don't suppose you know somebody — a good one we can trust?"

She shook her head uncertainly.

"Actually, I think I might," Victor hinted, "but there's just one little problem."

7

What incomprehensible misfortune. This was his reward for denying further death? Such idealistic values once brought him to the top, but little did he realize they'd also mean his downfall. Much less could he have estimated the pace of what would follow — or that his patient would malign him to the Court.

Yet right until the end, Ross didn't lose integrity, treasuring the one possession they could never hope to steal.

With introductions nearly finished, he had to focus on survival, so he eyed the other convicts nervously, shaken by their battle-worthy statures.

Though all were masked for decency, Ross caught the gaze from one of them.

Combatant Number 12, as denoted by the marker on his jumpsuit, appeared to watch him from across the Field of Deliverance.

Ross quickly looked away, but he could feel the attention linger.

It wasn't long before a trumpet blared, signaling commencement of the show, officiated by none other than Overseer Hardwin.

A misty fog arose while they scrambled off to arm themselves, their PODs being televised across the city for everyone to see firsthand.

Cheers erupted from the spectators, the grisly action amplified on giant monitors.

The fracas further escalated as reflective panels popped about the stadium.

Knowing himself to be no match for hardened criminals, Ross avoided confrontation, hastening across the arena's bloody grounds.

What did any of it matter, though? Safeguards precluded every possible escape, and where else would he go, after soundly losing everything?

The only chance he had was to win this deadly game, for as the rules made clear, only one man leaves alive. Yet even to save himself against the lowest of society, Ross couldn't bring himself to betray the oath he took. Regardless of the cruel dilemma faced, he was determined to survive.

Darting through the labyrinth of mirrors, he struggled to distinguish from threats illusory and genuine. Others fared little better, charging Ross on sight, only to be met with shattered glass as they struck with all their might.

At least he managed to stay relatively hidden, as the broadcasting drones eschewed him for more notable engagements. Combatant Number 12, for instance, fought with particular finesse, and on more than one occasion, caught Ross's assailant handily by surprise. The doctor would have thanked him, but he knew he'd soon be next.

Sure enough, once the protracted bloodshed reached an ominously still respite, only the two of them remained.

Raising a simple bludgeon, Ross prepared to defend as best he could, but the capable opponent lowered his weapon, purposefully approaching.

With a sudden clumsy backstep, Ross tripped upon a nearby corpse. Now disarmed, he could only scurry away, bumping into a terminal pane of glass.

Ross braced himself in panic for the looming blow, surprised to find the mist increasing all around him, enveloping them both. He thought they would prefer a clearer view for the coup de grâce, forthcoming either way.

"Hold on," warned his adversary.

"What?" said Ross, thoroughly confused.

Suddenly, the floor collapsed beneath them, and both went for a fall.

Clamoring to his feet, Ross continued struggling to comprehend what was happening.

In addition to the other convict, an intriguing woman stood there, observing him with a laptop at her side.

Another figure soon emerged from the shadows, notably with a strange, rippling aura surrounding both his hands.

Their heads were well concealed under hoods, seemingly of the same variety that was then placed on his own.

"W-who are you?" he asked, able to see them through the finely woven mesh.

"Whatever you do, kid, don't take that off," instructed Number 12.

"Officer Talos?!" Ross exclaimed, quite sure he knew the voice.

"Not anymore — and for the last time, call me Victor."

Ross looked back toward the girl.

"As for who *we* are," she answered, "call us Libertas, though the name's not set in stone."

"In any case," the other spoke, "welcome to the fight."

8

Days had passed since Lucas formed his crew, so they now prepared retaliation against the broken system. Though undeniably small in numbers, his fellow outcasts burned with equal ardor, for each one had a score to settle. Thus united by a noble purpose, they plotted in the fashioned headquarters of Victor's large apartment.

"We don't have the manpower to go after Draconis, Rinehart, *and* Foregrave," argued Victor.

"What about the overseer?" wondered Ross. "Isn't he as much a problem?"

"You'd be surprised just how irrelevant he is," Carrie scoffed, absent-mindedly touching the ribbon in her hair. "Trust me when I say that Xul's Executors really run the show."

"You've got that right," said Lucas. "Besides, even with any real authority, he'd be powerless without their backing."

"Speaking of which," Victor noted, "the Vanguard have us pretty well outgunned. Not only that, Capstone has its own security force — and don't forget the Temple Guard."

"Without the public on our side, it wouldn't matter anyway," Lucas added. "As long as they control the narrative, they control perception, and before the truth can be accepted, it will be violently opposed."

"Then, how do you suggest we reach them?" inquired Ross.

"Before we can appeal openly," Lucas outlined, "we need to eliminate what barriers we can. The Executors, of course, present the most conspicuous impediment, but there are other, more subtle mechanisms of manipulation."

"Full-spectrum dominance," replied the former officer.

"They target our biology to suppress what makes us human, but it doesn't stop at genomancy. One convenient side effect for them is the impact on behavior, which helps to guarantee a relatively manageable population."

"How do they pull that off?" asked Ross.

"Many different ways," Lucas answered. "Among the more nefarious tools, I'd say, is Capstone's blend of industrial pollutants, dumped into everything from pharmaceuticals to the food and water."

Carrie had to shudder with disgust, aware of quite a few by name. "They've been *inside* us this whole time?"

"Accumulating every day since birth."

"I can't say I'm surprised," she reasoned, "given Rinehart's pathological efficiency. I just wish I'd known it sooner, for whatever good that might have done."

"For your safety, it's probably best you didn't," warned Victor. "You know how they react to those who threaten their agenda."

"Don't forget about the Zen," Lucas added.

"So much for 'free of side effects'," groaned Ross, profoundly nauseated.

"The neurological imbalances are often overlooked, but along with destabilizing mood, it greatly dampens the flow of aether."

"They've really got it all figured out, don't they?" Victor commented.

"And, unfortunately, there's more than just the chemical component. Our DNA, it turns out, is a remarkable antenna, making us vulnerable to certain electromagnetic frequencies."

"From what?" asked Ross.

"Everything, I'm sure," said Carrie with a sigh.

"You're not far off," admitted Lucas, "but the worst would be their telecom array. PODs are bad enough, but from their weapons to surveillance drones, the network is extensive. I won't bore you with voltage-gated ion channels or cyclotron harmonics, but such pervasive radiation eventually takes its toll."

"Not something they focus on too heavily in med school," said Ross in retrospection.

"Or electrical engineering," added Carrie.

Lucas nodded gravely. "The net result not only suppresses higher consciousness but amplifies the lower brain."

"The seat of reflexes and fear," Ross expounded.

"Primed for full submission," concluded Victor.

"But why aren't *we* affected to the same degree?" Carrie wondered.

"Some innate resistance?" Ross hypothesized.

"There's certainly a chance," Lucas granted, "but it could also be psychology. Sufficient trauma, after all, can lead to growth for those who overcome it."

"True," said Carrie, "but even if we could address all this, how long before we'd see results?"

"Well," considered Ross, "the body doesn't repair this damage overnight, if it ever can. I'd say, at the absolute minimum, it might take several weeks."

"They'd probably catch on to us by then," said Victor.

"That's why we can't leave any traces," Lucas emphasized, "or else it will be for nothing. On that note, we'll need to wipe the access logs before they're archived, or else their algorithms might detect irregularities."

"How often is the backup?" Carrie asked.

"At the top of every hour."

"That's all the time we have to infiltrate, sabotage, and withdraw?" Victor summarized. "We'd also need credentials to get anywhere near those targets."

"My informant will provide those."

"I hate to state the obvious," Ross reminded, "but only one of us can show his face in public."

"Good point," acknowledged Lucas. "Carrie, did you get anywhere repurposing those NOVA PODs?"

"Indeed, I did," she boasted. "They should really come in handy."

"Excellent," said Lucas. "In that case, we just might have a plan."

9

Once everything had been prepared, Libertas began what it called Operation Nona. Split up into pairs, they took positions under nightfall, ready to make a change. Though the teams were separated physically, their minds remained in sync, as the Subverse now afforded them a modest means of contact.

"I'd feel better if we had some way of testing these credentials," Ross mentioned as he and Carrie approached the Capstone entrance.

"My forgeries are solid," she snapped at him. "As long as the mystery contact gave us valid POD IDs, we have nothing else to worry about."

"*Nothing*? That's more than optimistic."

"Fair enough, but in spite of all that might go wrong, you'd be well advised to trust my work."

"Tweaking our facial models to match some photos is more art than science," he opined. "You really think it'll be convincing?"

"To human eyes," she answered confidently. "Stay away from biometric scanners, though; it's only a hologram, after all. Provided that we're out before the juice runs dry, nobody will recognize us."

"Yeah," Ross acknowledged. "You really couldn't make it any longer? It's not like we needed another ticking clock."

Carrie became defensive once again. "I used the largest battery I could. You didn't want a brick hanging off your neck, did you? The whole point is to be discreet."

"I realize that, but it won't mean much if they shut down halfway through."

"Look, I may not be an official fugitive, but they want me dead all the same — if not more — so I appreciate your concern."

"I didn't mean to suggest you weren't also taking a substantial risk," Ross clarified. "I know we're in this together."

Neither having any more to say, they remained in awkward silence, waiting for their cue.

«go,» Lucas promptly signaled, and so began the countdown.

Taking in deep breaths, the two stepped through the doors, collectively exhaling as they made it past security.

Disguised as Vanguard officers, the others entered straight into the Pillar of the Sky, a massive central obelisk and seat of High Command. Even in the dead of night, it bustled with activity, helping to maintain control within an iron grip. Fortunately, nobody paid them much attention as they headed toward the top.

"You're thinking about Capstone, aren't you?" asked Lucas, remembering their argument.

"I still say it would have made more sense to have me there," insisted Victor. "I was supposed to be on duty, anyway."

"Which is why they would have noticed if you'd up and left your post. Besides, you're the only one of us who's been through here before. You know this plan is the way to go."

"If you say so."

"Look," said Lucas earnestly, "I promised you Rinehart would pay for what he's done, but there's far too much at stake tonight."

Victor turned abruptly to respond. "You think I'd jeopardize the mission for a personal vendetta?"

"Of course not," Lucas reassured. "I just don't want you to have regrets. When the time is right, a reckoning will come. You have my word on that."

After curtly nodding, Victor brought his focus back.

"So many memories," Carrie muttered as they walked the mostly empty halls.

"Any good ones?" Ross inquired.

"There were — until I learned what I was really doing. Now all I can think about is how much better it would be if I never had existed."

Ross recalled his own career, finding it rather easy to commiserate. "You're not alone," he stated. "I've caused my share of harm, as well."

"At least you can say you acted with the best intentions," she countered. "All too often, I never bothered to consider the implications right in front of me."

"None of us could have known what was really going on."

"*I* should have," Carrie stressed, "and in the end, even if a medical license could have afforded the same destruction, you can still point to one life saved for each one lost."

"Not as many as you'd think," he admitted to her glumly.

Soon, they reached the Zen production facility and, once covertly inside, scrambled to their respective goals, Carrie logging in to the nearest computer and Ross heading for the vats of chemicals.

Without any major issues gaining access, Carrie wirelessly transferred the payload from her POD. "All right, my worm's inside their network," she reported. "Now I should be able to redirect the waste flow to the sewers, where it belongs."

"And you're sure that nobody will notice?"

"It's a mostly automated system, so not for quite some time, once I spoof the onboard sensors and diagnostic checks. They shouldn't get suspicious until people start to think more clearly, and if everything goes as planned, they'll have bigger problems to worry about by then."

Ross nodded with enthusiasm and, after a few moments more of searching, identified the label for his task. "Here we go," he noted. "This should be the precursor — I'd say at least a month's worth."

"And you're still sure that altering a key ingredient won't change the appearance or something?"

"Not entirely, but anything visible would be masked when it's encapsulated. Another credit to automation, I suppose." He knelt down before the vat, but then he quickly froze.

"What's wrong?" asked Carrie, becoming aware of his untimely hesitation.

"I can't help but feel a tad hypocritical," Ross confessed. "All the tough days it got me through, and now we're just taking it away from everyone on their behalf. Is that really fair of us?"

"*That's* how you see the ethics of the matter?"

"I was just wondering . . . Even if they knew the real cost, how many do you think would make the same call?"

"Well, right now, we're the only ones in a position to make it," she answered frankly, "and I don't think philosophizing will bring us any closer to giving them that option. Detoxing might be rough, but you can't deny they'll be better off in the end."

"Fair enough," he conceded.

"Besides," Carrie added, sensing Ross's continued rumination, "they say over half a drug's effect is placebo, so who's to say they won't be able to have their cake and eat it, too?"

"That's a good point," Ross considered, clearly more at ease. "Even if that's not the case, they'll have plenty to be happy about once they understand their true potential."

"We can only hope."

Holding a vial of water in one hand, Ross moved aether through it so as to copy the subtle signature, which he then projected into the larger vat. Slowly but surely, his energy spread to fill the whole container, soundly reconfiguring its contents.

"That should do it," he confirmed, sampling a cautious whiff of the now inert reagent.

"Then, what say we get the hell out of here?" Carrie pressed.

"Right behind you."

Across the city, Lucas and Victor had smoothly infiltrated the Pillar's comm center, where they now stood within its mobile switching station amid machinery to retrofit.

Wishing he could smash it all to pieces, Victor had to recognize the ultimate futility, for a total outage would no doubt get them caught before they'd even left the room. Even disabling their drones or weapons would make no lasting difference.

Although not fully comprehending sympathetic resonance or Schumann oscillators, he could plainly see the changes in their blood samples, assured the plan was more than theory.

Trusting in the savvy craft of his more educated cohorts, Victor chose the smarter play, passing many rows of servers to find the base transceiver unit.

Lucas, meanwhile, now with superuser access to a nearby terminal, cycled through the various root-level settings: Diagnostics, Perimeter Defenses, Personnel, Security Status, and finally System Logs.

Discovering his designated target, Victor withdrew Carrie's biomod, a flat pentagonal device with rounded corners, then opened the cabinet door to install it.

"Shit," he said, examining the unexpected setup.

"Problem?" Lucas called.

"The ports don't match," Victor answered. "Looks like they've upgraded recently."

"Is that something you can handle?"

"I'm no engineer, but I'll see what I can do."

After a brief assessment, Victor drew his knife to carefully strip the cable on the biomod, then removed the obsolete adapter while making careful note of the wire sequence.

Next, he grabbed one of the live connectors and channeled his awareness into it, hoping to avoid any signal interference. In his other hand, he steadily manifested a perfect match.

Once finished, he attached the new part to their gadget, sure to maintain the wire layout, then hooked it up to the appropriate component.

"We're good to go," he reported. "The lights are flashing, so it should be working."

"Nicely done," said Lucas.

Ensuring that the biomod was well concealed, Victor closed the cabinet and went to join his friend.

Having received a go-ahead from Ross, Lucas checked the clock, noting little time to spare before their coming deadline.

After capitalizing fully on such access to their systems, which involved the planting of his own worm, he concluded with a cleanup, surgically erasing every record of their presence.

Soon thereafter, he nodded that success to Victor, and the duo took their leave.

«heading back,» Lucas conveyed to the other pair. «mission accomplished.»

10

Days passed, then weeks, and after a full month of waiting, the fledgling resistance had to painfully accept that their grand uprising was not forthcoming.

"Nothing," said Carrie bluntly, "unless you count the rise in hospitalizations."

"It could be just a Herx reaction," suggested Ross. "The body needs its time to heal."

"Even if that's the case, it's hard to feel like we accomplished anything."

"You saw the biomarkers," he reminded. "Those changes are more than wishful thinking. Clearly, *something* is happening; I think we just overestimated the implications."

"Does any of it matter with the Curtain always running?"

"I'm sure more time is needed for any impact to be made," considered Lucas, "but by then all of our efforts will no doubt be undone. That likely goes for future actions we might take, as well."

"So, what's the solution, then?" asked Victor.

"We need to strike them at the top."

"I thought we ruled out targeting Executors?"

"I'm not talking about them," Lucas clarified, "since they'd only be replaced without disrupting much. To free ourselves for good, we need to take out Xul, the hydra's immortal head."

"You think that would be easier?" Ross questioned in bewilderment.

"Not by any means, but given our limited resources, it would be the most efficient move."

"Assuming we could pull it off," said Victor, "how does that deal with the ones who do his bidding?"

"Xul is the mastermind — the Architect. Everything they've done here has been by his design. Without him, the system falls apart."

"But if his agents can be replaced, couldn't he be, too?"

"There are no others like him," answered Lucas. "I've been reliably assured of that."

"And everything else just works out in the end?" asked Carrie.

"Once he's gone, we shut the Curtain down, and the public will awaken. Without any backing, the powers here will crumble."

They entertained the gravity of his proposal.

"Aren't there about a billion miles of space between us?" Carrie noted. "That seems like quite the trip."

"Which is why we wouldn't fly," acknowledged Lucas. "Thanks to a process they call Subverse tunneling, matter can be converted into analog data, passed through a quantum bridge, and then reformed on the other side in seconds."

"So, . . . teleportation?" she inferred.

"Basically," he granted. "The technology drives not only their communications but an interplanetary gateway network."

"Where do we find an access point?" asked Victor.

"There's an outpost in Antarctica, but getting out of the city would be challenging enough. That means our only option is the one deep under Capstone."

"Why would it be there?"

"Mostly to exchange research materials across their various facilities."

Carrie brooded with annoyance. "Is that where all my labor went?"

"It's very likely," answered Lucas. "Of course, the area is pretty well guarded, so we'll need a bolder approach this time."

"What does that involve?" asked a nervous Ross.

"Precise coordination, which means I'll have to travel through alone."

Carrie scoffed at the idea. "You plan to face him by yourself?"

"My contact will be waiting once I get there."

"And you're sure that you can trust her?" Victor wondered.

"She hasn't faltered yet," said Lucas in defense, "and when it comes to stopping Xul, her motive is undeniable."

"So, you really think we have a shot?" Ross inquired hopefully.

"The strategy entails a rather monumental risk, and the only way it works is with absolute commitment. That's why I'd never ask this of you if I saw another way, but if anyone objects, I'd fully understand."

A heavy silence lingered as everyone reflected.

Victor was first to speak. "If this is what it takes, I'd rather die than live a coward."

"I'd be dead without you anyway," Ross added, "and the city deserves its freedom."

Their eyes then turned to Carrie.

"Compared to my life before," she considered, "it's not the worst fate I can fathom. Let's do the best we can, no matter what the cost."

Lucas beamed with pride. "Okay, then," he concluded, "let's get right to work."

11

From a distant vantage point, Lucas watched as flames engulfed the Temple, thus markedly commencing Operation Decima. On any other night, it would only be another 'senseless act of terror' to galvanize the public, but he expected this to soon permit a far more lasting victory.

Such brazen desecration would, of course, enhance the faith of many, which is why success was needed here and now, no matter what the cost. They had to break the cycle and tear the lies apart, laying the foundation for a brighter future.

Nearly at his target, he focused on their daunting mission. Decades of hardship he distilled into a single charge, where all the trials and tribulations would finally count for something.

Whether more would rally under his banner of truth and freedom, there certainly was doubt, but he stayed committed to opening the gates for any who might accept the call. If nothing else, Marlowe proved the embers of hope still burned inside their hearts, so now was the time to enkindle that desire into an inextinguishable fervor.

«nice work, ross. are you in position, carrie?»

«ready on your signal,» she confirmed.

«then, let's begin.»

Lucas joined with Victor, stepping boldly through the doors of Capstone. He couldn't help but appreciate the irony after fighting so hard to escape it.

The high director sat behind his desk with a usual drink in hand. After a busy day like any other, he hardly expected to be disturbed by the distant sounds of gunfire — or the alarms that promptly followed.

For some odd reason, security personnel could not be contacted, so he checked the CCTV feed, finding many of the cameras now offline.

Before he had much time to think, however, a guard burst through his doors, shouting, "Director Rinehart, we're under heavy attack!"

"By whom?"

"It's unclear, but they seem to be well trained. They're advancing quickly through the building, and we can't do much to slow them down. We need to evacuate now."

"Out of the question," said Rinehart firmly. "Alert the Vanguard for reinforcements."

"We have, sir, but they're dealing with a situation of their own. Apparently, we're not the only target."

"What could be more important than protecting our research here? Kindly advise the commander to reassess priorities."

"Yes, sir." The guard reached for his POD, but he couldn't send a message. "They must be jamming us. We'll have to hold them off right here."

"I'm not waiting around to be slaughtered like an animal," spat the high director.

"With respect, sir, I don't see another option."

Rinehart paced his office while working out a plan, but his own POD flashed a message, which stopped him in his tracks. "Impossible." He stared in horror at the notice, sheer panic washing over him.

"Sir?"

"The Dark Sector's been compromised!"

"The what?"

"How the hell would they even know about it, much less gain access?" wondered Rinehart, ignoring the guard's confusion.

"They seem to be quite capable."

Rinehart hurried to his desk, where he pressed a button underneath.

Consequently, the watchful marble owl went moving with its bookcase, which parted to reveal a private elevator.

"You're coming with me," Rinehart ordered after fumbling for a pistol.

"To the Dark Sector?"

"That's right."

"Sir, are you sure that's wise. We need to—"

"The only thing that matters is protecting what's down there," Rinehart interjected as he opened the elevator door. "If they get their hands on it, death will be the least of my concerns."

Once inside, Rinehart withdrew a card and swiped it on a strip. A series of sweeping lasers then projected across his face.

"High Director Ceros Rinehart," he stated clearly.

A keypad next appeared, and he swiftly entered his authorization code.

"Executive clearance approved," a voice confirmed, and the elevator began its descent.

"We must secure the area at any cost, but avoid collateral damage if you can."

"Understood."

"And above all else," Rinehart stressed, "only target human threats."

"What other kind would there be?" asked the guard, but his question went ignored.

Finally, their ride came to a steady halt, the door then opened, and they both were met with stillness.

Profusely sweating, Rinehart stepped into the low-lit hallway, his lone companion close behind.

The two moved expeditiously, approaching the foremost laboratory.

At the entrance, the director pressed his hand against a panel. Access was approved, a few short breaths were taken, and into the room they charged.

Rinehart waved his gun around, aiming for intruders.

Looking back were eyes of deep obsidian, annoyed at the disturbance, for with experiments underway, those attending worked intently. They matched the dismal atmosphere, thanks to their gray and scaly skin. Of concern was not their presence, though, but that all appeared in order.

"Director," growled the nearest one, "we were not expecting you this evening. Is anything . . . amiss?"

As he struggled to assimilate the uneventful scene, Rinehart fell unconscious by a sharp blow from behind.

Before the others could react, a concussive sonic charge erupted, followed by a spray of blaster fire that slayed them all in seconds.

The guard then crossed the broken glass and bodies on the floor, scanning for survivors.

«i'm in,» Lucas finally reported, deactivating his NOVA mask. «everyone head back.»

He walked along a sturdy railing, stopping briefly to glance over at the sewage waters rushing below. How much of that filth would the city soon be drinking once again? He quickly moved away, trying to ignore the disgusting thought.

Thanks to their concerted efforts, Lucas arrived at his objective: a spanning arch atop a metal dais. After initializing the terminal beside it, he input the destination. The request was then transmitted, and he awaited a response.

The gateway shortly activated, beckoning him forward with an eerie glow.

Appreciating the weight upon his shoulders, he stepped boldly up the platform, ready for whatever might be waiting.

Once the timer finished counting, a translucent barrier encased him. The chamber then emitted whirring noises, and he became enshrouded by a veil of prismatic light.

With a remarkably bizarre sensation, everything disappeared.

12

Reconstituted on the gateway's other side, Lucas descended from its platform, coming face to face at last with his shadowy informant. The energy she gave him proved a welcome change indeed, and, judging by the sparkle in her eyes, such sentiment was mutual.

Even so, he hadn't quite anticipated their passionate embrace, which inspired further confidence in the strength of them together. Yet despite the concrete presence she now bore, her fragrance elicited almost mystical impressions, as it wasn't anything he recognized from a city in the sky.

"It's hard to believe we've never truly touched before," said Lucas as they parted.

Nevara smiled faintly, though his words had clearly troubled her. "If our plan succeeds tonight, there should be plenty more to come."

"All the more reason to survive," he said, getting down to business. "Speaking of which, how long before they're on to us?"

"The security disruptions will be discovered soon, so time is not our friend."

"Then, by all means, lead the way."

"First, I ought to give you this," she added, presenting him a dagger made of bone that curved inward like a talon.

Unsheathing it with reverence, he felt a strangely deep connection to the primitive aesthetic.

"It once belonged to a legendary warrior," she elaborated.

Lucas nodded, understanding readily. "The last to battle Xul."

"I thought it would be appropriate as we finish what he couldn't."

"I'll do my best to honor him," Lucas promised, securing the blade behind his back.

They proceeded through the immense facility, careful to remain unseen.

With his longtime goal now coming true, could he accept it as reality? So much about the recent past still seemed impossible, especially how all of this began in earnest, the moment when they met outside his dreams . . .

Time had little meaning in the hell where Lucas found himself. This untold land of darkness proved relatively barren, aside from eldritch forms that would arise and fall at random. Accompanied only by these phantoms and many haunting memories, Lucas wandered hopelessly across his wretched world, suspecting that the ever-creeping madness could not be stalled forever.

Brooding through his torment, Lucas one day met a visitor. Though emerging from the shadows, her origin lay elsewhere. With flowing void-spun hair and amethystine eyes, she bore a certain mysticism suited to the realm of dreamland. Did such beauty serve to mock him, or was it more than just a nightmare?

"In spite of all this grief, do you remember who you are?" she wondered.

"Lucas Corvin," he replied. *"I know that much for now."*

Her face grew rather somber, but she continued to approach. *"You fought against their tyranny,"* she noted, *"searching for some higher life along the way."*

"Fate had other plans," Lucas bitterly remarked.

"Why should that stop you," she countered, *"when your will is so much stronger?"*

"It hardly seemed to matter with so few options left."

"A phoenix rises from the ashes after going up in flames." Her youthful countenance belied a timeless wisdom and conviction. *"If you change your bleak perspective, I can show another way."*

"And who are you to bring me such an offer?"

"My name is Nevara, . . . biologically the progeny of Xul."

"Yet you came so far to help me?" he asked in disbelief.

"Don't hate me for my father; I seek the same as you."

"Well, who am I to judge?" said Lucas. *"But what is it you want?"*

"An end to the enslavement, which spans further than you realize. Together, I believe we have a chance to break the cycle."

"That might be expecting too much of me."

"We both know what lies inside you, but the true test is one's resolve. It's encouraging that, despite such unfavorable conditions, your being remains intact, memories and all."

"I remember only failure," he considered, *"and those who let it happen."*

"You must learn to forgive them."

"They're the reason for my hell!"

"Is that where you think we are?" she asked him.

"What else could it be?"

79

"Neuro-ocular virtualization and augmentation," she *cryptically responded.*

He felt around his temple. "Yeah, what about it?"

"Those portable omnifunctional devices are but a taste of its potential. The world in which we're standing is a product of your mind."

"I created this?" Lucas looked around in horror.

"'Populated' would be more accurate," Nevara clarified.

"Then, how can you be here?"

"My position grants me certain access, though I'm limited on time."

"Can you change the simulation?" he inquired.

"Not without alerting Xul."

"So, what is to be done?"

"Continue to endure," she ordered, "and prepare to fight again."

They navigated quietly thus far, but the halls were long and winding, so anything could change that.

"How big is this place?" Lucas had to ask.

"Several times the size of your entire planet," replied Nevara.

"Now, that's what I call a megastructure. It must have taken quite some time to build."

"Once you solve the obstacle of aging, time is all you have."

"And what do they need with so much space?"

"Xul keeps many projects to himself, especially from me. I shudder to think what he might have done by now with the full potential of this facility."

"What do you mean?"

"He and the Elarch have had . . . disagreements in the past," she explained, "so to rein in his ambitions, Velroth set restrictions."

"Still, for the size alone," considered Lucas, "I'd expect more of a colony."

"They keep their numbers well in check, owing to the price of immortality. Thanks to technological supremacy, fewer boots can run an empire. Also, without the looming fear of death, they don't need offspring to secure a legacy."

"Is conquest really all they value?"

"It certainly consumes them."

They rounded yet another corner, hitting the first outstanding roadblock: a lone technician loitering near a laboratory door.

"Shouldn't they all be gone by now?" Lucas whispered.

"Honestly, I'm surprised there aren't more."

"Well, we don't have time to wait around politely." With open palms extended, he shaped an aether javelin of indigo.

She took a glance in both directions and nodded her approval.

"Then, after you, my dear," he playfully suggested.

Nevara smiled again before walking onward to get into position.

The Anakhari greeted her with relative surprise, and when she came to pass him, he turned his back to Lucas.

In response to light then piercing through his chest, she conjured violet blades to finish him.

Thus did they remain clandestine, with others none the wiser.

"We make a worthy team," Lucas granted as they quickly hid the body.

"I should hope so," said Nevara, "because this fight is far from over."

As they pressed toward their target, her long hair flowed beside him, adding substance to his dream, for though they'd been so close in spirit, their bodies were only just united.

Even more surreal, her proficient use of genomancy left Lucas quite impressed, evoking thoughts of way back when she first instructed him . . .

"Will this power be enough to stop them?" Lucas asked with skepticism.

"Yes," assured Nevara, "but not without a wider understanding of it. Those applications more familiar to you, while effective in the proper context, barely represent a sliver of the Subverse."

"What exactly is the Subverse?"

"That which underpins existence — the primordial canvas of life," Nevara spoke profoundly. "To draw forth and transform its latent energies grants the power of creation. With it, you will have the means to undo all the damage brought upon your world."

"So, how do I control it?" Lucas asked intently.

"Start by expanding your awareness and narrowing your focus," she instructed. "Banish from your heart all uncertainty and fear, and recognize intention as by far your greatest weapon."

To demonstrate, she unleashed a violet orb of energy from her open hand.

"What the hell are you doing?!" shouted Lucas as he dodged it.

"Training you," she answered bluntly. "Aether can be channeled into matter, but it's also rather potent in the raw. Though not requiring the same finesse, it has a higher chance of causing spiritual exertion, especially when casting. There is, of course, a spectrum of infinite variety."

"*Well, what am I supposed to do?*"

"*Reflexes are valuable, but they only help so much,*" Nevara cautioned. "*Without the balance of a wakened mind, you'll meet with certain death.*"

"*Then, how do I block an attack like that?*"

"*I already told you: focus your intent.*"

"*What about technique?*" asked Lucas. "*It can't just be that simple.*"

"*Why jump straight to such complexities? You must first identify the spark of genomancy deep within. For now, merely trust the process, and soon, the rest will follow.*"

Another blast flew toward him, so Lucas held his hand straight out as if commanding it to stop. His effort made no difference, though, and he slammed into the ground.

"*It didn't work,*" he snapped, getting hastily to his feet.

"*Of course not,*" said Nevara. "*I told you not to fear.*"

Lucas glared in protest. "*I wasn't—*"

"*I saw it in your eyes,*" she countered. "*Your spirit froze, if only for a moment.*"

"*Fine,*" he begrudgingly conceded, "*let's try that again.*"

For the third attempt, however, Lucas ducked in haste.

"*Coward,*" she responded. "*You doubt your own ability.*"

He grew even more annoyed. "*How can I resolve that?*"

Nevara stared impassively. "*Take a leap of faith.*"

"*Faith?*" he scoffed. "*You mean like—*"

"*In yourself. That's what remains when all else fades, because no matter what, your final voyage will be made alone, and without commitment at the deepest level, prepare to lose everything you are.*"

Lucas shook his head. "*And here I always thought that death would bring me peace.*"

"*Ignorance is a blindfold, not a shield,*" said Nevara. "*If you wish to stand against the inevitable, you must embrace the truth wholeheartedly.*"

"I know," he readily accepted. "I've never shied away from that."

"Prove it, then."

A globe again flew toward him, but with intense determination in his eyes, Lucas raised his hand, sending a ripple through the air. As the energy scattered around him, he filled with awe and courage.

"How did I do that?"

"You don't ask how you walk," Nevara pointed out. "It's really not much different."

"So, how do I improve?"

"How did you learn to run?"

Lucas reflected. "I couldn't do any of this before," he noted, "but not for lack of trying. There has to be something more — something I was missing."

"You were held back by many factors, both natural and contrived. A limited awareness, bounded by the senses, had filtered all experiences to prevent true awakening."

"Then, what's the point of training here? Even if I can escape, will any of this matter?"

"Don't expect to be returning as you were," she informed him. "Once perceived, the hidden can't be so easily forgotten."

"What about my body?" Lucas wondered. "If it doesn't adapt—"

"Consciousness transcends all else. In time, you'll see the changes propagate."

"But will I have a chance to make it count? What are the odds of getting all the way to Xul?"

"I'll do everything I can, Nevara promised, "but you must have greater foresight. The road ahead is long, and it calls for more than vengeance."

He nodded pensively. "If you believe that path exists, then count on me to do what must be done."

* * *

Sneaking along a spanning hallway window, Lucas finally had a chance to glance out into the raging hexadic storm.

"The Black Sun," he uttered, marveling at the scene. "Too bad we can't see the rings from here. I bet they're something to behold."

"That's putting it mildly," replied Nevara. "His ingenuity is not to be underestimated."

"And there's nothing to be done about them?" Lucas wondered. "If we could disable the Curtain at its source—"

"Sabotage on such a scale would be too readily discovered," she had to interject, "and inconsequential while Xul is still alive. Once he's been removed, there'll be plenty of time to dismantle all his handiwork, starting with that huge antenna."

"Will it really be that easy?"

"Without his careful guidance, they will quickly lose control. Velroth can appoint another, but I'm confident that there's no suitable replacement."

"Even so," reminded Lucas, "the Elarch is sure to intervene directly, and though lacking in Xul's intellect, he does have quite an army."

"Once humanity is freed, we'll deal with the rest," she promised. "The Mechagen incursion has spread their forces thin, so they've never been more vulnerable."

"I hope you're right," considered Lucas. "How far left to go?"

"His private lab is just ahead."

"You're sure that's where we'll find him?"

"He spends nearly all his time in there. Tonight is no exception."

They soon advanced along a different corridor, flanked throughout by strange containers, and preserved inside among this gruesome gallery were distorted specimens, all disturbingly humanoid to varying degrees.

"The methods of his madness," Nevara noted grimly.

"To accomplish what, exactly?" Lucas asked her, pausing briefly to examine one.

"Hybridization," she replied. "Xul's been trying for millennia, but much to his dismay, it seems that nature can't be rushed."

"Then, all this byzantine manipulation — it really was the only way?"

Nevara nodded solemnly. "Their greatest obsession has been harnessing the Subverse. With unmitigated access, there's no telling what they'll do. You already know the horrors they've committed, and many more will follow."

Preferring not to dwell upon the recent qualifying misery, Lucas redirected his attention, instead recalling the dark agenda's far more distant origins . . .

Years passed in the tenebrous domain, which may have only reflected months back in the waking world. The trials Lucas endured by no means lessened, but he overcame them with the passion of a man driven by destiny.

Nevara visited whenever she could, imparting her wealth of knowledge and expertise. Lucas learned with remarkable ease, and so the time had come, she finally determined, to tell him the painful truth.

"Long ago, I told you of my lineage," Nevara prefaced, "but I never explained the origins."

"There's more to it than being Xul's daughter?"

"My birth was but a means to an end."

"How so?"

"The Anakhari's use of genomancy relies on artificial methods, and the lack of inborn faculties has always been their greatest shame. When they came across your distant ancestors, it seemed as though they'd found the answer."

"So, where do you come in?"

"Xul created me to gain their trust — to study them in ways he couldn't. As a being of hybrid form, I was able to help explore the compatibility of their genetics."

"And it worked?"

"All too well," she mournfully confessed. "I hid the full extent of my abilities, but he ascertained enough, and once he had his proof of concept, he sought a living specimen. Since I had grown close to a worthy candidate, Xul demanded I deliver him."

"Did you?"

She slowly shook her head. "I warned them all instead, but the damage had been done. They spared my life but could not forgive my betrayal. With nowhere else to go, I returned to Xul, failing in my mission. Elarch Velroth feared the power of the Zephyrans, especially as the Revelation neared, so he put an end to the experiment. In desperation, Xul made one last bid to get his target."

"But he didn't win," concluded Lucas.

"Not entirely," confirmed Nevara, "but the Zephyrans lost far worse. Their bravest champion led the final stand, hoping to secure an exodus."

"To where?"

"No one can be sure," Nevara pondered. "They believed the Revelation would allow for their ascension, but after Velroth ordered global inundation, little evidence remained to study. All we know is that they simply disappeared."

"You think they're gone for good?"

"Xul would disagree," she answered. "He believes they still exist, and these higher-form Stellarans, as he calls them, are enough to convince him of what the Subverse might achieve. That's why he's prepared to stake everything on his research."

"And what do you believe?"

"Although I can't explain it, there is a faint connection. Perhaps it's just my guilt, but I feel they still are out there."

"They might be valuable allies in our cause," suggested Lucas.

"Indeed, they would be," said Nevara, "but I doubt they'd accept my invitation. Even if they did, I'm sure the Curtain would be an issue for them."

"How many could there be?"

"That I cannot say," she considered. "Those who stayed to fight chose death instead of capture, knowing the dire consequences if Xul were to succeed."

"Even with their DNA, he couldn't find the key to genomancy?"

"Laboratory efforts failed, so he let nature take its course . . . to the extent that was required. After wiping the planet clean, he engineered the genesis of man, and his tendrils have pervaded every facet of society."

Lucas reflected on the epic tale.

"If only we had another champion," he smiled softly.

Instinctively, Nevara reached toward her upper chest, stopping abruptly once aware.

"Did you really see the same in me?" Lucas wondered.

"More than I can say," replied Nevara.

She smiled faintly, too, but a sadness lingered in her eyes. Lucas knew she held back more, but for now, he simply enjoyed her company.

13

"Well, here we are," Nevara finally proclaimed. "Security is tighter, so we'll need to push aggressively before we cut him down."

"Can we really hold the station by ourselves?" Lucas wondered.

"Once we gain his access to their systems, the rest will be quite simple," Nevara reassured. "Xul will be the real challenge."

"I'm ready, then, if you are."

Nevara turned to Lucas, adopting a somber tone. "Whatever happens next," she whispered, "please forgive them. Forgive *me*."

"I never blamed you," he replied.

She smiled faintly, betraying a hint of guilt. "Just remember what we planned, and everything will work out in the end."

Together, they marched their final gauntlet, unleashing all they had.

Xul's guards contested the intruders, and though struck with blaster bolts and aether, they held their ground quite well — at least until a shock wave knocked them off their feet.

Lucas and Nevara charged, projecting burning blades of light, which proved remarkably effective at striking down their targets.

Once the obstacles were slain, they motioned for his lab, but before they could proceed, two more arrived behind them.

Taken by surprise, they could barely shield the barrage, but Lucas grabbed a fallen rifle, piercing through their armor.

After they were dealt with, he glanced back at Nevara, only to find her lying on the floor.

Quickly rushing over, he attended to her wound, but as he moved to heal, she grabbed his hands in protest.

"More will come," she warned, "and we need to stop him now."

"I won't let you die like this," he countered. "Just let me try to save you."

"If you don't finish what we started, then all will be for nothing."

Lucas glanced at the heavy metal door. "How do I even get in? Nevara? Nevara!" he shouted, but her consciousness already faded.

He had prepared himself to face the worst, but with it now before him, what was to be done? Just as promised long ago, she brought him to the heart of darkness, which rested in his hands. The choice, at last, was his to make and his alone.

Resolute, he rose, approaching the door to make a declaration. "I think it's time we met," he stated, sure that he was watched.

The path ahead soon opened, and inside stood the Architect, leaning against a workbench as the human promptly entered.

Wearing sleeveless robes of ivory as he waited with amusement, Xul had more than one distinction prominently visible.

His haggard form connoted age beyond the others just encountered, and the mechanized life-supports across his chest only heightened that impression.

Most notable, however, was the artificial limb, evidently packed with advanced abilities, given the display upon his forearm.

"I can easily surmise her purpose in coming here," Xul responded with a calm, ethereal supremacy, "but yours is more equivocal, I suspect."

Lucas blinked, but silent he remained, choosing his words carefully.

"She really did believe in you," Xul continued, "but I know better than one so blinded by emotion and self-righteousness. Fortunately for you, I am a man of practicality and reason."

Lucas couldn't help but scan the curiosities in view. Among them was a rack of loaded vials, which held viscous pewter fluid that almost seemed alive.

Nearby sat two creepy jars, housing side by side a jet-black eyeball and a twitching dusky hand. Both were cybernetically infused, though their Anakhari essence remained apparent.

"Clearly," Lucas noted, "but I came here with a job to do."

"Well, then? You've made it this far." Xul made a sweeping gesture. "Hardly a throne room, but if need be, I'm sure we can find some place more befitting a final showdown."

Lucas didn't move. "But that was her plan, . . . not mine," he revealed with dramatic weight, staring pointedly at Xul.

Though hidden behind another cold appendage, the viceroy's mouth betrayed a telling smirk. "If that really is the case," he said, "I wonder what might yours be?"

"I trust that you're a man of reason," Lucas granted, "so I doubt you'd go through all this trouble needlessly. You must be proud of just how far you've come, despite the tremendous cost."

"Means to an end," said Xul dismissively, "but the results are undeniable."

"And you're rather close to that end, aren't you?" asked Lucas.

"Is that what my daughter told you?"

"It was obvious enough," concluded Lucas, "based on the escalation of your strategy: the Blight, the Havens, revealing your involvement. To some, these might be signs of desperation, but I tend to think they were calculated measures. Not much remains of Earth, after all, so the grand finale must be near."

"Very astute of you."

"Then, perhaps you'd want to improve your chances?" suggested Lucas.

"Go on," said Xul, impassively studying the man before him.

"I've already proven what can be accomplished with a ragtag band of rebels. Imagine what further damage could be done, should the movement be allowed to grow. Humans are a stubborn lot, and other malcontents will soon arise, under the banner of Libertas or not."

"Might you, then, present me a solution?" asked the Architect, genuinely intrigued.

"Put their fate in my hands, and I'll make your vision a reality."

"And what about your friends? I doubt they'd be amenable."

"Indeed, they pose a threat," said Lucas. "Do with them what you will."

Xul considered for a moment. "So quick to turn on those who swore their lives to you? Understand why I might have some reservations."

"They were my own means to an end, so if you think I'd shed a tear for them, you'd sorely be mistaken. If your concern is in my loyalty, however, you know I couldn't possibly succeed without support from you."

"Your words fail to entice me."

"I disagree," said Lucas, boldly undeterred. "You could have killed me long ago, so you must have thought I held some value. If I had to take a guess, you're after my genetics."

A stir gave confirmation.

"Accept this offer," Lucas vowed, "and you'll have my full cooperation."

Xul certainly was curious. "And what is *your* prize in this arrangement?" he inquired.

"While apotheosis might entice me," admitted Lucas, "it would be rather foolish to expect an equal share. Fortunately, the only recompense I seek is having justice realized."

"How pragmatic," Xul observed. "You're quite unlike your kind."

"So I've come to learn," said Lucas.

"No doubt she underestimated you."

Lucas reflected silently, unable to argue against the notion.

"It appears, then, that there's no one better to oversee my enterprise. Consider their fate now yours."

* * *

Ready for his bold return, Lucas had a final meeting with Nevara in the confines of his prison world.

"Now that it's all becoming real, do you still believe in our chances?" he asked about their current outlook. "I mean, it's only just the two of us against their entire system."

"We may not have the numbers now," she acknowledged, "but there are soldiers out there waiting for the call."

"Do you really think they'll answer?" Lucas wondered cynically, remembering his past.

"They may need time to understand," she warned, "so you must have proper patience."

He reflected on the challenge. "It won't be easy without you there."

"We still will be connected," she reassured herself as much as him, "so you shouldn't have to feel that alone again."

He smiled back emphatically, but her apprehension gave him pause. "You still blame yourself, I sense," he broke the heavy silence.

"How can I not?" she answered woefully. "I gave Xul total confidence to execute his plan, betraying both sides in the process, and in the end brought only death."

"You did everything you could," he stressed, attempting to console her.

"That doesn't change the past," maintained Nevara. "Nothing ever will."

"Then, we'll have to right the present . . . and shape the future as we can."

Cautiously inspired, she forced a smile of her own. "One can only hope."

"I'll make it a reality," promised Lucas, "just you wait and see."

After bidding a warm farewell, Nevara left to take position.

Shifting focus carefully, Lucas felt the other side, and as he reached on over with awareness, vibrations rang throughout his body.

Moments later, he was gone.

PART TWO

14

Long ago, on the banks of the Rubicon, a troubled man paced methodically about his tent, shrewdly weighing his options at this momentous crossroads. Meanwhile, Nevara's floating shade lurked among the darkness, beyond the torchlight and perception of unexpected callers.

"The decree is clear:" — he motioned toward the scroll upon his desk — "I am to disband my forces and return home immediately. Any deviation would undoubtedly be deemed insubordinate and treasonous, if not outright casus belli."

Nevara considered the implications. "And without the immunity of your position," she inferred, "they may seize the opportunity to strike against you."

"Of that I have no doubt," he agreed, "but what is the alternative? Compliance would surely mean the end to our endeavor, and if all you say is true, then I fear the Republic may not endure the coming storm."

"I sense a tide is now upon us," she said portentously, reflecting further. "Rarely in the grander scheme are men given a chance to become the masters of their fate, but it seems that such a current flows, ready to be taken, if you would be so bold."

99

He pondered the gravity of her words. "I am no coward, for when I taste of death, it shall be but once. Matters of pride notwithstanding, the commonwealth is fragile enough already, making civil war all too likely. Is disintegration of the social order to be my legacy?"

Though the prospect made Nevara dread, it was one of comparative triviality, given the larger stakes at play. "The order and unification needed among these lands can come from no one else," she stressed. "His influence over the Senate grows with each passing day, and his puppets lie eagerly in wait to do his dire bidding."

"Even so, such open defiance would also mean betraying my once trusted friend and ally. How much audacious action can be justified for the greater good?"

The mention of betrayal forced Nevara to recall certain deeply unpleasant memories, which she quickly sought to bury by rallying her conviction. "We cannot afford to lose our venture," she avowed with vigor. "The Demiurge will stop at nothing to achieve his twisted vision, and I assure you that full consolidation can be our only hope of thwarting him." She spoke as though she needed to convince herself, as well. "You alone, one as constant as the Northern Star, possess the august character and force of will necessary to defy a god."

Silently deliberating, he knew her cogent reasoning could not be faulted.

"The initiative is yours to seize," she summarized, "and the 13th Legion stands at your command, . . . Imperator."

"Indeed, your counsel has favored me well thus far, and your wisdom is unimpeachable. Alas, owing to the current affairs of men, I suppose that what will come will come regardless, and as one who can direct its course best of all, what choice do I then have?" After careful consideration, he stated the unavoidable conclusion, "Let the die be cast!"

* * *

Rain continued falling as the Libertas trio awaited news of their endeavor. Though well into the night, sleep was far from consideration, given the stakes involved. Having played their roles, they could only trust in Lucas to make the final stretch.

"I can't take this," Carrie moaned, feverishly pacing their headquarters. "How do we know they're even still alive?"

"Give them a fair chance," Ross reassured. "If anyone could pull it off, . . ."

"That doesn't make it easier to sit around here doing nothing," she snapped.

"It's out of our hands now," Victor stated. "All that we can do is be ready for what comes next."

"Speaking of that," Ross noted, "shouldn't we start reconsidering the insurance policy? I mean, we made it back, right?"

"It's not just insurance for *our* lives," reminded Carrie. "If they fail, I really don't see what other option we have left."

"We're not talking about a resonator anymore. Once you start altering gene expression, you might just cause more damage in the end."

"I agree that it's a bit extreme," reiterated Victor, "but like you said, we need to give the plan a chance."

Ross nodded in concession.

"Besides, we don't wanna be caught on the streets at this hour, especially with the Vanguard out in force."

Back at Capstone offices, Director Rinehart feverishly investigated the unprecedented breach, Commander Draconis working closely with him.

The former, jacket tossed aside and sleeves rolled up, scoured intently through the servers for any trace of evidence. With blame for such a catastrophic blunder falling squarely on his shoulders, he desperately sought hope of earning some redemption, such that not even the throbbing head injury had entered his awareness, fearing far worse might await him at the wrathful hands of Xul.

"It should go without saying that I expect your complete support going forward," spoke the director candidly.

"You mean as it pertains to any forthcoming repercussions?"

"We're in this together, after all."

"Is that how you see it?" Draconis wondered, free from liability. "I was rightly attending to the Temple. With these premises well under your purview, any lapse in security is entirely on you."

Rinehart's panic increased at the unavoidable truth. "Might I remind you that, without me," he sternly countered, "there would be no one to provide your precious antidote. How do you think the Architect might react upon learning your little secret? Or have you truly deluded yourself into believing that a distinguished record is enough to buy forgiveness?"

Draconis glared at him, resentful of the blackmail. "You have my cooperation," he granted nonetheless, unable to refuse, "but surely, you must realize that, once he sets his mind, there is nothing I can do to save you."

"Fair enough," conceded Rinehart. "Just keep his judicar in line."

"Of course," agreed his colleague with a sneer. "Now, regarding our predicament, . . ."

"Right," the director said, attempting to refocus. "Their efficiency suggests a high degree of training, and the attack itself, a zealous motivation."

"I can't argue there."

"It's also worth noting that all on-duty personnel were accounted for, and all were fully clothed."

The commander raised his eyebrows. "Meaning what, exactly?"

"You saw the footage," reminded the director. "He entered the building in that uniform. Where do you suppose he managed to acquire it?"

"It could have been stolen anytime," Draconis noted. "This was clearly orchestrated, as you say."

"Perhaps," considered Rinehart, "but getting into our systems would have taken more than skill. They knew exactly what they were doing — not only shutting us down, but triggering a false alarm from the Dark Sector."

"Then, you're convinced it was an inside job?"

"I just ran a computational analysis of my staff, and two names jumped straight to the top for subversive tendencies. Seems quite plausible, no?"

Draconis checked the monitor. "You may have something there, Director," he acknowledged. "Frankly, though, I'm surprised it took an algorithm to uncover them."

Rinehart glowered at the insult while Draconis promptly dispatched a unit. "Not going to handle it in person?" he asked.

"She's perfectly capable," asserted the commander, "and I'd rather not risk losing our only solid lead."

Soon thereafter, the men were interrupted by calls through both their NOVA PODs. Upon discovering the source, they exchanged looks of great bewilderment.

* * *

High atop the city in a lavish apartment suite, the ringing of a NOVA POD broke through the silent bedroom. After cursing himself awake and learning that it was not to be ignored, the weary owner mustered as much composure as the situation granted. Sliding to the edge of his bed, he answered it through thin lips tightly pursed.

"Speaking."

". . ."

"What the hell does he want at this hour?"

". . ."

"Fine, I'm on my way."

". . ."

"Yes, of course I'll bring it," he irritably confirmed, ending the conversation.

Still venting under his breath, he quickly changed into more appropriate attire.

Before departing, he walked over to the safe concealed behind his bedroom wall and prompted the authentication protocol. "Vice Overseer Anson Pryce," he hoarsely spoke, still groggy from the unforeseen disturbance.

Once its lock had disengaged, he grabbed the most important item, transferred it to his pocket, and headed out the door.

Soon making his way through the narrow streets toward his office, he suddenly paused at the approaching pair who blocked his path.

After abruptly turning, he stared agape at the worst face to be seen in such a context, a face now quite a bit more scarred than usual.

An arm was raised, then a single shot was fired, dropping the official before he could react.

Sevro knelt beside the body and reached into its coat, swiftly locating the object he was after. Stowing it securely, he signaled his associates to proceed with their disposal.

"Job's done," he reported through his POD. "Where do you want it delivered?"

Elsewhere in the shadows, a horde of masked Disciples had surrounded the rotundal city hall, readying their incendiaries. Concurrently, other crews arrived to swarm the Pillar, several hospitals, and other institutions. Vanguard patrols were nowhere to be found, even around their own headquarters, despite the conspicuous presence of surveillance drones nearby.

As coordinated units of chaotic force, the firebrands unleashed their volleys, accomplishing the goal instructed. In no time at all, the city burned, dwarfing fires from the Temple hours earlier. The perpetrators, having served their purpose, fled unimpeded amid the cover of the night.

The authorities would come eventually, of course, but not before sufficient damage had accrued. It was therefore passersby, helpless to respond, who watched the conflagrations roar. Uncertain of the cause, they could only stare in fear. Civilians, both young and old, would be demanding answers to be sure.

Shortly thereafter, more distressing news then made its way to the sanctum of the overseer's private quarters.

Bursting through the door, a pair of guards disturbed his peaceful slumber. "Overseer! Forgive us, but we just received word of an urgent threat to your life."

"What? Now?" he grumbled himself awake.

"Yes, sir. Please, we have to lock down until reinforcements arrive."

Marcus Hardwin wasted no time in rolling his portly frame out of bed and following them closely. "Who's behind this?" he demanded.

"We don't have the details, but we've been assured that it's credible and imminent."

"What's the point of coming after me?" said Hardwin in a panic. "You'd think anyone with the means to do so would know better."

Arriving at the safe room, he briskly rushed inside, leaving his guards posted at the door. "The commander must be losing his grip," he ranted, stopping moments later at the sight of his backward-facing desk chair, clearly not the way he left it.

"Actually, I'd say his grip has never been stronger," mocked an unseen voice, causing the blood to drain even further from his face. "Wouldn't you say so?"

Hardwin wheeled around in horror to realize that he was trapped by his own guards. With no escape, he looked back to the desk, watching as the chair began to turn.

"Good evening, Overseer — well, *Former* Overseer," said the bold intruder.

"You? What the hell is this?" Hardwin blustered.

The young man glared at him, strange burn marks extending from beneath a patch that covered his left eye, and the penetrative cobalt of the other made his visage all the more intense. "Isn't it obvious?" he responded.

Hardwin blankly stared, his face crossed with a mix of rage and terror.

"Revolution," stated Lucas Corvin.

Though still in shock, a sense of indignation rose from within Hardwin, spurring a rebuttal. "You really think Draconis — let alone the Architect — will stand for this insanity?"

Amused, the usurper simply grinned.

Hardwin shook his head with a faltering sneer. "You won't live to see the morning," he threatened, but a wavering inflection belied his false bravado.

Undeterred by empty posturing, Lucas gestured grandly around the room. "How do you think I got this far already?"

"Let's just say they won," Carrie reasoned, continuing her restless motion. "Xul is dead. Now what? Even if they're still alive, there's no guarantee they'll be able to deactivate the Curtain, which leaves us right back where we started. I know I didn't expect everything to come crumbling down overnight, but we have to start thinking about our options."

"We'll figure it out," Victor reassured.

Carrie laughed in sheer exasperation. "That doesn't help. Aren't you even the least bit worried?"

"Until we know more about the situation, obsessive speculation won't do us any good. Just give them time."

"That's really not in my—"

Carrie suddenly halted. Ross lifted his head. Victor snapped from his idle contemplations. Each one had the same expression of concern.

"So, I'm not the only one who felt that," Ross was the first to voice.

"Something's definitely wrong," Carrie surmised.

"We have to move," said Victor, springing to his feet. "Grab whatever gear you can," he ordered.

The trio frantically collected from about the dark apartment.

"Where are we supposed to go?" asked Carrie.

"We can go to my place," suggested Ross.

Before the notion could be further entertained, a blinding light came flooding through the window. Taken by surprise, they stood frozen as the door was subsequently breached.

"Drop your weapons, and get on the ground, all of you!" shouted Vanguard officers entering the room.

Swiftly outnumbered and outmaneuvered, the warriors of Libertas had no choice but to surrender.

With her hungry eyes of jade, Lieutenant Alicen Pryce made a fleeting search before reporting her success. "High Commander," she spoke into her POD, "we have them all in custody. How shall I proceed?"

The three exchanged uneasy glances, anxious to learn their fate.

"Very well," she acknowledged, turning to her men. "We're taking them back to the Pillar."

Before the prisoners could breathe a sigh of relief over their deferred execution, a series of electrical bursts rendered them unconscious.

15

Dressed in stark white robes iconic of the office — his duties represented by the all-seeing eye upon a gilded brooch — Lucas formally addressed the three Executors of Xul, now gathered in his briefing room.

"You are all undoubtedly surprised to see me here, but you have hopefully received sufficient evidence regarding the authority with which I speak."

The others curtly nodded.

"Suffice it to say that my presence should not be viewed as threatening to any of you, now that we serve the same agenda."

"You'll forgive us for distrusting your intentions," the commander stated bluntly, "considering the troublesome insurgency you spearheaded up to an hour ago."

"I simply sought an audience with the Architect," explained Lucas. "As gatekeepers to that end, you stood in my way before, but since that goal has been achieved, I see no reason to maintain hostilities."

"And now that we have apprehended your cohorts, I'm sure you expect their prompt release?" Draconis asked him.

"That doesn't concern me at the moment, though they may still be of some use, so try to keep them intact for now."

"Since you mentioned our history," said Foregrave cautiously, "are we really to believe that you bear no resentment at all against us?"

Lucas watched him with a piercing stare. "Now is not the time for pettiness," he impassively replied. "A new era dawns before us, and if you trust in Xul, there is no need to question my appointment. Besides, you still have a role to play in this, and I wouldn't dream of jeopardizing it. That goes for all of you," he directed at the others.

"And what might that entail, *Overseer*?" Rinehart wondered stiffly.

In response, Lucas placed a metal briefcase on the table, capturing their curiosity with its platinum finish. "I'm so very glad you asked," he said, relishing the buildup.

The setting sun cast a long shadow across Victor's mostly empty apartment. This day was bound to come, so he couldn't be surprised, but that didn't make him any readier to face it. Sitting at the edge of his bed, he held Lenore's hand, knowing the end drew near.

"I always tried to make the world a better place for us," he lamented, "but I didn't expect to fall this short. I thought there would at least be something to show for it by now."

"I know you did your best," she reassured, "but it's never too late to try a different approach."

"What other options could be left?" he asked in deep despair.

"You always had a good heart, Victor, but I hate to see it wasted chasing ideals doomed to fail. If you could only see the potential of the system, flawed as it may be, you could reshape it for the better, instead of trying to burn it to the ground."

Her words weighed heavily on Victor.

"People will always need order of some kind," Lenore continued, "and with the right leadership — someone like you — it can be guided for the better."

Victor considered what she said. "And what happens when I'm no longer there to steer it?"

"Others will follow your example."

He reflected further, spirits not improving.

"Please," she squeezed his hand, "I don't want to leave this world knowing you're headed down such a hopeless path. Give me that peace, at least. Don't you love me enough to promise you won't destroy yourself?"

Tears welling in his eyes, Victor reached behind his back.

"Throughout my long, miserable life, I have never loved another as I do Lenore," he responded.

She smiled, leaning closer.

"Which is how I know you aren't her," he added with a darker tone.

Before she could respond, he raised his gun and fired, unable to watch the deed.

Victor then walked over to the window, staring blankly at the sunset.

After waiting several seconds, he closed his eyes defiantly. "Fine," he said, "I'll end this travesty myself."

With the gun pressed to his temple, he once more pulled the trigger.

* * *

Awaking with an awful headache, Victor found himself confined inside a bland and stuffy room, bound by electromagnetic restraints.

As his vision came into focus, he noticed two guards posted opposite the table that sat before him.

Soon, an interrogator entered, viewing a report he held.

"You sick bastards," Victor noted with disgust. "There's nothing sacred to you, is there?"

The man looked up indifferently. "I provide a valued service, which allows me certain leeway in the details of execution."

Victor glared in silence.

"They usually prove effective, but you are a stubborn one indeed," he confessed, sitting at the table. "But now that the ruse is over, I suppose we could try a more direct approach."

"I'm not begging for your mercy, and if you expect a show in the arena, you'd better kill me now."

"And what a waste that would be, especially with such a record. Tell me, how *does* a man like you fall so far from grace?"

"By having dignity," retorted Victor.

"Be that as it may, your skills, while perhaps underutilized in the past, just might find a place here, after all. The fact you're still alive should give some indication of your worth. For everyone's best interest, you shouldn't be so quick to pass on this opportunity for redemption."

Victor continued glaring. "Whatever happened up there last night," he replied morosely, "I can be damn sure nothing's changed down here, so why would I suddenly be anything to you but a complication?"

The interrogator smirked. "You know, it occurs to me that you probably haven't heard the outcome of your nocturnal escapades. Aren't you the least bit curious?"

"Not really," Victor answered. "Either our mission failed and the powers reign as usual, or Xul is dead, in which case it's only a matter of time before you are, too. Either way, I served my part, and there's nothing left to do about it now."

The smirk became a grin. "If that's the way you see it, then you might be in for a surprise. In any event," he paused before leaving, "you'd be well advised to keep an open mind."

Expecting better luck, the interrogator proceeded next to Carrie's holding cell.

"Welcome back, Miss Hardwin," he announced, her simulation ending. "I hope you were able to gain some valuable perspective."

Carrie looked around, returning to her senses. "Is that what became of NOVA tech?" she bitterly inferred. "I should have known it wouldn't stop at simple 'entertainment'."

"None of it would have been possible without your contributions," he noted.

"You don't have to remind me," she snapped, scowling with regret.

"Nevertheless, it seems that your mind constructed rather powerful scenarios, and I'm here to tell you that they're possible as more than mere illusion."

"Bullshit."

"Well, professional advancement can certainly be arranged, but that other little fantasy . . ." He winked. "You'll have to work it out with *him*."

Carrie averted her eyes, trying not to blush. "Why should I believe anything you say?"

"What other option is there for one in your position? After all, it would be a real shame to lose your precious intellect."

"Rinehart didn't think so," she rightly pointed out. "Neither did the Court — or those who tried to kill me."

"There's been a recent change in management, but I suppose you didn't hear. Without your father's shadow, the opportunities are bright, and there just might be a place for you, if you're willing to comply. Everything you saw and felt can now be your reality."

Carrie reflected on the offer with longing in her eyes. What could he possibly mean? Had Lucas overthrown them? If so, why was she imprisoned?

After careful deliberation, she defiantly responded, "I've already found my place, and I don't think I'll be moving."

The inquisitor faltered in his courtesy, then rose to leave the room. "Perhaps you'll reconsider," he warned her, "if you wish to have a future. Try to do it quickly, though. I wouldn't test the overseer's patience."

16

Victor continued to reflect upon the cruel fantasy imposed upon him. Securely restrained and under the careful watch of a pair of guards, he could do little else. Soon, the door opened, providing a welcome but perhaps equally grim distraction.

Expecting the inquisitor to return with a fresh round of questioning, he was mildly surprised to see just another Vanguard grunt.

"I've been told to get the prisoners ready to move," said the officer.

"I wasn't aware they were finished questioning."

The officer shrugged. "That's just what I've been told."

"Whatever." The guard motioned his partner toward Victor. "Remember, one funny move, and we have orders to kill." He looked back to the officer. "Where did they say we were—"

The guard approaching Victor turned abruptly, finding a knife inside his partner's throat.

Seizing his moment of opportunity, Victor grabbed the restraints and used them as a garrote to subdue his captor.

The officer then removed his helmet, revealing a strong-featured face with an earnest gleam in his eyes. "You don't know me, but I'm on your side, and I'm not letting Libertas die today," he explained, offering a sidearm.

Victor, still bewildered, accepted the weapon, and the two hurried through the hall, doing their best to avoid additional personnel. "Where are the others?" he whispered, fearing for his friends.

"They're down this way — both intact, last I checked. Once we free them, we can head up to the hangar and grab a cruiser."

"Shit!" They spotted another pair of guards stationed down the hall. "We can't trigger an alarm, or else we're gonna be in a real tight spot."

"Here, follow my lead," said Victor, tucking his blaster into his waistband.

"Hey, what are you doing with the prisoner?!" one of the guards shouted as they approached. "They're supposed to be under heavy lock and key. Draconis made that clear."

Blake maintained his calm. "Didn't they tell you: we're moving them for processing."

"I didn't hear anything like that. Let me check with the commander."

As the guard passed, Victor swung around and firmly grabbed ahold of his neck.

Before the other could respond, the friendly officer had again employed his blade. "You handle yourself pretty well there, Talos," he noted.

"Thanks. Call me Victor. You're not too shabby either, uh, . . ."

"Blake — Blake Warner. It's my pleasure to help in any way I can."

After reaching the nearby holding rooms, they wasted no time in rescuing and arming their still-unbroken allies.

Unable to restrain himself when once more seeing Carrie, Ross greeted her with a fleeting hug, surprised that she reciprocated in spite of clear discomfort.

"I thought for sure we all were finished," Ross admitted as they parted.

"No kidding," Carrie said uneasily, unable to make eye contact. "Who's this?" she asked, noticing their extra member.

"A friend," said Victor, "but we'll have time for introductions later. Right now, we need to keep on moving."

Rinehart carried out his task inside an empty lab, whose only other occupant was Foregrave, diligently scrutinizing everything he did.

"Your time is wasted here," insisted the director.

"If only the Architect could trust you unattended," the judicar responded. "Frankly, I'm surprised he needed you at all for this."

Rinehart glared defensively. "There's more involved than simply mixing chemicals. Any scientist would know that." He gazed upon the amber fluid. "This one in particular has a rather fleeting half-life, so proper timing is required."

"Then, wouldn't it be feasible to wait until we're ready?"

"Preparation is needed to achieve ideal balance; otherwise, the results could be disastrous. As long as he intends to use it by tonight, you need not be concerned."

The platinum case lay open on a nearby table.

"Do you think it really is his blood?" asked Foregrave, glancing at the contents.

"That hardly matters, does it?" Rinehart said indifferently. "But if you truly are so curious, I could always run some tests."

"Not a chance," the judicar forbade, remembering his duty. "I won't incur his wrath because of your fixations."

"Have it your way, then," said Rinehart with a frown.

Soon thereafter, the delicate components had been carefully combined.

"There we are," the director said with confidence. "The rest is up to him."

Thanks to the familiarity of the massive headquarters between the two officers, past and present, the quartet made their way to the hangar bay undetected, though their escape was far from assured, thanks to the heavy presence of patrolmen.

"This doesn't look good," said Carrie.

"We still have the element of surprise," reminded Victor. "As long as we take them out before anyone can trigger an alarm, we'll make it out of here."

Slowly, they crept along cover, fanning out beneath the rows and rows of docked cruisers, steadily converging on the group of Vanguard.

Before they could reach optimal positions, however, a siren began to blare.

"Shit, they must have realized we're missing," Victor noted. "Open fire!"

Still able to catch their targets off-guard in the confusion, the fugitives managed to secure the hangar with minimal delay.

"We're gonna have a hell of a time getting out now," said Victor. "They'll have authorized a lockdown." His hunch was then confirmed, as the hangar doors could not be opened from a nearby access terminal. "Damn." He turned to Carrie hopefully. "Do you think you can hack your way around it?"

"It doesn't really work like that," she answered, somewhat irritated.

"I can try a few administrative overrides," Blake offered, heading up the closest ship and sitting at the helm.

"Better make it quick," urged Ross, as further troops arrived.

"We'll hold them off," said Victor. "Just get us in the air."

They took defensive positions around the ship, returning fire at the Vanguard reinforcements.

"How's it going?!" he inquired.

"Still working on it," Blake responded. "Here, these might help for now." He tossed a belt of sonic charges to even out the odds.

After setting them to maximum intensity, Victor lobbed a few.

The Vanguard barely stood a chance, and soon their numbers were reduced until the blaster fire ceased.

Tentatively, the three poked out from cover, sure they'd got them all, but their troubles weren't over, for across the hangar now emerged another to stare them down.

Once more they opened fire, but it did little good this time, for the approaching high commander made a barrier of aether.

They then tried genomancy of their own, but he brushed aside their efforts with a wave.

Halfway to their ship, Draconis channeled fire through his hands, matching well the madness in his eyes.

Almost out of options, Victor held the final charge, desperately searching for a way to make it count. At last, he found a worthy target, then aimed at the underside supports of the upper docking platform.

The ensuing detonation brought a crushing weight down onto the commander, but he narrowly braced it up with rippling waves of aether.

Seemingly overstrained, his face contorted in a manner most unusual, and as the energy flowed forth, a rather gruesome transformation occurred before them. Once finished, it left him barely recognizable as human.

He suddenly erupted with a deeply primal roar, scattering the vehicles about in all directions.

The group stood terrified and frozen as he menacingly neared.

"Got it!" shouted Blake. "Everyone onboard!"

Nobody needed telling twice, so they scrambled up the cruiser and quickly sailed from the hangar, leaving Draconis in their wake.

Once allowed to catch his breath — and realizing the ghastly effects of his exertion — he withdrew a leather pouch, then promptly injected himself with a turquoise fluid, returning his appearance to normal before backup soon arrived.

As he stared out after his elusive prey, Lieutenant Pryce appeared beside him, leading a small retinue not far behind.

"Made you work for it, did they?" she questioned playfully, noticing the syringe clutched in his fist. "Will you be needing more from the director, then?"

"Our new overseer should be apprised," Draconis growled, and the lieutenant watched him turn to leave.

Throughout his years of service, she had never seen another man eclipse him, but rising now was a greater power, and something told her that it sought beyond this realm. Time would make the truth apparent, perhaps before too long a wait.

17

Though they had narrowly escaped, no victory could be enjoyed, for the giant screens across the Pillar's face alerted all to watch for them, reminding Libertas they had nowhere left to hide.

"Nice work back there," Victor complimented their skillful pilot.

"Happy to help," said Blake. "As soon as I heard you guys were caught, I knew I had to do something. I only wish we had more support."

"Yeah," lamented Victor.

"Not to put a damper on our escape, but where exactly am I going?"

"Well, we can't return to our apartments," Carrie noted.

"We still don't even know what happened to Lucas," Ross considered. "What if they're holding him somewhere?"

"Who?" asked Blake.

"Lucas Corvin," Ross replied. "He's the one who created Libertas and brought us all together. Last night, he went to confront Xul himself and end their tyranny for good."

"He confronted a god?"

"A mortal," revealed Victor.

"So, the conspiracies are true?"

"You'll get the details later, but right now, we need to find Lucas."

"There was nothing official about other prisoners," Blake reported, "captured or killed."

"Something must have happened," Carrie reasoned. "Why else haven't we heard from him? I mean, every contingency was—" A pressing thought arose. "The biomods!" she suddenly remembered.

"Shit! That's right," said Victor.

"The what?"

"Our fail-safe," Ross clarified. "We knew our plan was a long shot, so we hid them around the city as a final countermeasure."

"What exactly are they?"

"They emit a special frequency," said Carrie, "one that can neutralize the expression of Anakhari DNA."

Blake turned his head in sheer bewilderment. "I'm afraid I don't quite follow."

"Again, it'll make sense later," reiterated Victor.

"We were hoping to undo some of the damage they've done over the years," Ross explained.

"Then, why just a fail-safe? Seems like a good idea regardless."

"Well, we couldn't really know how the majority would react. The hope was to jumpstart a mass awakening, but . . ."

"It could just as likely kill them," Victor stated bluntly. "Our past efforts didn't exactly go as planned, and this would be aggressive escalation, to say the least. Between Capstone and the Pillar, I've seen some pretty nasty results of bioweapons testing."

"It's a *modulator*," Carrie protested.

"Even so."

"I get it," Blake responded, "but now that we're all exposed out here, our options might be limited. Are you sure—"

"We'll find another way," asserted Victor, making his position clear.

"Fair enough. And how long before they activate?"

Victor checked the time. "Less than an hour."

"That doesn't give us long," worried Ross.

"Especially not with the entire city looking for us," added Carrie.

"So, where are they?"

"One of them is at the mall," said Ross, "but we'd never make it past the surveillance drones."

"Don't worry," Blake assured. "Just tell me where to look, and I'll take care of it." He tapped his helmet pointedly.

The high commander finished his report while silently beside him stood Lieutenant Pryce.

Staring out his office window, Lucas weighed the implications. "You said it yourself: they weren't talking, anyway."

"Be that as it may," Draconis protested, "I'm confident that with more time—"

"Time, Commander, is running thin. The Architect made it clear what he expects and when, or do you not appreciate the gravity involved?"

Though replying with a stalwart glare, Draconis quivered faintly at the thought of such a failure. His lieutenant's eyes upon him, he recovered his composure, but the momentary fear had already been betrayed.

"In any case," continued Lucas, "the trackers are in place, the asset's been deployed, and the situation is being closely monitored. I just hope your man knows what he's doing."

"Of that there is no doubt," the commander said with pride. "I expect we'll hear from him at any moment, though I still must question the need for such a stratagem. The full force of the Vanguard is exceptionally capable."

"As are *they*," Lucas noted, "which is why a bit of subtlety is warranted. The threat must be contained, and we can't afford sympathizers complicating matters."

Draconis took offense at the implication of disloyalty — the impugning of his leadership, in front of a subordinate — though chose to stay professional. "They may well cause greater damage in the process," he advised the overseer.

"What could they really do?" Lucas countered. "They have no resources or shelter; we'll catch them soon enough."

"And once they lead us to the target, I trust you won't object to speedy executions?"

"Why ever would I, now?" said Lucas, not showing much concern.

As the Age of Enlightenment drew to a close, Nevara mulled her latest revolutionary efforts.

After witnessing the breadth of her incidental handiwork, she decided to end her sojourn at the Tuileries Palace, aiming to confront a certain statesman.

She found the solitary man inside his office, then spoke to him through spectral form, "Your heartless reign has brought only terror."

Taking offense at the narrow-minded viewpoint, he pompously responded, "What you dismiss as 'terror', I call nothing short of justice, so only fitting that it be prompt, severe, and unwavering. Can you not see that everything I do is a consequence of democracy itself? It has all been in service of the most pressing needs of those whose voices rose to unseat tyranny."

Nevara was unswayed by his articulation. "And when do the beheadings end?" she inquired harshly.

"When I have rid us of the demon spawn," he answered, baffled by the tone of his former patron. "Conspirators lie in wait around us, aided by complacency, and you suggest reprieving the oppressors of humanity? To punish them is clemency, and forgiveness would be the truest cruelty of all, lest any leniency granted impede our noble cause."

Her exasperation mounted. "Senseless bloodshed cannot be the only path!" she cried in vain.

Indignantly, he rounded on her. "How content you are to judge me — high above your perch, divorced from such affairs of men — while it is not only my head being wagered but the many of my countrymen. Why, then, at this juncture, should I trust you, for whom the gravest outcome would be but a minor setback, when so much lies at stake down here amidst the mortal realm?"

"Misery awaits us both, should his plan succeed."

"Not entirely commensurate. As one descended from the heavens, what could you not endure, compared to we of flesh and bone?"

Nevara briefly considered the ways in which Xul might respond to knowledge of her deeds. "A punishment far worse than yours, I promise," she bitterly replied, "beyond constraints of time and magnitude familiar to man."

"Nevertheless," was his retort, brimming with self-righteous confidence.

126

Sensing the futility in any further argument, Nevara ceded all her hope in stopping his crusade. By now, she knew full well of the inevitable conclusion, having seen it quite enough already.

"Then, at the very least," she wondered, "do you not fear swift reprisal coming from the populous you claim to champion?"

"Why should fear be allowed to stay my mission?" he haughtily declaimed. "Whatever fate awaits me, I embrace it as a paragon of patriotic virtue that others may embody. Rest assured, I do not walk to some eternal sleep of death, eager to cast aside my responsibilities and ideals, but onward to the commencement of immortality, where I might bolster them in the next life."

The 'next life', thought Nevara. She might as well begin to plan for that, knowing not when the opportunity might arise. How long would she have to wait again, and could the outcome still be somehow worse?

Sadly, there was no other option, so she continued elsewhere in her raison d'être, desperate to believe that prospects would be kinder someday.

After not so long an absence, Blake hastened back aboard the cruiser, handing Carrie a flat pentagonal device with rounded corners.

"With the way you hyped it up," he said, "I expected something bigger."

"It had to be discreet enough; we couldn't risk them being found."

"So, what kind of range does it actually have?" he wondered.

"Enough to do the job," she defensively replied before disarming it.

"Okay, then."

Blake made his way to the cockpit and powered on the craft.

"Everything went smoothly, then, I take it?" Victor asked him.

"As far as I could tell. It's still pretty early, so there wasn't much traffic."

Victor nodded silently.

"We should probably see what they're up to," Blake suggested, scanning the radio for news reports. "I don't know how you guys manage life offline." He tapped the empty space upon his temple, where his POD was just removed.

"I thought the same at first," admitted Ross, "but you'll get used to it eventually."

"Especially when you consider the alternative," Carrie added.

It didn't take long to find something of interest. "Looks like there's an executive proclamation coming in," Blake noted.

Upon hearing the unexpectedly familiar voice, the other passengers bolted upright, struggling to believe their ears.

"Citizens of Empyrea, you may rightly wonder why a convicted heretic is addressing you today, but regardless of my past, the words I speak are true, and you'd be well advised to heed them. Last night, the violent extremist group known as Libertas conducted their campaign of terror across our city — with no shortage of callous disregard for property and human life. In light of this unprecedented threat to our safety and security, I have been appointed your new overseer by the absolute wisdom and authority of Xul himself, and I promise to succeed where my predecessor failed miserably.

"Thanks to the swift and tireless actions of our Vanguard forces, key members of Libertas were identified and apprehended shortly after their attacks, but that victory was regrettably fleeting. Before their motivations or the full extent of their network could be ascertained, they managed to escape from custody, due in no small part to sympathetic elements operating covertly within The Order.

"These fugitives are to be considered armed and extremely dangerous, and those found harboring or assisting them in any way will be deemed enemies of the state, subject to the appropriate punishment. To resolve the dire crisis we face, I hereby sanction full emergency powers of the Vanguard, effective until further notice, and I urge everyone to cooperate however possible.

"Although these measures may no doubt appear unwarranted to some of you, rest assured the need is just, for the moment we have long awaited is at last upon us — our *final* ascension — and I was duly chosen to help ensure it . . . by any means necessary. Foremost in anticipation, we must cleanse ourselves accordingly to be worthy of his holy blessing, or else our fortune will be lost forever.

"It is no secret that long-standing complacency has allowed certain impurities to fester among our ranks, but why should they be allowed to sully our worth in the eyes of the redeemer? In order for us to rise unfettered, I therefore call upon our noble protectors to begin the culling of those who would only serve to damage the collective. Thanks to the comprehensive efforts of our medical apparatus, all the necessary data is available to make such judgments with the utmost confidence.

"If you happen to be among the unfortunate few below the purity threshold, know that your sacrifice is the highest honor you could hope to earn in this life, and it will not be soon forgotten. All others, prepare yourselves for an experience unlike anything you could possibly imagine. Glory unto Xul."

18

Speechlessly they sat, struggling to comprehend the sinister announcement.

"I don't believe it," said Ross, breaking the painful silence. "What does he mean about a 'culling'?"

"It seems obvious enough," said Carrie. "What the hell do we do now?"

"We still have two more biomods to disarm," reminded Victor, devastated by the unequivocal betrayal yet determined to stay their course. "Once we've taken care of that, we'll figure out what to do about *him*."

"Wouldn't Lucas have told the Vanguard where to find them?" Blake inquired.

"I doubt it."

"How can you be so sure?"

"Because he doesn't know."

"What do you mean? I thought he was running things?"

"It was part of the plan," Ross explained, slowly overcoming the initial shock. "Any one of us could have been captured and made to talk, so nobody could know all the locations."

"And what if one of you didn't make it back? Wouldn't that leave a biomod still out there?"

"It wasn't a perfect plan," admitted Victor, "but it was the best we had."

"Fair enough," conceded Blake. "So, where to?"

As the ship sailed off to its next objective, a hooded figure watched closely from the shadows, waiting for the opportunity to strike.

Once more gathered at the overseer's call, the Executors grew impatient over the disruption in their busy schedules.

"I do apologize for having to reconvene you all again so soon," Lucas prefaced, "but I'm afraid there is an urgent matter to discuss."

"Only one?" Draconis noted.

Lucas ignored the dry remark. "With Libertas once more on the run, I find it now a suitable time as any to conduct an audit of your administrative keycards."

The Executors exchanged concerned glances, though Lucas pretended not to notice.

"Do you doubt our competency?" Draconis wondered, barely suppressing his resentment.

"If you are so confident in your abilities," Lucas replied, "then you have nothing to fear."

"What makes you think they would even know about them?" wondered Rinehart.

"I did," stated Lucas bluntly, "which is why I have every reason to believe they would be targeted. You know what's at stake should they fall into the wrong hands, and I shouldn't have to remind you three of the responsibility you bear. At this critical juncture, the slightest disruption could upset the Architect's grand vision."

Foregrave rose abruptly from his seat. "I will not be accused of impeding his holy design!"

Stepping forward, he swiftly produced a darkly opalescent rectangle from his breast pocket, then laid it on the table self-importantly. "Do what you must."

With one hand holding the card and the other resting in his pocket, Lucas closed his eyes.

The unique sheen radiated even brighter as his focus illuminated it from within, forcing even the Executors of Xul to marvel at the sight.

After a few seconds, the glow receded, and he opened his eyes.

Evidently satisfied, he handed the card back to its bearer, who returned to his seat with a deferential nod.

Rinehart was next to present his card for inspection, and the process went much the same.

As the director sat back down, Lucas turned then toward the high commander, who stared back in defiance before begrudgingly complying.

When Lucas finally offered back the key, Draconis snatched it brusquely and marched behind his chair. "I trust we have satisfied your curiosity?" he spoke with an air of indignation.

"Perfectly," said Lucas.

"Then, if you don't mind, I have other matters requiring attention."

Draconis turned to leave, Foregrave bowing out in toe, but Rinehart rubbed his chin before raising a point of concern. "Not to pry, but what of the *other* cards, if I might inquire?"

The question clearly piqued the curiosity of his cohorts, who awaited the response.

"Shouldn't you be far more concerned about those falling into the wrong hands?" continued the director.

"Not at all," Lucas answered, brandishing the two companion pieces acquired the night before, reinforcing both symbolic and pragmatic consolidation of his office.

This time, the trio consciously avoided meeting each other's gaze, and whether out of respect or fear, they all beheld their overseer in a somewhat different light.

With the final biomod at hand, Blake lowered their transport into a relatively empty parking structure in the city's underlevel.

"So, this is it — the last one?" he asked.

"Yeah," said Victor. "Last one. I'm sure Lucas would have recovered his own already. If not, we'd have no idea where to look for it anyway."

"There aren't any cameras down here, so you might wanna stretch your legs," Blake suggested.

"Sounds good," said Ross, jumping at the chance.

The others quickly followed suit, eager to breathe fresh air for the first time since their bold escape.

Victor headed over to a nondescript recess in the wall to retrieve his hidden gadget.

"Not to be a downer," prefaced Blake, "but have you guys given any thought as to what we do now?"

"We need to find somewhere to lie low," said Victor.

"Easier said than done," added Carrie. "It's not like we can trust anyone for sanctuary, especially after a speech like that."

"If only we had more friends," Ross lamented.

Blake scratched his head. "I don't want anyone to get the wrong idea here, but I was kind of hoping there'd be more of you. I mean, is there really nobody we can reach out to for help?"

Victor looked askance at him. "You're not having second thoughts, are you?"

"Of course not," he reassured. "I'm deep in it now, but . . . are we really all there is?"

The others exchanged uneasy glances.

"Well," Ross began, "there was another one who—"

"All of you, on the ground!" a voice called out, surprising them.

They turned to find a pair of Vanguard officers advancing, guns drawn. A surveillance drone followed closely behind.

"Now!" the officer barked.

Caught off-guard and with nowhere to run, the group begrudgingly complied.

"Reporting in," the officer barked into his POD. "We have the fugitives in custody. Please advise."

". . ."

"Drones ID'ed the stolen cruiser, and we have visual confirmation. It's them, all right. How does the commander want us—"

Two shots erupted from the shadows, striking them down.

Before the drone could turn to identify the attacker, it too was taken out of commission.

A figure then emerged, cloaked in black and gun still raised.

The group stood watching nervously, not sure how they should react.

Blake responded first. "I suppose I should thank you, stranger."

The figure carefully assessed him before replying, "Don't."

A momentary pause, followed by a sudden shot, and the officer collapsed, dead before he landed.

The others froze in shock, only more confused.

"I'm on your side, so please don't be alarmed," assured the figure, lowering her gun.

Carrie promptly drew her own. "You've got a funny way of showing it. How does *that* factor in?" She nodded down to Blake as Ross examined him.

"Because he was a spy," answered Victor, "wasn't he?"

"Sent by the high commander," she confirmed, "on the orders of Lucas Corvin."

"They already had us," Carrie noted. "Why go through the trouble?"

"To track me down."

"And who exactly are you?" Ross inquired.

"My name is Nevara," said the figure, lowering her hood, "and I came to stop this madness. If you still are willing to assist, then I suggest we hurry."

War continued raging on all fronts as Nevara made her last appearance in the fatherland. Although the point of no return had long been crossed, disillusionment compelled her to find closure.

Noticing the sullen apparition, her ersatz champion looked up from his command-room table. "I did not think I would be seeing you again," he admitted. "Have you come to apologize, now that progress had been made?"

Nevara bowed her head in shame. "Tell me exactly how this brings us any closer."

"What would you have me do when the devil's blood infects humanity? As long as their tainted lineage can breed and intermingle, our race will never truly be our own. For the pure among us to thrive, that poison must be eradicated. I don't see how you could have lost your strength of will, when I simply do as nature has decreed."

"I never advocated genocide!"

"What else was to be done? They dominate the wealth of every nation, and no institution is free from their control. Only a final solution could rid us of the scourge, once and for all."

"Was is not enough that you already set the world alight?"

"How else was I to end their stranglehold? No matter how grand my vision or noble my intent, it would count for nothing if confined within our borders, and given the complicity of global interests, I don't see how you could argue that diplomacy would have possibly been viable."

"There had to be another way," she claimed. *"All you've done is lay the groundwork for the next phase of his plan."*

"Why do you think of only failure? Can you not see that we are winning this fight?" He gestured toward the battle lines across the map.

"If that's what you believe, then I shudder to imagine your victory."

"There was a time you called it 'our' victory," he reminded her.

"Long before I knew what you were after — what you would become."

The enmity between them could not be reconciled, so there was little more to say.

Thoroughly dejected, Nevara posed a closing question that she desperately needed answered, even if she didn't expect to hear one. *"How can you ever justify what you have done?"*

He glared at her defensively. *"If I succeed, I won't have to,"* was his curt reply.

And so she left the world to burn, understanding that, in the wake of devastation, Xul would rebuild it even worse, all thanks to her.

Wallowing in despair, she couldn't help but entertain that he might know more about her actions than she ever had suspected, simply allowing them to unfold without obstruction. After all, how could he have asked for a better scenario than the one she thus delivered? Truly, she was his angel of darkness, willing to serve or not.

19

The remaining few of Libertas had narrowly escaped the Vanguard reinforcements, but rest could not be entertained.

"Are you sure we're not being followed?" worried Ross, looking frantically out the window.

"They're not looking for this cruiser, so that should buy some time," said Victor, now the acting pilot of a freshly stolen craft.

"We can't just fly around forever," Carrie argued, fidgeting absent-mindedly with the incapacitated drone. "Eventually, we'll need to find a new hideout."

"I know a place that should suffice," their new arrival interjected. "Keep to the lower levels, and you should avoid detection."

"So, you're the mystery contact," said Carrie, glaring suspiciously at Nevara. "Any reason we should trust you after what went down?"

"Besides the fact I saved your lives," reminded Nevara, a trace of guilt nonetheless crossing her face.

"To be fair, so did the guy you shot," said Ross, drooping his head. "I still can't believe he was only using us. We really don't have any friends, do we?"

Nevara's eyes began to fill with tears, but no one seemed to notice. Why had she ever thought this iteration would be different? Born of little more than desperation, of course it ended in disaster. Now the faded memories of a time long past gave way to the stark reality before her. On and on the carousel continued to spin, though she felt a dark tranquility in knowing that, one way or another, it would soon be coming to an end.

"Oh yeah," Carrie suddenly remembered, rounding on Victor. "You still haven't explained how you knew about Blake — and did nothing about it, either."

"I didn't *know*," defended Victor. "There was a voice that kept warning me not to trust him, but I figured we weren't exactly in a position to turn down help. Also, I didn't wanna raise concerns without more actionable evidence."

"A voice?" wondered Ross. "Like an auditory hallucination?"

"Nothing like the NOVA tech," Victor clarified. "In hindsight, I know it sounds like just a cynical hunch, but I could have sworn it came from . . . outside of me." He turned to the mysterious passenger. "I don't suppose that was you?"

Nevara stirred abruptly from the reverie of sorrow. "Despite my efforts," she admitted, "I failed to contact you at all beforehand."

"Maybe it's a kind of heightened intuition," Ross considered.

"Or full-blown paranoia," Carrie added. "I certainly wouldn't blame you."

"In any case," continued Victor, glancing at their guest, "I'd like to hear how *you* would know about their spy."

"I witnessed Lucas orchestrate the plan," she stated.

"How is that possible?" asked Carrie.

"In astral form," Nevara clarified. "At the time, I was in no condition to do more than intelligence gathering. I'm still not exactly at top strength."

"Did you learn anything else?" Victor pressed.

"You no doubt heard his speech?"

The others nodded gravely.

"It would appear," she continued, "that Xul has entrusted Lucas with overseeing the final stages of his grand design."

"Which is?"

"The harvesting of humanity."

How far he had come from such lowly depths, Lucas pondered while gazing out the window of his private cruiser. Never could he have imagined the power in his hands, yet it felt so familiar — so fitting. Could it really be the path of destiny?

The inner voice then promptly warned, «vipers lie in wait for you, so do not think of resting.»

"Everything has been arranged for this evening," Lieutenant Pryce reported next to him. "Baron Eisencroft sends his regards."

Lucas nodded. "Hopefully, this will put to rest any lingering concerns about the new regime."

"Also," she continued, "in light of recent issues, he requested more security."

"He can have it along the perimeter and the grounds, but only high-ranking personnel are to be allowed inside. If he raises further objections, remind him of the premise for our gathering, and I'm sure he will appreciate the need for utmost discretion."

"As you wish, Overseer Corvin."

But before she could relay the message, an urgent call came through her POD, quickly changing her expression to one of consternation.

"Is it confirmed?"

". . ."

"Shit!"

Lucas raised his eyebrows.

"I'm afraid I've got some bad news."

"They escaped again?" he guessed.

"It would seem to be a bit worse, actually."

"I see," said Lucas, understanding fully. "That does make things more interesting."

«they have not given up yet, and she will guide them to you.»

Lucas turned back to look outside, factoring the development into his arrangements.

Too absorbed in thought was he to notice the escort cruiser ahead of them abruptly raise its turret. Alicen did, however, and so she threw herself against him as it spun around to face them.

"What the hell?" their pilot wondered, failing to react before a burst of plasma struck him.

The backseat pair avoided injury, but those in front were not so lucky, which caused the ship to take a nosedive.

Alicen climbed forward, attempting to course correct as they fast approached the ground. "The controls are damaged," she reported.

Lucas joined her silently and extended out his hands. With a violent gust of energy, he cleared the broken windshield.

Channeling a counter thrust then helped to slow descent, allowing both to survive the crash that swiftly followed.

Before either could recover from the impact, the hostile cruiser landed, and soon emerging to encircle them were three masked figures.

In position, they unleashed a storm of gunfire straight into his ship, forcing its two passengers to once more dive for cover.

"It has to be them," Alicen inferred. "How could they have mobilized already?"

Lucas held his hands together, again without a word, and he pooled a ball of aether directed to their flank.

One of the attackers aimed his gun into the window, but Lucas fired first, blasting off the door.

A second reached the front, priming a grenade, but as he raised his arm to toss it in, the lieutenant answered with her sidearm.

The gunman fell aside, but so did his munition, resulting in a fierce explosion that flipped them upside down.

Heavily disoriented, they crawled out from the wreckage.

Only one man lay alive, still reeling from the shock wave.

Staggering to his feet, Lucas watched the nearby ship. Since no more intervened, it was likely to be empty.

Out the corner of his eye, he saw Alicen approach the downed combatant.

"Wait!" cried Lucas, but she already pulled the trigger, leaving him unable to stay the execution.

"You wanted them to have another chance?"

"We could have questioned them!" Lucas shouted angrily.

"I doubt they were the talking types."

He rushed over to the body and removed its balaclava. "Those are Disciple markings," he then determined, now a little calmer.

"Impossible," said Alicen. "The Baron might be cunning, but he'd never pull a stunt like this."

"Who's to say he did?" Lucas pointedly inquired. "We know of other masters they often like to serve."

She caught the implication, becoming more concerned. "In that case, we must proceed with caution . . . and be careful whom we trust."

20

Barely clinging to consciousness, Nevara could only lay still and listen to the words piercing like a knife. Had this been his plan from the start, and how could she have not foreseen it? Was there any hope at all?

Perhaps the other freedom fighters, she considered, would be made of better temperament.

Regardless, there was clearly nothing for her here, and she could take no more of his depravity. Barely having stabilized her wound, she knew that it was now or never.

Remaining still, she pooled a ball of aether in her hand, though neither seemed to notice.

Once it reached sufficient potency, she rose to hurl it straight at Lucas, grazing him across the face as he turned in shock.

Before he or Xul could react, she fired another at the door, triggering the fail-safe to slam it shut. Desperately, she ran back through the station, eluding reinforcements as they threatened her escape.

Sheer determination kept her moving, and at last she reached the gateway. With only seconds left to act, she used her mainframe exploit, establishing a passage with unilateral control.

Just as they arrived behind her, the prismatic veil shone, and Nevara found herself in the Dark Sector laboratory of Capstone Industries.

Unfortunately, waiting for her was none other than the high commander, accompanied by a Vanguard squad, all aiming their weapons directly at her.

"You? What the hell is going on?!" Draconis barked.

Her mind raced.

"The intruder has been dealt with," she answered calmly as she could. "I'm here to assess the damage from your appalling lapse in security."

They lowered their weapons as she stepped forward, doing her best to hide the pain.

"An extent most certainly avoidable, had protocol been duly followed." Draconis glared at Rinehart, who leaned against a desk while holding the back of his head.

"What was I supposed to do?" the high director protested. "How could I have expected them to even know about this place?"

"A valid point," considered the commander. "Moreover, how could one traverse the gateway by himself?" he inquired of Nevara.

Overcome by pain and growing faint again, she braced herself against the nearby railing.

"Something the matter?" Draconis noted.

"Nothing to concern you."

"If the threat has been addressed, I would advise you to have a seat."

"You do seem to have the situation under control," she acknowledged with a grimace.

"Quite right," agreed Draconis, "but you would have no way of knowing that." He eyed her more suspiciously. "I have to wonder why, then, you would come here on your own — and in your current state, no less?"

Rinehart glanced between the two, arriving at a sudden understanding. "He knew exactly how to get in — that he needed me alive."

"Another excellent point," said Draconis, moving closer. "Such observations are rather curious, aren't they, . . . Nevara?"

They stared each other down, but there was no answer she could give. Behind her back the waters loudly rushed: the only option left.

Aside she threw her body, disappearing with a splash, and off somewhere unknown she went, truly at her low.

Nevara's captivating tale thus concluded, the city's gloomy underworks concordant with its tone. The others now sat crestfallen, unsure what to say or do. The harrowing account, combined with his own haunting words, left little doubt as to the totality of betrayal.

"That's some story," Ross acknowledged.

"What happened next?" Victor questioned.

"I ran deep into the sewers, eventually collapsing here. By the time I awoke, you had already been captured and subsequently freed, so I tracked you, waiting for the proper moment."

"Why does Lucas want you badly enough to risk our actual escape?"

"Because of why Xul sent him here," replied Nevara. "I stand to be a significant obstacle to both of their agendas."

"Aren't they on the same page?"

"Officially, perhaps, but I know Xul well enough to suspect an ulterior motive. As for Lucas, I can't claim to understand him anymore, but he's clearly after one thing: retribution."

"What did *we* ever do to him?" asked Ross. "We've been right by his side through all of this, fighting the ones responsible for his misery — the ones he up and joined."

"I don't think those distinctions are of concern to him," Nevara pondered. "He sees humanity as irredeemable, collectively a scourge."

"Well, I'm not one to argue that," Carrie bitterly confessed, "but wouldn't he be the last person Xul puts in charge?"

"Lucas represents a curious anomaly," Nevara speculated, "evidently enough for Xul to justify the risk."

"They've been ruling from the shadows for thousands of years without having to resort to such measures," Victor noted. "Why the sudden rush?"

"Time was needed for the seeds to germinate, and they're quite eager to reap the bounty now that their crops bear fruit."

"Enough to wager everything?"

"With only one Haven left in service, they've become increasingly impatient. More pressingly, however, the Revelation is upon us."

"Lucas mentioned that," said Ross, "but he never told us why it mattered."

"It matters because the permeability of the Subverse will reach its peak, thanks to the rare alignment of certain cosmic bodies. This presents a tremendous opportunity to exploit, and Xul now has the means to do so. This is when he hopes to finally seize the talents of your kind."

"Can't they already perform genomancy?" Carrie asked. "How can that be possible if they lack the trait?"

"They may not have the genofactor to interface directly with the Subverse, but they do have a high capacity for aether — even greater than humanity's. That's what makes their workaround so daunting, contrived as it may be."

"Then, why are they so eager to copy us?"

"Because their solution has a price," explained Nevara, "namely genetic instability. Xul found ways to delay the long-term damage, but circumventing nature takes a toll eventually. Through perfect hybridization, he aims to combine their raw destructive power with your natural autonomy, and there wouldn't be such side effects."

"So, what can we do now?" asked Victor.

"As a critical step in Xul's plan, Lucas arranged a gathering with the chosen families for tonight. At the Eisencroft Manor, he will be collecting biological samples from them."

"And what makes *their* DNA so special?" wondered Ross.

"These dynasties, especially the Eisencrofts, have much more in common with the Anakhari genotype compared to the general population. By still retaining some connection to the Subverse, faint as it may be, they serve as valuable subjects for isolating the bridge that Xul so desperately seeks. Understandably, he's kept them under careful watch throughout the years."

"Does that mean they have abilities like ours?"

"Not quite, which is why, for the samples to be of use, a chemical catalyst is required to awaken and sustain the underlying genes. I suspect it will be administered as part of a ritualistic blood-drinking ceremony."

"The blood of Xul?" Victor guessed.

"Exactly," said Nevara. "Although symbolic more than practical, the pretense reinforces their fanatical devotion."

Carrie furrowed her brow at so much needless pageantry. "With such technology available, why not a more scientific method?"

"Tradition can be addictive," answered Victor.

"Indeed," confirmed Nevara, "but that's not the only reason. For all his cunning, Xul has never succeeded in replicating genomancy under laboratory settings. It seems there's far too much complexity in the molecular and subatomic interactions. That's why any specimens of value need to be acquired and preserved in their biotic states."

"If they're that important, we can't let Xul get his hands on them," said Ross.

"Unless we could manage to kill every single guinea pig," surmised Carrie, "wouldn't they just try the ritual again?"

"Not anytime soon," assured Nevara. "The catalyst is highly mutagenic, and overuse would mar the DNA's utility. Fortunately, they won't have another chance before the Revelation ends."

"In that case, I think it's clear what out next target has to be," concluded Victor.

Lieutenant Pryce returned to the overseer's office to give her latest updates, wishing that more were positive.

"We found Private Warner's body," she reported, "and the trackers have gone offline."

"It seems he blew his cover," Lucas thoughtfully surmised.

"Perhaps, though the commander disagrees."

"How else could it have happened? Few had known our plan."

"I'm afraid I can't answer that."

"No matter," conceded Lucas. "The odds she survived are slim enough, and it's not like any of them can hide for long."

"We did retrieve your biomod." She handed him the small device.

"Very good," he replied, pocketing it promptly. "At least that's one less thing to worry about."

"Regarding the attempted assassination," continued Alicen, "we've hit a dead end, it seems. Those men were just low-level thugs, always up for contracts. Anyone could have sent them."

"I presume the Baron denies any knowledge or involvement?"

"Yes, but he assured us that the matter is being investigated."

"Of course he did," said Lucas, weighing another possibility. "To be honest," he candidly disclosed, "I might have suspected you, had the situation been only slightly different."

"Oh? And why is that?"

"Avenging your father, perhaps?" he suggested. "It would be an understandable motivation."

"It would be," she acknowledged, "had I not been so relieved to see him gone."

Lucas responded with a look of mild surprise.

"As it turns out," she bitterly explained, "the superficial pomp and circumstance can make one turn his back on more important matters. In a way, I suppose it couldn't have been a more fitting end, so if anything, I really should be thanking you — or does that seem too insensitive?"

"Not at all," said Lucas. "I almost feel guilty that I deprived you of the pleasure."

"What's done is done," she said, smiling at the thought, "so it will simply have to do."

"Then, on that note, lieutenant, any other news?"

"Nothing, sir."

Lucas nodded, allowing her to leave.

Before she did, however, there was one more thing to say. "Unofficially, I've never seen fear in his eyes until you came along."

"But you don't share that fear, I gather?" he asked with a trace of wry amusement.

"The high commander clings to dying ways," Alicen confessed. "His loyalty is admirable, but it holds him back from greatness of his own. You bring something different, that's for sure. I don't know exactly what it is, but I can't help being intrigued. Frankly," she concluded, "I think we could do interesting things together."

"Such audacity," Lucas commented. "What makes you think I've any need for you?"

"I acquired more than combat skills from serving him so closely. In addition to my wealth of classified intelligence, I have other certain assets."

As a demonstration, she summoned a subtle ball of energy between her outstretched hand.

"I'm surprised the Architect allows this in a human," said Lucas, joining her beside his desk.

"He doesn't," Alicen informed him.

"Then, I'm more surprised at your superior. No doubt you learned from him?"

"You could say he's had a soft spot for me, but it was never generosity." She looked away reflectively. "I always pay him back somehow."

"So, he uses you?"

"Not any more than I use *him*."

"That's a dangerous game," Lucas warned her.

"What can I say?" she countered impishly. "I like a little danger."

He began circling around her. "And what of the poor commander?"

"Before you, I thought I knew what power was, but true power has no place for fear. I've helped bury many revolutionaries for The Order, but you . . . Well, there's a reason you've made it this far. If they could be rid of you so easily, you wouldn't have that pin right now." She nodded at the gilded eye upon his chest. "The Architect saw more in you — that much is clear to anyone."

Her shrewd assessment flattered him. "Have you considered they're just using *me*?" Lucas asked in turn.

"Now, you don't strike me as the kind of person to be used by anyone."

"We do have that in common." He grinned mischievously, but his expression faltered at the sight of a curiously bulky drone over her shoulder, just outside the window.

"Get down!" he shouted, this time being the one to tackle her as the payload exploded into his office.

21

Later that very night, an air of mystery and tension filled the quaint palatial ballroom. Xul's Executors attended, along with many hooded guests, and all were deathly still as Lucas delivered his address.

"I know you are looking for some assurance of stability in this time of great upheaval. Well," he prefaced, raising his voice over the choking noises, "let me start by saying: there will be none of it."

An outburst from the crowd below ensued, forcing him to orate even louder and with more authority. "Your unrivaled wealth and power signify a bold allegiance that has endured for centuries, but in these more recent years, you have since become complacent with certain limitations."

Lucas had to readjust his stance for better leverage. "For too long," he emphatically continued, "man's history was mere survival. Even at your place atop the pyramid, you could not evade so many laws of nature. Well, I say the time has come to aspire somewhat greater."

The resistance faded, allowing Lucas to speak more steadily.

"Now, you would be justified in questioning my legitimacy to guide you on this path, but you know that I would not be standing here without divine mandate. It is therefore by his will that I invite you to commence the final stage of his design together."

Upon finishing his introduction, Lucas lowered his gaze to the would-be assassin — a rogue Vanguard ensign pinned against the banister by his throat.

Soon, the struggling terminated, and Lucas eased his grip, allowing the body to fall beside the soldier's blade, which had already been relinquished.

After flashing an accusatory glare to the high commander, who responded with a look of pure disdain, Lucas turned back to the crowd and proceeded with his speech.

"I must, of course, give credit to our so graciously accommodating host, Baron Oswald Eisencroft, whose loyalty is beyond reproach and whose legacy is without equal."

He walked to the edge of the banister, nodding to Director Rinehart, who tapped the platinum case to indicate his readiness.

"Can we have some atmosphere?" Lucas called.

The exquisite chandelier then dimmed its lights to create a more intimately solemn tone. He began descending the staircase, his flowing white mantle trailing close behind.

"My purpose here tonight is not merely to provide assurances of our bright future . . . but to decisively commence it. To that effect, I offer you a potable taste of what is shortly coming."

Lucas approached an elevated altar at the forefront of the room, across which lay a crimson satin sheet concealing one rather hallowed object.

They watched in silent anticipation as Lucas took his place behind it.

"The age of man is ending, as anyone can see, and I am here to prove that your unwavering adherence will not be soon forgotten. Your bloodlines, always kept so pure, have been instrumental to his vision, but even while indulging in the gamut of earthly pleasures, you patiently awaited the true prize beyond all measure."

A restless hunger stirred throughout.

"And now, at long last, your service will be rewarded in a manner most befitting."

Lucas pulled the sheet away to reveal a jewel-encrusted chalice, archaic yet immaculate. Lights from nearby candles gleamed around the surface, elevating its ethereal mystique.

Their desire became insatiable.

"I present a token of the Architect himself. Drink it, and you will imbibe the essence of his rarified nobility."

As a show of trust, Lucas was the first to sip.

He then passed the goblet to the nearest hooded cultist, who brought it ravenously to his own lips.

"Once he's finished here, you may finally claim your seats among the stars, where they will honor you as benefactors of their transcendence."

Sitting patiently against the altar, Lucas watched the avid patriarchs until the cup returned to him.

"And thus, the true ascension has begun. Sleep well and be ready, for tomorrow the rest will come." He raised the chalice. "To the legacy of Xul!" he boasted, and the room erupted in applause.

"But as you know," he continued on a heavy note, the commotion soon subsiding, "nothing comes for free."

He descended from the altar and approached the center of the group.

The circle of 13 enclosed him as a drum beat steadily, and those observing from the sidelines began to chant in unison.

Lucas raised his arms above his head, pooling a ball of glowing energy that well outshone the flames.

Others followed suit, channeling their own brief powers and watching as the ball expanded.

The ritual continued as the drum beat faster, culminating in a frenzied ecstasy of bloodlust.

"Step forth to make the final pledge, assured that your sacred covenant may be renewed and sealed."

Lucas procured an ornate knife, which he drew swiftly across his hand before collecting the blood in a vial from his pocket.

Drawing ceremonial blades and vials of their own, each hooded elder repeated the same act one by one.

Once all had reached their limits, Lucas released the energy, sending ripples out through space, and the process was complete.

With every specimen at last collected, Rinehart closed the platinum case.

"I trust there won't be storage issues?" wondered Lucas, now back atop the stairs.

"You'll have perfect genostasis," the high director boasted.

"Excellent. I'll be sure to note your contribution."

Stony-faced as ever, Rinehart ignored such hollow praise, turning at once to head for Capstone.

For a moment of reflection, Lucas leaned against the banister to watch the scattered acolytes.

One stood isolated in the center, staring up at him.

After catching his attention, she pulled back on her hood.

He didn't recognize the girl, so her hostility surprised him, but then she powered off the NOVA mask to unearth amethystine eyes.

Before he could react, she threw a sonic charge toward the chandelier, blanketing the room with copious debris.

Just as all hell broke loose, Nevara took the case from Rinehart, who lay beneath a fallen beam.

She turned to locate Lucas, but he'd fled and barred the door, leaving her to plot some alternate escape.

Unwilling to abide the loss, however, Draconis was already on his feet.

With an escort flanking him once he stepped outside, Lucas crossed the rooftop landing pad.

They led him to his ship without intrusion, and the boarding hatch then lowered, but from inside, his path was blocked by a gun aimed at his head.

Before he could react at all to Carrie's icy glare, Lucas was confronted by his guards, who raised their guns, as well. Their smokey visors cleared, revealing the expressions of his disaffected friends.

"Well played," Lucas granted. "Indeed, I taught you well. I take it that you're here to kill me?"

"We came to hear it for ourselves," Victor stated. "At what point exactly did this become your plan?"

Lucas looked on him with pity. "You would never understand."

"You could have put a stop to it," said Ross. "You could have freed the world."

Lucas turned to him now. "Slaves will never break their chains while the prison is their mind."

"So, that's enough to justify betraying everyone?" asked Carrie.

"Though forced to share the company of man, I was never truly one of them." He seemed to bear no guilt at all. "They chose their fate already, and after everything they did to earn it, why should I object?"

Victor lost his calm, striking angrily at Lucas, but he passed on through the target — a double made of aether.

"Coward!" he shouted to the night. "This isn't over, you bastard!"

"We have to go," pressed Ross. "Nevara needs our help."

Reluctantly, Victor yielded and joined them on the ship.

Fleeing from the sedulous commander, Nevara raced along the many winding halls. Despite his close pursuit, she wouldn't turn to genomancy, fearing Xul might gain a greater prize than even what she stole. The only hope for now was to rely on natural agility.

Her flight soon ended at a narrow empty corridor, so with nowhere else to go, she charged toward the spacious window straight ahead.

Through it promptly crashed a Vanguard cruiser, and much to her relief, Ross was hanging out the back, beckoning her forward.

Draconis then arrived behind her, but instead of continuing the chase, he simply raised his hand, blasting forth a gust of wind.

Slamming to the ground, she let go of the case.

Across the floor it slid, so Ross ran out to grab it. As he motioned for Nevara, though, the Vanguard got there first.

Unable to assist her, he could only turn and run, but he didn't make it far before they shot him in the leg.

No longer quite as mobile, he tossed the case to Carrie. "Go!" he cried.

And so, without another option, Victor sped away.

"You can't just leave them there like that!" yelled his passenger.

"There's nothing we can do right now," he logically concluded. "The only way to save them is to leverage what you're holding."

Once back inside the mansion, Lucas pensively investigated, unable to deny just how impressed he was with what had happened.

While others were preoccupied, Xul's high judicar approached him, hoping for a word. "This is quite a mess," he noted. "The Architect will not be pleased, I'm sure."

Lucas met his gaze, reluctantly engaging. "At least you have possession of the subsequent libation."

"Hardly reassurance," Foregrave snapped, looking carefully around. "We both know the real worth was obtained already here," he whispered, "only to be stolen by the heretics."

"And don't forget in doing so, they paid a heavy price. If they wish to see their friends again, they'd be foolish not to trade."

"Assuming that you're right, I doubt the high commander would forfeit hard-fought prey — or the director a scientific marvel."

"Then, rest assured it won't be necessary," Lucas calmly told him, "as desperation tends to make one ruinously trusting. The odds are stacked against them, and we have no need to bargain."

"How merciless and shrewd," the judicar admitted. "Perhaps you'll earn his favor yet."

"Time will tell," considered Lucas, "as there still is much to do."

"Indeed, there is. I shall begin the preparations for tomorrow, and with any luck, it will truly be a spectacle to remember."

As Foregrave took his leave, Lucas turned to Alicen, who waited silently nearby. "Have Draconis bring the prisoners to Capstone," he ordered.

"Isn't the Pillar more secure?" she asked.

"Perhaps, but we need to keep them hidden, just in case the others try their luck. Also, the director might extract more value there. He certainly is eager."

22

Bound securely to a chair inside an observation suite, Nevara sat alone with defiant resignation. Unlike the confining walls of interrogation cells, this room possessed a forebodingly spacious and clinical design.

Before she had much time alone, Lucas made his entrance, walking straight to her.

Gone was any trace of love or hope she once had seen in him, as the man who stood before her exuded misanthropy. The scabrous wounds beneath his bandage displayed the rift between them, and the resemblance that he bore was nothing but an insult.

Might this all have differed had she simply told him everything? Or was it well beyond her power to sway a heart of stone? Perhaps those dreams could never be, and in her fanciful pursuit, she managed only to defile them, leaving her with nothing. Regardless, now she had to face it — to stare it in the eye.

"I won't tell you anything," Nevara firmly stated.

"Understandable," the overseer granted. "You also won't use genomancy to escape, even if you could." He glanced at the empty syringe upon a nearby table, noting several others ready for injection.

"Just came here to gloat, then?" she inquired.

"You know I'm not that petty," Lucas countered, seemingly offended.

"Clearly, I know nothing of the real you."

"I'm sure that's not exactly true," he mused, staring off in contemplation. "After all, we spent quite a bit of time together, albeit mostly confined within a virtual reality."

Nevara lowered her head, eyes welling slowly. "You still don't remember," she muttered to herself.

"What might that be?" Lucas asked, turning back to her.

"So, why *are* you here?" she snapped, recovering quickly.

Lucas once more averted his attention to reflect. "We never got to say goodbye. I thought I owed you that, at least."

"Anything else?" she scoffed.

"I wanted to thank you. Though you may not feel quite the same, this was the only path ahead. Scarcity and suffering will soon be relics of a time forgotten. I wish you could see that vision, too."

"You may have one eye left, but you could not be blinder to the truth."

Lucas moved in closer. "I could say the same to you."

Was there a trace of pity on his face? Surely, she must have been mistaken, as had always been the case. Either way, the urge to strike him down had never been so strong.

"Won't you even try?" he wondered. "It could be your only chance."

"You'll get what you deserve," she promised, "one way or another."

"Oh well," said Lucas with a shrug. "There still are other options, but I hate to see such waste."

"I could say the same to you," she echoed with a glare.

He smiled at her wistfully, then headed for the door, leaving Nevara to whatever fate might come.

"I have to know!" she shouted angrily, stopping Lucas in his tracks. "What really made you do this? Was it hatred for the world? A selfish lust for power? Does it even matter that you're nothing but a servant?"

After a moment's consideration, Lucas turned to face her. "In all the time you fought for them, did you ask if they were worth it? Perhaps you lived among them long ago, but you were always just an outsider — a perpetual pariah. Born to be a weapon, you never had a place, but I was rejected by my own . . . at every opportunity. Neither of us failed them; they brought it on themselves."

He then departed scornfully, and Nevara sat in sorrow. Her heart was broken soundly, but at least she had no doubts.

From behind a one-way observation panel stood the trio of Executors. With Lucas out of earshot, they mulled the implications of the scene.

"Quite the mess indeed," Foregrave noted.

"Did you honestly expect for him to break her?" Draconis countered. "This is what you get when you leave it to an amateur."

"Just give *me* some time," Rinehart confidently boasted. "There's quite a few ideas that I'd rather like to try." The briefest flickering of zeal shot across his deadened eyes.

"You're not doing anything until the Architect approves it," Draconis ordered.

"I must heartily agree," the judicar affirmed. "With all that has arisen lately, we must be at the limits of his mercy."

"He would undoubtedly be grateful for any discoveries that follow," the director said in protest. "I never had the chance before to study a chimera — at least of this variety. Who knows what other secrets she might be hiding that he never even realized?"

"I hardly think that vivisection is the best way to dispose of her," Foregrave criticized.

"Then, would you rather she be wasted on the Field?"

"Certainly not. She's far too much a threat for that, assuming she would fight."

"Agreed," said the high commander. "We needn't push our luck."

"Nevertheless," Rinehart pressed, "we were given discretionary authority for situations of this kind. If the Revelation truly is upon us, then we have quite a narrow window to exploit it. As such, we cannot afford to wait around for every little permission."

Draconis raised his eyebrows. "I would call this a pretty big one, actually, considering her nature. Do you really want to be responsible for carving up his daughter?"

"Besides," Foregrave added, "don't you think that if he wanted her dismembered, he would have done it long ago himself?"

Rinehart shrugged. "I wouldn't dare to speak for him."

"Precisely," Foregrave snapped. "None of us can ever hope to guess his true intentions."

"And while we stand here arguing, they plan their next attack. Shouldn't that concern you more, in light of what they've done?"

"Their numbers have been cut in half," Draconis reassured, "and we have everything we need to hunt them down, so until we are told otherwise," — he fixed his gaze on the high director — "*nothing* will be done to her."

"Very well," conceded Rinehart, soundly overruled. He knew there was no getting through, so he walked away to focus on his consolation prize. "It's not as though she was our only catch this evening," he pointedly reminded.

"And what exactly might you learn from him?" inquired the commander. "He's proven quite resistant to your NOVA tech already."

"Perhaps a more direct approach will yield some results," hypothesized his colleague. "I trust you don't object on that front?"

"Fine," Draconis granted, "but I'm keeping a drone on him."

Rinehart waved his hand with marked indifference, sure that, in addition to intrinsic satisfaction from the work ahead, he would be the one to reap the graces of the Architect.

Back at their desolate new headquarters, the fugitive crusaders tried to cope, reminded that, for all the effort spent, their only compensation was a shiny metal case, which they couldn't even open.

Carrie set it on the ground beside her half-dissected drone. "Another two steps back and barely one ahead," she ranted. "We just can't catch a break, it seems."

Victor paced the grimy floor distractedly. "That's no excuse to give up yet," he stressed. "Too much depends on us."

"I haven't given up," said Carrie, "but I'd love to hear suggestions."

He slumped against the dingy wall, a painful look upon his face. "I could really use a drink right now," he lamented gloomily.

Carrie's frown intensified. "Even if that were an option," she retorted, "we need to have our wits about us. The odds are bad enough."

"Don't you think I know that?" Victor snapped, head buried in his hands. "It should be clear by now I'm not cut out for leadership. Say what you will about him, but Lucas was the mastermind."

"Get it together, soldier!" Carrie told him harshly.

Victor raised his head in shock at her simple yet effective order.

"We all have demons," she continued, "yet we've managed to survive. Even if we only made it this far because of Lucas, now's the chance to prove ourselves without him. More importantly, now's the chance to realize our full potential, and if we fail in the end, so be it, but we have to do our very best, because you know it's not in us to quit."

He nodded in agreement, pondering her words. "Forgive me if you'd rather not discuss it," prefaced Victor, "but do you ever think about the Jolt?"

"Sometimes," she admitted, "but not enough to miss it. Every now and then, I might wonder how much more productive I could be, but it's not like I would relapse. That past is well behind me."

Victor couldn't help but envy her. "How did you get over it?"

"At first, I couldn't imagine coping on my own, especially during the withdrawal. I was terrified of failure — of letting everybody down. It's not like I had a choice, though, with all of us being hunted. I just had to accept that limitation . . . and push on through regardless. Eventually, I learned to trust myself without it, and I haven't really looked back since."

He took a moment to reflect. "You're quite the inspiration," Victor said in earnest.

"Oh, thanks, I guess," she replied uncomfortably, "but I wasn't trying to brag or anything; I just did what was logical. Whenever the course of action is clear to me, I know I always have to take it."

"All the same," acknowledged Victor, "It's not a thing most people could endure."

"Well, we're not most people, are we?" Carrie stated bluntly.

Victor smiled. "I can't argue there," he granted, getting to his feet. Across the room he walked, considering for a moment. "If what Nevara said was true, they'll do anything to get this back." He tapped the platinum case. "Maybe we should take the initiative before they find it."

"If you're implying we make a trade," she gathered, "do you think it's wise to trust them?"

"Not at all," said Victor, "which is why we need to stack the odds a bit. Can you still get in their network?"

"All my custom software tools are locked up in the Pillar, but I might be able to get access through the cruiser," she considered, "assuming they haven't patched up their security. We'd have to grab a new computer if you wanna be more mobile. What did you have in mind?"

"A long shot, to be sure," Victor cautioned, "and it may well get us all killed, but I really don't see any other options."

"Well, then," Carrie reasoned, "I suppose it's only fitting we designate this one Operation Morta."

23

Long before the emergence of an empire, and before their ambitions carried them across the stars, the Anakhari dared to probe the depths of what had largely been inscrutable. Thanks to their brightest scientific minds, history was about to witness a monumental experiment, and for such a promising endeavor, even Velroth deigned to grant his presence. Thus were they all were gathered in the bowels of Solmar.

Second-in-command of the entire operation, Xul approached his elder brother Yenekai, having one last chance to reiterate concerns he had. "I implore you to reconsider."

"The Elarch requires a worthy demonstration to justify our research," Yenekai reminded, "and we have come too far to be stopped now. With these hidden energies revealing themselves before our very eyes, how could we not explore them?"

"Indeed," Xul contemplated. "The very understanding of life itself might be transformed forever, though I can't help but fear the application." He glanced up at Velroth, standing resolute on the observation platform. "In any case, we cannot afford to rush a matter of this magnitude, especially if it means putting you in danger."

"Our window is too fleeting to waste," Yenekai insisted. "I cannot leave us to wonder what might have been. Besides, keep the aperture within the range we determined, and the resonance should remain stable enough to gather the necessary data with minimal risk." In response to the lingering doubt across his brother's countenance, Yenekai placed a reassuring hand upon his shoulder. "We have every precaution in place."

Xul nodded reluctantly. "We should verify the integrity of the transducer housing. The last thing we need is energy leaking through."

Yenekai gave a reassuring smile, then began his preparations for entering the containment chamber.

Once completed, Xul took a nervous glance at the Elarch before setting the initial parameters.

"Please report," he requested shortly.

"I do not know how to describe it," Yenekai responded. "Vibration . . . Flowing . . . Expansion. I feel immersed within some kind of energy, but—"

"Can you control it?" Velroth interjected.

"Not that I can tell."

"The readings are unlike anything we've measured," Xul noted, marveling at their fortune. "Even our algorithms cannot detect coherent patterns. It could take ages to study this data and make any sense of it."

Velroth scowled. "I was promised armaments, not analytics," he barked, coldly unamused.

"Elarch, we have everything we need to begin material research into this event. Once we are ready—"

"An event that, by your own estimation, will not recur for generations, leaving you with nothing more than conjecture until that time. If you expect me to entertain your claims and continue to support this venture, prove them to me now," the Elarch ordered.

171

Xul turned at once to face his brother, who, appreciating the magnitude of the situation, firmly nodded after a momentary pause. Their eyes remained locked just long enough for the younger to carefully weigh his options, regretfully coming to the same conclusion.

"Increasing aperture to 25%. Resonant coherence intensifying. Please report any changes."

"The vibrations are stronger," Yenekai replied.

"And?" Velroth pressed impatiently.

"Still no perceivable response."

"Then, more!"

"Elarch," Xul objected, "I must advise you not to—"

"MORE!"

"Very well," conceded Xul. "Increasing aperture to 50%. Please report." The concern grew in his voice, but he remained committed to their cause.

"A burning, difficult to localize. The energy — I can feel it deeper, but still no integration."

Velroth glowered. "Well?"

"The equipment is not designed for this amount of power!" Xul fiercely protested. "We risk serious instability if—"

"Your project ends here if I do not see results this instant!" Velroth roared.

Noticeably shaken, Xul returned to the console. Now in a sort of trance, his brother failed to respond, leaving the decision to be made alone. "Increasing to . . . 100%."

Almost immediately, Yenekai burst out in pain, his body radiating a strange iridescence. Moments of bewildered curiosity transfixed them all, for none could ignore such otherworldly light.

Without warning, though, sparks erupted from the room's equipment, rendering key controls and gauges unresponsive.

"What is happening?" demanded Velroth.

"The resonance is too strong!" Xul answered in alarm. "It's changing his molecular structure."

"What does that mean?"

"It means I have to close the rift before it kills him."

"The experiment is not yet over!"

"If we allow it to expand, it might consume our world!"

Only now aware of the peril so created, the Elarch allowed himself to be swiftly escorted away by his retinue.

Scrambling to find operational controls amid a flurry of explosions, Xul shot a look of sheer disgust at the now empty observation platform.

Unable to intervene remotely, he ran to the containment chamber, only to find the door had jammed.

Desperate to save his brother and avert catastrophe, Xul grabbed a flickering oscilloscope, then proceeded to hammer at the protective encasement of the crystalline core.

Just as the instrument soon shattered into fragments, the hull finally gave way and cracked ajar. Though blinded by the radiance, he didn't hesitate to reach inside, attempting to remove the bridge component.

The protomatter, somehow losing physicality, allowed Xul's hand to effortlessly pass through it, resulting in a sensation indescribable with any words of science. Still, he couldn't let that stop him, as there was no one else around to help.

Frozen in place after hastily separating the inner conduit, his body began to unravel right in front of him. Starting with his fingertips, the very matter dematerialized into a series of wavelike ripples.

No amount of resistance could halt the process, so without another recourse, Xul fumbled for a piece of jagged metal, all the while unable to tear his eyes from the transcendental sight.

Makeshift blade in hand, Xul proceeded resolutely to sever the encroaching aether, far too much at stake to be deterred by such an agonizing action.

When the grisly job was done, he fell abruptly backward, having to brace himself against a nearby console with his remaining forearm.

Panting heavily, Xul then dared to glance at the containment chamber, where his worst fears were confirmed: nothing but emptiness endured.

After howling a cry of pure exhaustion, Xul finally collapsed, beholding the wake of devastation as the pain grew more intense.

In spite of it all, however, that vision beyond the fabric of this world failed to horrify as much as it enticed. None could now deny its destructive power, certainly, but a greater mystery lay beneath — an arcane beauty glimpsed by no one else — and with the seeds planted firmly in his mind, Xul swore it would one day belong to him and him alone, no matter what the cost.

The Architect flexed his metal digits, regarding them with an air of detachment while partly lost in reverie.

". . . and that's pretty much everything there is to say," reported Lucas, back within Xul's private lab but now by invitation. "The damage was less than I expected," he confessed, quietly observing the subtle changes from his prior visit. Though unable to recall every peculiar detail, he noted the glaring absence of certain jars and vials.

"A setback to be sure," the Architect agreed, now giving his full attention, "but a calculated one at least."

"Then, there is another option?" Lucas wondered.

"I might have one or two."

"How does it hurt your chances overall?"

"More than I would prefer," conceded Xul, "but as you said, she had the potential to do far worse."

"While we're on the topic, any request for how to handle her?"

Xul considered briefly. "Let them have their spectacle. Her misery is hardly worth protracting, and the energy of the crowd would certainly be useful." He allowed the idea to linger momentarily. "I trust we are in agreement?"

"Perfectly," said Lucas. "Foregrave should be pleased to hear it, but I'm not so sure about the high director."

"I would suspect as much," responded Xul. "Make it clear to Rinehart that he is only to *contain* the subject. We cannot allow such curiosity to welcome undue risk."

"I'll pass it along," Lucas promised, following Xul's meditative gaze toward his dark prosthetic.

Silence followed, their official business apparently concluded.

"Was that by choice?" Lucas finally inquired. "It's hard to imagine that a guy like you couldn't simply grow a new one?"

Xul seemed to find the notion quite amusing. "Do not mistake what is possible for what is optimal," he cautioned. "Far from any burden, it proves to be more useful and secure than alternative solutions. More importantly, however, it serves as a reminder of what might go awry, should such forces not be dealt with properly."

"If you say so," Lucas granted.

The Architect reflected further. "Perhaps you'd care to witness a fitting illustration?" he suggested.

Lucas grinned with intrigue. "How could I refuse?"

Readying the equipment necessary, Xul provided context. "Though calling it by other names, many have recognized the presence of the Subverse, even among your kind, but never could they grasp its enigmatic nature."

"I take it you know more than most in that regard."

"Indeed, I do," boasted Xul. "Though sometimes interpreted as just another spatial dimension, it functions more as the blueprint of our known reality — a hidden substrate, if you will. By aetheric transmutation, it can be harnessed and shaped into energy or matter, achieving feats impossible through any other means."

"It loses a bit of the magic when you put it that way," said Lucas.

"All mysteries are meant to be uncovered," Xul asserted. "'Magic' is a term of willful ignorance used by those who cannot comprehend."

"In any case, I learned all this already."

"I suspected as much, but you cannot appreciate the full significance without proper visual aids."

Xul retrieved a sample vial of Lucas's DNA, placing it on a rack inside one of the many devices upon his workbench. Shortly thereafter, a familiar double-helix form appeared illusively above the apparatus.

"Familiar enough, I trust?"

Lucas nodded, prompting Xul to reach across the table and activate another machine, which beamed a focused ruby light straight into the vial, outlining the contours of the floating hologram with a glowing aura.

"Nothing of particular interest yet," Xul continued, "until the specimen is removed." He withdrew the vial, but the coiled glow persisted, totally absent of any visible foundation.

"What kind of laser is that?" Lucas had to ask.

"Incidental," Xul assured, "as this phantom residue phenomenon arises from the DNA, specifically through its unique entanglement with the Subverse."

"How so?"

". . . For some unknown reason," Xul answered with a pause, betraying a hint of bitterness in his tone, "the genetic material of your species just so happens to resonate perfectly with it."

"What are the odds?" Lucas wondered, staring at the winding pattern. "Remarkable, undoubtedly, but I sense you have even more to show."

With the laser still engaged, Xul placed another vial in a vacant slot next to where the first had sat, then filled it with his own blood, prompting a second, minutely different hologram to soon appear beside the outline. He powered the laser down before rotating the specimen rack, positioning the new vial in the location of the first.

Before their eyes, the second hologram began to slowly alter in response.

Xul eventually reversed the rack, and once again the laser shone into the space now empty, resulting in two identical projections: one solid in its core, the other a bright red outline.

"The phantom strands of DNA imprinted on the physical," was Lucas's deduction.

"Quite astute you are."

Lucas then looked at the holoscope, speculating further on the empty slot. "The residual signature — how long does it remain?"

"Without an anchor," Xul explained, "it will quickly fade away."

"And with one?"

"That depends greatly on the medium, of course."

The presentation's purpose became a little bit more clear. "How about something like protomatter?" asked Lucas rather pointedly.

"A clever boy indeed," the Architect acknowledged, grinning at his understanding. "Or perhaps you already knew?"

"She didn't mention every aspect," Lucas clarified. "This may have been too technical."

"Strange, considering that you would have had all the time required."

"I guess she didn't see the relevance."

"I wonder why," Xul offered as a final thought, forcing Lucas to ponder the same.

24

As the morning sun stretched across Empyrea, devotees flooded to the Temple Paramount, ready for a service unlike any other. In the aftermath of Overseer Corvin's proclamation, many now sought reassurance from the Architect's high judicar. With martial law in full effect, those unable to attend had nothing else to do but watch the coverage from their homes.

"Long have we prospered by the grace of his almighty providence," Foregrave spoke, standing tall upon his chancel. "Were it not for the gift of this great city itself, we would have perished in the barren lands below. Today, we are finally deemed worthy . . . to join him in the higher plane."

Excitement roused throughout the congregation.

"Understand, my children," he proclaimed while backdropped by a thick red veil, "that such an honor cannot extend to all. There are those among us who would besmirch the flock, but why should many suffer on behalf of such unworthy few? Thus did he ordain his emissary to vanquish any fears, ensuring by the overseer's holy mission that the strong and pure will rise above."

179

* * *

The staging grounds beneath the stadium, where Libertas became complete, now served to host the tentative transaction. Anxious to be sure, Victor waited for his guest to arrive at the designated venue, which not only sheltered from surveillance drones but disallowed surprise attacks, as well.

Right on time, Commander Draconis appeared in the solitary entrance across the Field of Deliverance.

"You came alone?" inquired Victor, holding the platinum briefcase at his side.

"That was the agreement," Draconis answered calmly.

"That isn't what I asked."

A look of slight amusement filled the martial countenance. "You don't think I can handle you on my own?"

"Where are my friends?"

"Nearby," Draconis assured without concern. "They will be delivered once I verify the integrity of what you've stolen."

"I want to see them first," demanded Victor.

"You would really gamble with their lives? Bring me the case or you will see them in pieces," threatened the commander.

Victor stared him down with skepticism. "They're not here, are they?" he concluded. "This never was an *exchange*."

The malevolent grin then widened as Draconis marched ahead.

After yet another sleepless night in custody, now blindly dragged to who knows where, Ross could only guess the end was near.

Planted firmly in a chair with his blindfold fast removed, he was thus confused to find a lavishly appointed office. Before him, the high director leaned attentively upon his desk, unnerving Ross with his calculating stare. Hovering above his shoulder, an observation drone made the cold reception all the more disquieting.

"You may leave us," he told the posted guards.

Uneasily they turned, knowing better than to question his directive.

Once the door was locked behind them, Rinehart waited silently a moment longer, never breaking from his thoughtful gaze.

"Dr. Avalon . . . ," he spoke at last. "So far from the noble calling you once followed."

Ross did not reply.

"Do you ever miss those days?" continued Rinehart. "Do you ever wish to be once more helping others, instead of only spreading senseless terror? You might truly believe in the misguided cause that so passionately drives you now, but at the end of it all, what do you really have but fruitless ideology?"

"I have the truth on my side," Ross shot back defiantly.

"Perhaps," acknowledged the high director, "but it's not quite the same, is it? What if I could offer you something more substantial?"

"Your faith been well tested," Foregrave continued, "but many questions may yet arise, even if you dare not ask them. With our greatest trial now at hand, I hope to banish any doubt. To better help you understand what lies ahead, I now present the means of our salvation."

With grandiose panache, he unveiled the jewel-encrusted chalice, arousing a reverent enthusiasm as it twinkled by the nearby candlelight.

"Clever, Mr. Talos," granted the commander, "though not enough to realize the futility of your efforts. You certainly have heart, and that I can respect. Too bad it had to be so grievously misplaced."

Steeled and undaunted, Victor stood in silence as his adversary neared.

"One way or another, I'm leaving with that case." His tone grew in austerity. "You and your friends needn't suffer any further because of it — or other matters well beyond your control."

"And you're really just gonna let us walk away?"

"I'm afraid, Mr. Talos, there is nowhere left for you to go," Draconis readily confessed, "but that doesn't mean I can't make this quick and . . . relatively painless."

"Is that right?" Victor considered. "Well, if you want it so bad, come and get it."

"So be it," said Draconis, lengthening his stride, but before the distance could be closed, the room began to shift.

Smoke billowed upward, and mirrored panels erupted across the floor.

"Have you nothing more than cheap theatrics left?!" Draconis shouted. "You're still trapped in here with me, all on your own, with no one left to save you. What must it take for you to accept your fate?"

"The time of man is coming to an end," said Rinehart. "I'm offering the chance to have a future in this great transition."

Ross indulged the offer.

"With your help," Rinehart continued, "the keys to the very fabric of our universe may be acquired. Allow me to study your abilities, and we will usher in a golden age for life itself. Consider the wondrous possibilities, not only for yourself, but for all the good that might be done — an end to famine, poverty, *disease* . . ."

The word hit Ross profoundly, letting Rinehart know his argument had worked. "You're asking me to betray everything," the doctor said reluctantly.

"I'm asking you to carefully weigh your options," reasoned the director. "Trust me, you will not soon find a better offer. We'll catch your friends eventually, and I'm going to study you lot all the same. Your cooperation in these matters is simply easier on both of us."

Ross deliberated.

"I know it's tempting to preserve delusions of the past," said Rinehart, "but now's the time to think about the future."

"To commence our final ascension," spoke Foregrave grandly, "I welcome the elders of our foremost distinguished families — pillars of this great city, embodying the truest virtue and devotion that Xul may ask of us."

Foregrave gestured toward the hooded figures kneeling in reverence before him, whose heads then rose in unison.

"As exalted paragons for all to follow, they shall proudly usher us forward unto glory."

Once more, the goblet reached the lips of the chosen few, and they consumed its nectar ardently.

* * *

Draconis blasted yet another wall of glass as Victor's likeness dashed across it, but with each attack, more panels promptly took their places.

When chance permitted, Victor would emerge from cover to fire at his foe, further enraging him.

"How long do you think you can delay this?!" shouted the commander.

"As long as it takes," replied the outlaw.

Pushed beyond his breaking point by the rather petty ruse, Draconis unleashed a sweeping aether shock wave, shattering every illusory diversion.

Panting heavily, he scanned their underground arena with his eagle eyes, spotting Victor lying sprawled. Mere feet away, the true objective sat, fortunately unscathed.

"I may not be a spiteful man," Draconis growled, swooping to retrieve the case, "but your death will give me pleasure. I hope this all was worth it."

Lost in thought, Ross continued blankly staring. Rinehart really knew just what to say, giving much to ponder.

After careful deliberation, he glanced sideways at the drone, then back at the director. "That sounds like an interesting future," Ross admitted, "but if you believe it has a place for *us*, then the only delusions are your own."

The director's composure abruptly faltered, and he returned a bitter scowl.

"You're out of your depth," Ross punctuated, "and I'd say you always have been."

"Is that so?" Rinehart snapped, abandoning all civility.

* * *

"To join in such celestial splendor," Foregrave heralded, "we must first imbibe the proper essence. It is therefore why, to achieve divinity, Xul bestowed his only child — a sacred bridge for us to cross."

With another lofty flourish, he pulled the veil wide. Behind it lay Nevara, strapped upon the tilted altar by her wrists and ankles.

"Pity not," he reassured the restless crowd, "for she did subvert his righteous will, and so her sentencing is just. Take this as proof of true benevolence, for through his equitable judgment, her sacrificial blood will raise us all."

The deacon handed Foregrave a ceremonial dagger, not unlike the goblet resting on the altar. Utter silence followed from the nave.

After casting a look of deep contempt at his former underling, Draconis opened the platinum case to inspect its contents, finding only his reflection staring back.

Waves of rage swept over him, for the chicanery was compounded by discovering that his face had become disfigured worse than ever.

A crack of blinding sunlight shone through the ceiling as it began to part, and the floor beneath him simultaneously rose, granting nowhere left to hide.

He reached inside his pocket, grasping for the leather pouch and turquoise medicine.

Rushing off the platform, Victor disappeared into the darkness, though the commander hardly noticed.

After plunging the syringe into his neck, the unsightly issue didn't fade, so he tried frantically again, though it could not help his plight.

185

With no more options left to try, he froze in horror at the sight of reinforcements lying in wait, aghast, and high above them circling surveillance drones. Displayed on monitors throughout the stands, his alien disfigurement could not be missed. Around him, inexplicable destruction lay, and guilty there he stood, exposed for all to see.

"Do you think it was by chance alone we made it to this point?" chided Rinehart, stiffening his spine. "Was it by coincidence that each calamity only added to our control? Wars, and plagues, and revolution — all arranged to serve his will."

"Even the Blight?" asked Ross, surprised at the forward honesty.

"Of course," the high director boasted. "The greatest consolidation of all time. Nothing in his grand ambition would be possible without it, and I assure you, Xul does not forget his gifted, chosen few. Despite our differences in race, his loyal stewards have more in common with his kind than we do among the rabble of our own. Those simple minds who hold him as a god could never reach the heights of his design. Your hopes and dreams, your vice and virtue, your every thought and deed — all meaningless by any metric. But if you insist, you may die among the rest as cattle, the most you could ever hope to be."

Completely stunned, Ross turned his head toward the drone, which had inched ever slightly closer without Rinehart ever noticing. "Did you get all that?" he asked, grinning rather cheekily.

"You must be joking," Rinehart scoffed, confirming Ross's POD was gone.

"Really? I suggest you turn around."

The director then looked out his window and quickly filled with dread, for upon the Pillar's great facade, he found himself on show. Agape he stood, still broadcast by the drone. "Impossible," was all that he could say, unable to comprehend.

"Clearly not," Ross noted from behind.

Rinehart charged, indignantly enraged, but the drone discharged a shocking blast, knocking him soundly to the floor.

The guards called out, hammering the door.

Ross was trapped inside.

Suddenly, the drone then smashed into the window, creating a narrow gap before returning to him.

«jump on,» Carrie ordered.

"What?" said Ross aloud.

«jump! on!» she repeated in his head.

With no time to think, Ross complied, just as the doors were breached.

«brace yourself,» she warned, and he went careening through jagged hole. Though nearly falling off his wild ride, he held on firmly, free once more.

Before the sanguinary ritual could be completed, a chorus of priority POD alerts intrusively disturbed the gravitas, halting Foregrave with vexation. Pompously, he turned, ready to reprove the masses and fast restore the mood.

Nearly every face across the crowd flashed brightly with activity, making Foregrave wonder what on earth could merit blatant sacrilege. His unease grew, as shocked they sat, unable to believe their eyes.

Confusion and disgust soon turned to anger, directed now toward the altar. The hooded acolytes could sense the ire, so they nervously receded.

With a final desperate act, Foregrave raised his dagger high, trying to regain control. Poised above Nevara's heart it sat, ready to finish the show.

Suddenly, however, a piercing cry erupted from behind, drawing every eye. A black-robed votary hunched over deep in pain, pressing both hands to his head.

Without warning, his cohorts caught the same affliction, and like dominoes they fell, one by one in agony.

Upon their naked hands, the lambent flames revealed fierce mutations, and as the horror climaxed, a demented urge then drove them to attack each other. In the savage scuffle, ghastly faces were uncovered, causing panic to ensue.

Bewildered beyond words and action, Foregrave stared in shock. Much too late, awareness came, and he focused on the empty cup. How, sealed and secure, could the blood have been contaminated? Surely, the Architect had not intended this, and Rinehart well knew better. That left the only culprit as . . . But how—

Before he could ponder further, Xul's high judicar was tackled to the ground.

Dagger still in hand, he drove it well into his crazed assailant.

The Temple Guard soon tried to aid, but too unruly was the crowd.

Nevara seized her chance at last, conjuring a blade of light. Down it cut her tight restraints, with none around to see or care.

By the time she disappeared, her flight was but a trivial concern.

Back upon his feet, Foregrave glanced at all the watchful drones, then likewise made a hasty exit.

25

Nevara stumbled wildly through the back alleys, desperate to avoid the pandemonium erupting in the streets.

From the lowest levels of Empyrea to the highest, the truth could now be seen, and the Vanguard struggled to contain the outrage from all strata of society.

In the short time since her last fortuitous escape, she had witnessed shocking barbarism from every group, leaving her afraid to entertain the logical conclusion. Before such thoughts could build momentum, though, a familiar voice broke through the noise.

"Nevara!" Victor shouted, rushing over with the others. "That was a bit of luck back there. Sorry we couldn't help more directly. Why didn't you let us know where you were sooner?"

"It's too risky using genomancy while they can study it. I'd rather die than give Xul any such advantage."

"I didn't even think of that," Ross realized. "Good thing you got me out of there in time," he said to Carrie. "You really are my hero."

She nodded somewhat awkwardly, unable to hide her blushing.

"You hacked the drones?" Nevara surmised. "How did you manage that?"

"I reverse-engineered the communication protocol from the one we'd snatched," Carrie happily explained. "That part was a little tricky, but after cracking it, I also found a glaring vulnerability in their network."

"I thought they would have patched them all."

"It wasn't there before, so maybe luck really is on our side for once."

"You didn't hand over the samples, did you?"

"They're still on the ship," said Victor, "until we can properly dispose of them. We were hoping you could help us out with that."

"Gladly," she agreed, but the anarchy intensified, distracting her once more. "They won't last long against the Vanguard," Nevara worried. "Firepower is not on their side."

"I'm not sure it's on anyone's side right now."

"What do you mean?"

"I sabotaged their weapons with a simple firmware push," said Carrie. "It's not foolproof by any means, but by the time they realize, they'll be caught right in the thick of it."

"You got that deep into their system?"

"We still had access through our worm inside the Pillar. I guess Lucas never got around to having it removed."

"He probably didn't think much of our abilities without him," suggested Ross.

"Well, he'll be thinking twice now," Victor added.

"I'm sure he will," Nevara distantly replied.

"This is really happening," he noted, fairly puzzled by her hesitance to share in their elation. "People finally know the truth — what we've all been fighting for. Isn't this what you wanted?"

Far from reassured, she glanced anxiously down the alley at the sounds of growing discord. "I always thought it was."

As Lucas watched the bloodshed through his office window, which had promptly been repaired, a sergeant barged into the room, Lieutenant Pryce arriving next with two armed guards in tow.

"Due to current exigencies, the high commander bids your abdication, 'Overseer' Corvin," he spoke with great professional contempt, "and we are to ensure that you comply."

"Is that so?" asked Lucas, keeping his back to him. "What a truly fragile system. Just look at how it bleeds when tested under load. I bet you never thought you'd live to see the day."

The sergeant eyed him closely, his haughty smirk now faltering. "Are you coming willingly or not?" He motioned for his holster.

"You've served amid stagnation long enough," said Lucas, ignoring the request. "With so much raw potential out there, don't you think it's time for change?"

"I think it's time that your psychotic tenure ends," the soldier spat, drawing forth his weapon.

Lucas turned around to face him. "Not *you*," he scoffed. "And they say I'm the one deranged."

The sergeant's look of brief confusion then gave way to utter shock, as a glowing aether blade plunged swiftly through his chest.

"Does this answer your proposal?" inquired the lieutenant, grinning from behind.

Her guards glanced at each other, but that was all they did.

"Perfectly," said Lucas, and she let the body fall.

"Think it counts as notice? I don't much care for paperwork."

"I'm sure they'll get the message loud and clear. No doubt Draconis will be heartbroken."

"Maybe if he had one," Alicen remarked as she joined him at the window.

"You did betray his confidence," reminded Lucas. "I couldn't have done this on my own."

"He should have kept such secrets closer — or at least learned self-control."

"And what a mess it made," Lucas noted of the spectacle below.

"Well, there certainly is no going back now."

"Agreed," said Lucas, reaching toward his chest, "so instead, we shall advance." He removed the gilded brooch and tossed it on the floor, then cast aside his mantle in favor of mobility. "Gather all the troops you can," he ordered, "and prepare to make some history."

His gaze now fixed upon the crescent in the sky, which beckoned with a call that he could not refuse.

Retreating deep into his chambers, Foregrave dropped the dagger on his desk. What was to be done now? Could he escape from this?

The deacon quickly followed in, trying to make some sense of the bizarre affair he witnessed. "I never would have suspected the commander to be guilty of such deviancy," he confessed. "How could one be so impure yet serve atop The Order?"

"For some, no power is enough," Foregrave bitterly replied. "I have to give him credit, though: he's kept that secret well."

"And revealed it quite disastrously," said the deacon.

"How long have I served with the utmost loyalty," Foregrave muttered, mostly to himself, "yet fortune favors that impious boor."

"Favors? With such a taint of blasphemy? I'm afraid I don't understand."

Foregrave ignored the confused remark.

"In any case," continued his credulous assistant, "I have some thoughts as to how we might provide reassurance and distance ourselves from the . . . unsavory public perception. We can prepare an emergency mass in time—"

"Can't you see what's happening, you idiot?!" Foregrave snapped, wheeling around to face him. "The city's fate is sealed. There is no divorcing ourselves from this wretched mess. Our only hope now is to flee and beg for mercy. Then, we might be spared his holy wrath."

"Leave? Our duty is to guide the city spiritually. How could such an act of desertion be forgiven? This surely is our greatest test of faith, and now of all times, we must hold true in honoring his divine intention."

Foregrave turned once more toward his desk, lowering his head for a moment of reflection.

"You're absolutely right," he acknowledged, "and you have my eternal gratitude for holding me to the path when I might go astray. In fact, why don't we pore through some of my homilies together, and perhaps we'll find proper inspiration?" He motioned across the room toward a venerable tome.

"That sounds like an excellent idea," agreed the deacon, but as he turned his back, Foregrave plunged the dagger in, holding on until the deed was done.

Without a second thought, he quickly left the room, focused only on escape.

Rinehart paced his office, wondering how he was possibly to salvage the mess he'd helped create. This was no mere breach in protocol, for he had blown it all wide open, with no one else to blame. The Architect would not forgive him twice, so what was he to do?

Before a solution could be devised, his doors burst open, and Overseer Corvin marched inside, flanked by a pair of Vanguard officers.

"Hello, Director," greeted Lucas. "Not having the best day, huh?"

"What the hell do you want?" Rinehart took a swig from his decanter.

"I was hoping to borrow a few engineers. Where better else to find the best?"

Rinehart glared with sheer contempt. "I don't have time for this nonsense."

"Yeah, I thought as much," said Lucas, "so I helped myself already."

Rinehart slammed his desk in anger. "No matter what title you may hold, I am still in charge here!"

"Well, about that," Lucas prefaced, "there's only one use that I still have for you — and really just your face."

His intention slowly dawned upon the high director, who couldn't stop from glancing toward the marble owl. "You still need the access code, remember? Please, let's work something out like gentlemen."

"You're not in much of a position to withhold anything from me. I'll get what I need, one way or another."

The blood drained from his face again as Rinehart swayed uncomfortably. "What exactly do you expect to accomplish here?" he pressed. "Do you really think the Architect would let you pull the same shit twice? In case you don't remember, you can't rely on that whore's treachery again. You're on your own this time."

Lucas narrowed his gaze but remained composed. "I wouldn't say it's the same as before," he clarified, "and while it's true that I don't have my former access, I'm certainly not alone."

Lieutenant Pryce used the cue to make her entrance.

"You?!" was all that Rinehart uttered.

"Quite the upgrade, wouldn't you say?" Lucas gloated at the irony of life only now appearing in those eyes.

Out of cards to play, the high director simply watched as Alicen closed the door behind her.

"Remember, Lieutenant," noted Lucas, "we're going to need his head intact, but anywhere else, . . . do as you will."

Together once more aboard their cruiser, the Libertas crusaders took stock of what they'd set in motion.

"Why is it always two steps back for us?" Carrie grumbled.

"We knew it was gonna get worse before it got better," Victor answered.

"Not this much," said Ross. "The city's tearing itself apart. What happens when there's nobody left to save?"

Nevara stared out the window sullenly, haunted by the question.

"For now, at least, you should really do something about that," Carrie noted, pointing at the laceration on his leg.

"Shit, I didn't even realize." He took a closer look. "Is there anything I can use for a tourniquet around here?"

"Here, try this," Carrie offered, untying the ribbon from her hair.

"Is this actual silk?" Ross marveled at the texture.

"Yeah," she responded flatly.

"And you don't mind getting blood on it?"

"By all means; that rough exit was mostly on me. Besides, it was a gift from my father — really the only thing I have left to remind me of him now. I wouldn't mind being rid of it."

"That's too bad," said Ross. "You wear it rather well."

"Thanks," she muttered, averting her eyes uneasily. "So, does anyone have a plan?"

"Well, we can't just wait for everything to resolve itself," Ross argued. "What if the Vanguard regain control, then crack down even harder, if that's possible. It won't matter what people believe if they lose all means to fight."

"How the hell are we supposed to stop mass rioting by ourselves?" asked Carrie.

"I'm not sure appealing to their reason will get us very far," considered Victor. "As much as I hate to admit it, Lucas was right about one thing: before the truth can be accepted, it will be violently opposed. We tore the mask off something big, and now it's out there, laid bare for all to see."

* * *

High above the Earth, disturbing news continued flooding those among the Anakhari lunar outpost.

Unrest grew widespread in the city far below, yet no official explanation had been offered. Afraid to apprise the Architect without sufficient intel, the staff persisted in their efforts at establishing contact.

Finally, a response came through — not to the control room, but to the transit cabin well across the station.

"Director Rinehart is requesting access," a security attendant reported.

"He'd better have some answers. Let him in."

A barrier soon formed around the dais, ready to allow his passage.

Prepared to face the high director, the operator found his expectations only partly met, as Rinehart's face stood poised atop a younger frame, donned in overseer garb.

Before he could react, a sudden burst of energy then knocked him to the ground.

As others turned in shock, the Vanguard retinue emerged and quickly shot them down.

Once the gateway was reset, further waves of troops arrived, fanning out aggressively to deal with resistance.

Lucas raised a hand to remove his NOVA mask, returning his face to its natural appearance. "She really is a clever girl," he remarked to his new partner, pocketing the innovative gadget.

"Everyone has their uses," Alicen replied.

"Isn't that the truth," said Lucas, and the two continued on their conquest, clearing one corridor after another with brutal efficiency.

197

By the time their onslaught reached the center of control, emergency distress alerts were flashing everywhere.

"Looks like they know we're here," Lucas noted. "Couldn't be helped, I suppose. Still, now that the place is ours, we should get to work at once."

"You think you accomplished anything?" a voice asked from the floor.

Lucas glared at the lowly grunt who sounded the alarm.

"Your suffering will be equal to your arrogance."

Alicen drew her sidearm, but Lucas intervened, halting her enthusiasm successfully this time.

"We seem to have been locked out of their system," he responded to her look of irritation. "He may yet be of use to us."

"Only Xul can restore it now," the Anakhari scoffed. "There's nothing you can make me do."

Lucas shot a glance at Alicen before lowering himself to eye level.

Their hostage's bravado, though backed by superior physique, faltered against the piercing steel gaze that fell upon him.

"I think we both know that's not true," said Lucas with a cadence both menacing and calm.

26

Lieutenant Pryce watched carefully as her captive spoke with Xul. Not a speaker of their native tongue, she had no way of deciphering their exchange, but the severity of Lucas's persuasive methods left little doubt of his compliance. Even so, she was not about to drop her guard.

Suddenly, all the flashing red on the consoles disappeared, replaced by graphical interfaces.

Her nonverbal confirmation allowed Lucas to end the conversation.

Alicen then attempted exploration through the main computer terminal, though it proved unfeasible regardless of the lockdown lifting. "We might have to keep him alive," she warned, "unless *you* can make any sense of this."

Lucas glanced at the characters and symbols foreign to any human language. "Actually, I can," he said, deftly navigating through the system.

"Where did you learn that?" she asked him in surprise.

"There were many things I learned in exile; I had nothing else but time."

Deciding not to pry, she moved to change the subject. "I have to admire your technique," she noted, glancing at the now unconscious prisoner.

"Somewhat different from yours," he mused, "but no less effective, it would seem."

"You're far too modest," countered Alicen. "The director hardly needed much persuading, and these guys have quite a bit more nerve."

"Indeed, they are not to be underestimated — the Architect least of all."

"What chance is there he's on to us?"

"I can't really say," considered Lucas. "I'm no expert in recognizing coded Anakhari signals of distress, but he did restore access, apparently."

"Still, we should prepare for their eventual response."

"Not just from Xul," he added. "If the Elarch becomes aware, retaliation will certainly be in force."

"Do you think he'll be a problem?"

"A nuisance, maybe, as I've been assured this outpost is impregnable, now that I disabled the gateway passage."

"It's also a bit enormous," Alicen expressed, noting the lingering hostile presence while cycling through the cameras. "You sure we have the numbers to hold it, even from here?"

"I'll take care of that," Lucas guaranteed, walking across the room to the nearest ventilation duct. "Kindly ensure that all the men are wearing helmets," he instructed before then removing the protective panel.

Once she relayed the command, Lucas began channeling a dark miasma into the air stream from his hands.

As she turned to watch the monitors, the station filled with noxious vapor, exterminating the occupants room by room.

"I think you've done it," she eventually announced, no longer able to detect enemy signs of life.

"So," said the lieutenant as Lucas returned to her, "now that we've taken the Moon, what could possibly be next?"

"I'm so glad you asked." He procured from his breast pocket a trio of thin, iridescent keycards. "I have a rather important job for you," he stated, offering them to her.

"I see," she responded. "If it's what I think it is, you might be a little short."

"No worries," he assured, reaching into a side pocket for an additional pair, which, though perfectly matching the shape of the others, lacked the same alluring sheen.

"Now, that's more like it," Alicen remarked, pleasantly surprised.

"Nobody would listen to anything we say," asserted Victor, debating a solution. "They don't want answers — only retribution."

"There has to be a way to buy some time," Carrie urged, "at least while everything's up in the air."

Ross, looking at the sky, offered a suggestion. "If we can raise the city high enough," he theorized, "the altitude would induce unconsciousness. I know it sounds risky, but with the right balance, we should be able to avoid fatalities."

"Assuming we could even move it fast enough," Carrie warned, "all that g-force is gonna put some serious strain on the architecture."

"Not to mention the human body," realized the doctor, now doubting his idea.

"That wouldn't be an issue," said Nevara, breaking her contemplative silence. "The engines produce an artificial gravity field, which helps to evenly distribute the acceleration."

"Inertia negation?" Carrie reasoned.

"Effectively."

"Well, then," Ross concluded, "unless there's any better plan, . . ."

After weighing the implications and recognizing they were largely out of options, the group tacitly accepted the desperate measure.

"Navigational controls are way up in the Pillar," Victor noted, "which is probably on lockdown, considering the riots."

"Could we even get in?" Carrie wondered.

"It wouldn't matter without the keycards," he reminded. "I doubt we'd get our hands on one, let alone all five."

"Is there really no other way?" asked Ross.

"Xul has remote access to the city's infrastructure," replied Nevara. "Quite some time ago, I installed a backdoor channel that should allow us to exploit it."

"That's great."

"I'm afraid it's not that simple, as the cards hold more than just encryption: they provide the extra power necessary through embedded protomatter fragments."

"Protomatter?" Carrie noted.

"A uniquely biphasic mineral, concurrent across dimensions. Though tremendously unstable if not properly controlled, it's connection to the Subverse is integral to most Anakhari technology."

"So, the override is useless," Victor summarized.

"Not completely," said Nevara. "Though there are a few distinctions, we do all have another way to generate that energy."

"You mean genomancy?" Ross inferred.

"It's worth a try, but I would have to be the one to do it, as the likelihood of aetherburn could result in lasting damage."

"Okay, then. We'll be there to cover you."

"No," she readily objected. "I'll have to disable the atmospheric regulators to deal with its garrison. Oxygen won't be a problem for me, but you'll need to stay inside the ship to be conscious for whatever follows."

"Are you sure about this?" Victor asked. "We just got you back, and you're already taking a hell of a risk."

"I know their systems well, and this is how it must be done."

Attended by a small group of key personnel, Lucas wasted no time in making his way through the sterile white halls to the heart of the lunar base, the true value held within. Fallen guards lined their path, but no additional resistance was to be found, for his technique had proven quite effective.

Without delay, Lucas reached the nucleus of industry, stymied only by a thickly windowed door, though he readily gained access with administrative clearance.

Inside the massive chamber, Lucas walked across a grated catwalk, beholding the brilliant electric blue from the main reactor, a booming hum vibrating in his chest.

Among the intricate machinery otherwise bathed in shadow, there hovered overhead a toroidal pulse transformer, coiled like a snake around the cavernous core. Indeed, here was where the plan would really come to be.

"This is unbelievable," said one of the men behind him.

Lucas turned abruptly. "That's a shame. I was hoping it might be familiar enough."

"Well, I can't say much for that," the engineer nervously replied, pointing to the giant power source, "but we should be able to handle your request."

"Excellent. Inform me as soon as you make progress." Lucas headed back out the door, leaving a pair of officers behind. "And do try to hurry," he stressed. "We're on a very tight schedule."

Urgently, a messenger arrived before the lab of Xul, breaking routine solitude. Inside, he found the Architect inspecting vials of his pewter mixture.

"My lord," spoke the nervous deputy, "there still has been no update on the specimens. Furthermore, we've noticed mounting signs of lawlessness. Something must be very wrong down there."

"I don't doubt it," Xul agreed, focused on his task.

"I thought it might be time to notify the Elarch," his aide suggested, growing more uneasy.

"He doesn't need to know just yet."

"How long do you expect to hide it?"

"However long is needed," said the Architect emphatically. "He never was a man of patience, and now from dealing with the Mechagens, I know not how he might respond to yet another crisis. Once we have results to show, all will be forgiven."

"And if we fail in that pursuit?"

". . . Then, his rage would strike us either way," Xul concluded, "so better to control the situation by ourselves."

"Do you still believe we have a chance?"

"Empyrea may fall," Xul readily acknowledged, "but one way or another, there will be no further cycles."

As Nevara neared the engine controls within the Pillar of the Sky, her heart beat heavily to the pulsing lights and sirens. Rinehart's chemical suppressant had a lingering effect, compounded by her recent injuries, but she could not let anything interfere with what she came to do.

At last the dark agenda was exposed, but rebellion would count for nothing if humanity destroyed itself. What else could be expected, though? Their world now lay in tatters, leaving little chance for rationality to soon prevail. The bitter truth required a new story that could frame it, but would any endure long enough to write one?

Arriving at her goal, she found a pair of guards before the door. Thanks to their surprise, however, Nevara dealt with them, straining herself more. She hoped there were no further obstacles, but upon entering the room, she encountered yet another presence.

"The demon daughter of Xul," greeted Alicen, standing at the controls. "You don't seem to be in the best of shape."

"Lieutenant Pryce," Nevara stoically replied. "On whose orders might you be here? You seem to vary between allegiances."

A blast of aether nearly struck her as she dodged, instead shattering the windows all around them.

"It might seem that way to you," granted Alicen, the wind blowing loose her golden hair, "but ever since the commander showed his fear, I can promise you my loyalties have only lain within the man who put it there."

"You really think you know him?" snapped Nevara. "I have to pity you."

"Is that right?" Alicen launched another burst. "What would you know of ambition — one that exceeds the bounds of life itself? I can't imagine what he ever saw in you."

Nevara lunged from cover with a violet spear in hand, though its use was blocked by a manifested shield.

The lieutenant then responded with a rather fierce riposte, knocking down her foe.

"You traitors both deserve each other," said Nevara, trying desperately to stand. "You'll meet a fitting end, I'm sure."

Alicen sauntered forward. "You're the one whose path has ended," she retorted, pulling back Nevara's head to reveal a trigonal pendant inky as her hair. "Mine has only just begun." She then tore off the relic before kicking her back down.

"You're nothing but his lap dog," said Nevara in disgust.

Busy gloating at her triumph, Alicen dismissed the insult. "If only you could live to see how wrong you are," she entertained, "but we can't have that, now, can we?" In her open hand appeared a spartan blade of light, forcing Nevara to frantically weigh her options.

Too beaten and exhausted to counter back with much, she chose instead to roll right out the window, the only escape afforded.

Deafened by the winds, Nevara closed her eyes, for what remained in sight but an insignificant demise?

The roaring noise intensified, but much to her surprise, Nevara heard a friendly voice call out from a nearby falling ship.

"Grab on!" it shouted, snapping her awake.

With a momentary pause, she reached for Ross's hand, and back aboard he pulled her, away from death's embrace.

27

"What the hell happened up there?" asked Ross, healing Nevara's latest injuries.

"Lieutenant Pryce — she damaged the controls before I could use them."

"Why would she do that?"

"To move the city without interruption."

"By herself?" asked Carrie. "How's that possible?"

Nevara shook her head. "I don't know, but she seems to be working directly with Lucas. He must have found a way to copy the other keycards. Even a fraction of the protomatter in them would be enough to partially run the engines."

"What would that accomplish?" wondered Victor.

"By descending to the surface, they could be drawing Xul's attention before making their next move. I suspect it already involved disabling the Curtain."

"Now that you mention it," said Ross, "it does feel like a fog was lifted. How did that happen?"

"Lucas must be in control of the lunar base."

"So, he's turned on Xul," concluded Victor. "Was this all just a ruse to gain more power?"

"Perhaps, but there's a greater concern," she stressed. "That facility harbors the second largest protocore reactor in existence, and I fear what damage he might cause with it."

"Worse than he's already done?" asked Ross.

"Considerably. Many years ago, Xul tore the fabric of reality and exposed the Subverse, which threatened to warp all matter beyond repair, had it not been promptly closed. Lucas now has the means at his disposal for something similar, and I believe that to be his true goal. After all, what punishment could better suit the world he so despises?"

"Then, how do we stop him?" Victor asked, but Nevara just continued staring wide-eyed without response.

"Look!" Ross pointed out the window.

Down below, the rioting seemed only to intensify, with outrage now replaced by feral madness.

"I think the situation just got a whole lot worse."

"We need to get the hell out of the city," concluded Victor.

"I'm not abandoning them!" Nevara protested.

"Nobody said that, but there's not much we can do in our current state. We're not gonna be able to help anyone if we die trying."

"Did you forget about the perimeter defenses?" reminded Carrie.

"We'll have to chance it," he resolved.

"Is that really our only option?" wondered Ross.

"There's nowhere safe to land, and we'll get shot down regardless if we just keep circling around, assuming that our fuel doesn't run out first."

A few seconds of silence passed.

"Fine," agreed Nevara.

They sped toward the haven's border, a panoply of turrets looming in their path. None had broken through before, so this exception would be notable, to say the least.

"Look," Ross began, "if we don't make it out—"

"We'll make it," Victor promised.

With bated breath, the crew now braced themselves for impending fire as they drew closer . . . and closer . . . until . . .

The ship then crossed the threshold, but their passage remained unchallenged.

In disbelief, they all looked out the window, finding the spiral city slowly shrinking far behind them.

"Did it malfunction?" Carrie asked, more curious than relieved.

"Unlikely," responded Victor. "Those systems have multiple redundancies in place. I've never known them all to fail."

"Then, I guess we'll have to chalk it up to luck," said Ross. "But what do we do now?"

"If the city's really landing, maybe we can start evacuation. That should cool things down a bit."

"I doubt we'd manage by ourselves," Carrie noted. "We're on our own out here."

"Perhaps not," advised Nevara. "There may be one place left to turn."

Returning by herself, Alicen entered the control room of the captured station.

"I take it you succeeded?" Lucas asked, exploring the computer system.

"It's done," she boasted. "The city's on the move."

"Excellent work." He looked up to greet her. "You changed your hair. I like it."

"Thanks, but it wasn't by choice. I had to do some pest control."

Lucas raised his eyebrows.

"The half-blood arrived there shortly after I did."

"And?"

Alicen offered him the trophy claimed. "She won't be bothering us again."

Lucas remained impassive, slowly approaching to take it. "And the others?" he asked, staring at the pendant.

"No idea. They probably got caught up in the riots. I wouldn't worry about them."

Lucas placed his hand firmly at the nape of the lieutenant's neck.

She quivered momentarily, mesmerized by the penetrative cobalt. Deep inside that gaze, she saw the soaring heights of his ambition. Never had she witnessed one achieve so much in so brief a span of time. Together, they would surely rise to bask in glories few imagined. Together—

"Overseer," some technician interjected, "a colossal vessel just entered the system."

"Where?" inquired Lucas, finally breaking eye contact.

"Through the Saturn relay, it appears."

"Qel'therus, no doubt."

"Sir?"

"The 'Ark of Destiny'," said Lucas, "Velroth's flagship."

"How could they have responded so quickly?"

Alicen finally exhaled as Lucas retracted his hand.

"Word travels fast when you've harnessed the underlying framework of reality. It won't be long before they act, so we'll have to begin at once."

* * *

Aboard his massive ship, the Anakhari emperor stood furiously impatient.

"Elarch Velroth," Xul remotely answered, "to what do I owe the honor of your visit?"

"Did you really think I wouldn't learn?" replied the sovereign.

"I saw no reason to alarm you," Xul assured. "The situation is being managed."

"Hardly!" Velroth yelled. "I have indulged in this experiment rather long enough. You were always playing with fire, and now we're set alight." He turned toward his captain. "Do we still control the satellite?"

"It would appear so, Elarch, but it's not yet in position."

"Then, initiate the priming sequence," Velroth barked before glaring firmly back at Xul. "Once I clean this mess of yours, you will answer for such rank incompetence."

"As you wish," the Architect conceded. "I await your swift arrival."

"I thought Empyrea was all that remained of humanity," said Ross in disbelief.

"Not entirely," Nevara told him. "Once evacuation started, many distrusted the salvation offered, so they sought shelter in the woods, underground — anywhere they could. Enough of the population readily complied with Xul's agenda, so these renegades were deemed unworthy of pursuit, and nobody expected them to survive that long. If anything, he was glad to be rid of such potential agitators."

"You think they managed to eke out a living after all this time?" asked Carrie.

"I know they have," assured Nevara. "Xul is quick to dismiss those of little apparent value to his goals, so he has allocated few resources to tracking them. Fortunately, I conducted my own investigations under his radar."

"And you really think that they can help us?" wondered Ross.

"They certainly know how to handle themselves," she noted. "Also, being subjected to far less genetic manipulation than the Haven populations, they will be valuable allies on the road ahead."

"That doesn't speak much to their willingness," Victor pointed out. "They sound like quite the stubborn types."

"We'll have to be convincing; we're out of other options. Empyrea represents millennia worth of effort, and Xul will stop at nothing to reclaim it."

"I'm sure they'll understand the threat against us all," said Ross a bit naively.

"One can only hope."

"Where are we headed, then?" asked Victor.

"Here are the coordinates." Nevara leaned over the dashboard to input the numbers, setting course for their destination, the final source of hope.

With nothing else to do, Carrie used the brief respite to explore the contents of the platinum case. In addition to the collected samples of blood, it contained several carefully arranged items that piqued her curiosity — among them a syringe filled with unknown amber fluid.

"Would this one be the catalyst?" she inquired of Nevara.

"In unadulterated form."

"You mentioned that it could awaken latent abilities," reminded Carrie. "Is that something we . . . I mean—"

"You're not serious, are you?!" Ross exclaimed. "You saw what it did to those creeps."

"We still don't know exactly what happened to them."

"What else could it have been?"

"He's right," Nevara warned. "The effects are far too unpredictable. We should destroy it at the first convenient opportunity."

"Along with the samples," added Victor.

"Right," said Ross, glancing at the blood. "Is there a special protocol or something?"

"Thermal denaturation should be enough to destroy any usable data," replied Nevara, "but their energy signature may still be detectable this far from civilization. In fact, so might ours, I fear."

"Does that mean we can't use genomancy?" reasoned Victor.

"Caution would be wise, at least until after we've made contact. Even that may not suffice, though, so the best we can do is hurry."

Returning the syringe, Carrie sifted through the case with eager fascination.

"Even if these survivors don't outright kill us," Ross considered, "will they be enough to—"

From a distant point above, a blazing beam of scarlet burst across the sky, and once their eyes recovered, they witnessed in despair the target of its path.

As the majestic city crumbled, Nevara could only stare in horror at her devastating failure.

While the others continued to gape in disbelief, she broke the silence with an anguished wail after collapsing to her knees.

After holding her head for a few moments more, she rose abruptly to her feet. Without speaking a word, she turned and reached into the open case, grabbed the syringe, and before anyone could stop her, depressed the plunger straight into her neck.

What followed was an almost immediate sensation of pain and adrenaline. The intensity grew such that she quickly found herself bracing for support.

Finally, her constitution could take no more, and her consciousness began to fade. Ross and Carrie gently guided her to the floor.

"Damn it, Nevara, what the hell did you do?" asked Ross, examining the empty cylinder.

"What I always should have done," she whispered in a raspy voice. "For too long, I suppressed what lies inside me . . . Now I must embrace the truth of what I am."

28

Lucas watched the smoldering wreckage across the vast array of monitors, each one a different angle of the unforeseen atrocity.

"Scans aren't picking up any signs of life," one of his men reported.

"*None*?" asked Lucas, rather disconcerted.

"Not from the city, but it looks like several cruisers evacuated shortly before the blast. I'm not sure how they made it past the perimeter defenses, though."

"It hardly matters now. I'm more concerned about how they utilized the Beacon," Lucas noted angrily. "I thought it was controlled entirely from here."

"There would appear to be a secondary override. I'm afraid we can't do much about it — not without tearing the place apart."

"Of course." Lucas turned away and shut his eyes. "Why would he make anything so easy?"

Though shaken visibly, Alicen maintained her professional demeanor. "If they have that kind of firepower, . . ."

"This fortress can withstand all that and more," Lucas reassured.

She nodded somewhat cautiously.

"Besides," he added, "there's too much value to be lost here, and we'll be finished long before they could even mount a siege."

"Why would they resort so quickly to such a drastic measure? You said that Xul would do whatever it took to reclaim the city."

"Evidently, his command has been revoked," Lucas reasoned. "Velroth isn't known for patience, so if I had to guess, they're simply cutting losses."

"That might complicate the situation."

"Indeed, but not as much for us. The Architect won't be happy with his interference, which should work out well to our advantage."

"We certainly are playing with fire," Alicen considered. "Luckily, I don't mind the heat."

"Good to hear," acknowledged Lucas. "We'll need it to temper our resolve."

He continued to observe the absolute destruction of his onetime home, stopping only when his engineer abruptly entered the room.

"Has it been reconfigured?" asked Lucas hopefully.

"To your exact specifications. The frequency modulation appears fully stable."

"Excellent. We should now be ready for whatever comes our way."

After continuing their plotted course for not much longer, the Libertas crusaders descended into a forest clearing, where an already somber mood was further dampened by the dearth of sunlight able to penetrate the haze.

"This is as close as we can land to the coordinates she gave," said Victor.

"So, what do we do now?" Carrie wondered.

Victor glanced at their unconscious partner. "How's she doing?" he asked Ross.

"Still breathing," the doctor answered.

"Is she stable?"

"More or less. As far as I can tell, her condition hasn't worsened, but this really is new ground for me. Sorry that I can't give much of a prognosis."

"I'm sure you've done everything you could for her," Victor noted. "This is new ground for all of us." He looked out through the window at the uninviting scenery.

"Well, we won't accomplish much by sitting here," Carrie reasoned.

"Agreed. We should scout the nearby area, at least."

Ross then moved to join them. "I'll come with you," he said eagerly.

"No." Victor held his shoulder. "Someone has to keep an eye on her." He gestured toward Nevara. "You're the most qualified."

"You guys have no idea what's out there," argued Ross. "I can't just wait around while you might be in danger."

"We'll be careful," Carrie reassured him. "As soon as we see anything of interest, we'll let you know and head straight back."

Ross begrudgingly relented. "Just . . . be safe, okay," he warned them.

The two then disembarked, each grabbing a service rifle on their way.

Before departing, Victor emptied the contents of the briefcase on the ground, shooting the vials in turn with superheated plasma.

"That should do it," Carrie stated.

Victor tossed the empty case back on the ship, and they proceeded to survey the immediate vicinity before going on their way.

Ross then spent the next few minutes attempting to heal Nevara, intermittently checking her vitals for any sign of improvement.

Before long, however, he was interrupted by an overwhelming sense of doom. «carrie?! victor?!»

Nobody replied, so he hastened to his feet and quickly followed after them.

Outside, Ross frantically scanned for emergent threats. Isolating the distant sounds of distress, he dashed into the decrepit woods, hoping that it wouldn't be too late.

His frantic flight soon brought him to a riverbed, unveiling the sight of his friends now set upon by feral beasts.

With vicious teeth and claws to match, the mangy animals were menacing indeed, even for such a harsh environment.

Rolling through the dirt, Victor grappled with one champing for his throat.

Carrie, meanwhile, stood backed against a tree with naught but a fallen branch to guard herself. After a fearsome growl, the second creature lunged, pinning her as it gnashed the last line of defense.

Neither of the rifles remained within their grasp.

Instinctively, Ross charged forward, summoning a potent burst of energy. Surging to the brim, he tackled Carrie's assailant and, with unbridled strength, hurled it across the clearing into bramble.

The other turned toward the injured howl, giving Victor an opening to grab a rock and strike a well-placed blow.

Carrie could only stare dumbstruck at Ross, who seemed equally surprised.

"You okay?" he panted.

"I think so," she answered, still in partial shock.

"Good, 'cause I don't think I can do that again."

"Come on!" yelled Victor, another pack not far away. "We have to make it back."

Approaching at incredible velocity, their pursuers left them no choice but to run.

Moments later, their ship came into view, but the path ahead lay blocked by fresh arrivals.

"Is this really how it ends?" lamented Carrie.

All three stood back to back, slowly reaching for their sidearms, as there was little chance to do much else. Even Victor doubted whether he could land a shot before they were devoured.

Baring jagged fangs, the predators advanced, craving their welcome feast.

The alpha then prepared to lunge, but a blinding bolt of plasma struck it down.

Before any could react, a subsequent flurry dealt with the remaining threats.

Once the chaos had subsided, the trio turned to find Nevara standing atop the boarding hatch, holding a rifle while glaring at the scene before her.

"Nevara!" Ross called in relief. "How, uh, . . . How are you feeling?"

"I should be asking you," she replied, tossing him the gun. "Blightfiends can't be underestimated."

"We're still in one piece, thanks to you," Victor added.

Nevara scanned the area. "I take it you have yet to establish contact?"

"Not quite," he admitted.

"Then, let's get to work," she said, walking down the hatch. "We've wasted too much time already."

After welcoming the Elarch to his dominion, Xul proceeded to exhibit the merits of his research. Traversing an array of intricate biomes, vast enough to stand as worlds unto themselves, he unveiled a sublime expanse of nature, belied only by the hidden walls encasing them.

Despite the staunch indifference with which his creations were regarded, Xul maintained his measured pride along the tour.

"All of this was possible through advancements made in transmutational technology," boasted the clever scientist as they headed through a jungle. "With strong enough intentionality, one can even—"

"This is how you spent your time?" Velroth interjected. "Of what consequence are these hollow reproductions?"

"Merely a proof of concept, Elarch, as they demonstrate but a fraction of the means at our disposal."

"I fail to see how this can advance our conquest, should our resource limitations persist. I will not allow Solmar to be our tomb."

"The applications will become apparent soon enough, I assure you."

Velroth lost his patience, shooting from his dusky hand a fevered blast of aether, which gleamed across the jeweled crown to match his carmine cape.

A nearby tree exploded, and Xul glared silently at Velroth, though he'd long since grown accustomed to his ways of wanton violence. The royal guards, in turn, traded nervous glances.

"Time is not a luxury we can afford! We still don't know the source behind the Mechagen attacks, and now the humans openly defy us in the closing hours of this most fateful cycle yet. With blood in the water, our subjects have become emboldened, threatening to undo everything we have accomplished."

Xul allowed the Elarch to continue on his rant.

"My ambitions may offend your academic taste, but you must understand the call of destiny — not simply mine or yours, but that entitled to our kind. As elders of the galaxy who conquered death itself, I will not allow our long-fought journey to end in starvation. All that we have subjugated, from sentient spawn to natural laws, bears testament to our unyielding resolve. These nascent mongrels, blessed by chance alone, shall not extinguish our eternal flame, and it will burn brighter yet across the cosmic sea, even if I must bear it on my own."

"Mongrels as they are," Xul defended, "they were the most promising lead by far."

"And greatest threat," Velroth countered. "The path to victory does not lie in granting our enemy the very powers we desire, especially when you have yet to properly discern their limits. Have you forgotten your own wild theories concerning their progenitors?"

Xul remained silent.

"Once they had clearly surpassed your control, destruction was the only viable solution."

"Be that as it may," said Xul with veiled contempt, "they were not the only avenue explored. It would have been unwise of me to rely exclusively upon their potential, encouraging as it might have been."

"There is another?"

"Enough to proffer the results you seek, I dare say."

"I recall nothing mentioned in your latest reports," the Elarch noted with skepticism.

"Hardly worth addressing at the time, as it remains quite experimental. Organic integration was always the primary goal, but with that option lost — and given the pressing circumstances — duty compels me to inform of the alternative."

"Show me," the Elarch ordered flatly.

29

Heading deeper into the forest among the fading trees, the others followed Nevara's determined pace. Nobody had thus far acknowledged her sudden resurrection, for she had swiftly marched ahead along her quest.

"You should take it easy, Nevara," Ross tentatively prescribed.

"I said I'm fine," she snapped.

"Actually, you didn't," Victor pointed out. "That stunt you pulled was a tad bit reckless, and we were pretty worried you'd never come back."

"Well, I did," she stated flatly, "and I can assure you that I've never felt more capable."

"I'll say," Carrie agreed. "That sure was impressive how you saved our assess back there. We'd certainly be dead without you."

"We all need to make it through this together," Nevara stressed, "or else there won't be a chance in hell of stopping Xul."

". . . Yeah," said Carrie, taken aback by the aggressive tone.

Ross looked around uncomfortably.

Victor was quick to break the tension. "You mentioned that Xul never paid them much attention because they weren't as valuable to him as the controlled populations. Don't you think he might reconsider now that he's out of options?"

"I'm sure of it," Nevara agreed, "which is why we must find them before he does."

"I thought you said you knew where they were?" asked Ross.

"The Blight forces them to move around, so I narrowed down their most likely whereabouts. We should be close, but keep your guard up; in addition to the savage fauna you already encountered, environmental hazards are everywhere — quicksand especially."

"Can't we just do an astral scan of the area?" suggested Carrie. "We'd cover a lot more ground with lower risk."

"The atmospheric radiation poses greater difficulty. My energy body doesn't seem to have fully readjusted yet, and you need to conserve your strength for later."

"Do you think they'll believe us?" wondered Ross. "I mean, we all lived through it, and I'm not even sure I can fully process everything that's happened. So much of it just seems like a bad dream."

"We'll have to make them," Nevara insisted.

"Let's hope they don't just kill us on the spot," Carrie grumbled.

"They're civilized enough by what I gather, but don't expect them to be so trusting of outsiders," Nevara cautioned.

"So, how do we broach the subject?" asked Ross.

Victor shook his head. "I guess we'll figure that out when—"

The quartet found themselves quickly surrounded by half a dozen men, all camouflaged against the patches of foliage, and all brandishing primitive weapons ranging from blades to bows and arrows.

"Who the hell are you?" one of them barked through a heavy scarf, stepping forward warily.

"We're from Empyrea," Victor told the rough-skinned, shaggy man while pointing to the sky, "and we came to warn you."

"Is that right?" he replied in a gravelly voice, raising his goggles to better inspect their foreignness. His gaze focused on Nevara, whose face remained partially concealed beneath her ebon cowl. "You sure came a long way to send a message," he noted with suspicion. "What threat could there possibly be that we haven't faced already?"

How indeed could Victor best explain it? With far too many words that came to mind, he simply answered, "Annihilation."

Not entirely dismissive, the hunters traded glances of amusement, then motioned their captives forward, careful to keep them well in view.

Inside one of many testing grounds, the Architect prepared a demonstration to soundly prove his worth, the Elarch's battle-ready legion standing fully in attendance.

"My lord," said Xul, "I promise that my years of research were not all spent in vain. Aside from the progress made through recombinant DNA, I have engineered a synthetic symbiote — or *synthiote* — with promising results. This integrated nanoparticle may solve our need for protomatter, at least regarding genomancy."

The room erupted in a murmuring of whispers. Clearly, Xul had struck a chord.

"I hope you can substantiate such claims," insisted Velroth.

"With pleasure," the Architect assured. Turning to a nearby workbench, Xul retrieved a pewter fluid. He drew a full syringe, then beckoned a technician.

"No," Velroth halted. "Uldred," he motioned forth his trusted captain, who readily complied.

"Very well," Xul granted, injecting the solution.

The others waited silently, unsure of what might happen.

"How long before results appear?" Velroth asked at last.

"See what you can do," the Architect suggested, confidently watching.

Without apparent effort, the captain formed a glowing ball of energy larger than thought possible, unleashing it with fierce intensity against the metal wall.

The Elarch stared in awe as embers filled his eyes. With a sweeping gesture of his cape, he hastened to the vials. "Begin deployment," ordered Velroth, raising one expectantly.

"My lord," Xul protested. "As I said, it has yet to be fully—"

"The Revelation is upon us, and I've waited long enough to see the fruits of your endeavors," Velroth interjected, plunging a syringe into himself. "If such insolent defiance is allowed to stop us now, we may not see another cycle. This is not the time for hesitation. This is the day our legacy will be truly secured."

"As you wish," conceded Xul. "So it shall be done."

* * *

After arriving in a secluded sylvan settlement, the Libertas crusaders received an audience with Jerico, a scruffy-bearded, square-jawed man sitting before a large campfire in a dark brown coat. Efforts thus far to sway the de facto leader of the Remnants, as they called themselves, made little headway. Kurtis, the second-in-command who escorted them, glared distrustfully nearby, still fully armed beside his hunting party.

"You have no idea what we're up against!" yelled Victor. "Your ancestors were right to be distrustful, but they couldn't have possibly appreciated the true extent of the lies being sold. We've seen firsthand the damage these bastards can do, and you've experienced it for yourselves. This disease across the planet — you know what they're capable of."

"I admit, there has certainly been a recent change in the air," Jerico acknowledged, "but you come to us out of nowhere, spouting doomsday warnings and wild claims about magic, and you expect us to stake what little we have to join you in some grand war? We have survived by blood and steel, not sorcery and wishful thinking."

"I would expect more imagination from one so resourceful," Nevara finally spoke.

"And who might you be?" he inquired, addressing her at last.

Nevara lowered her hood to a wave of clamoring and gasps. Jerico seemed genuinely startled, but quickly recovered.

"I'm the one who can show you exactly what your future holds."

"So, you're a fortune teller? A prophet?"

"A harbinger," she replied.

Nevara pooled a ball of energy in her palm, then, without warning, spouted a stream of blazing scarlet high above her head.

It swirled into a violent vortex, dwarfing even the roaring bonfire below.

The searing heat caused many of the Remnants to recoil in alarm.

After a few seconds, she allowed the mystic flames to dissipate, leaving only singed treetops as evidence.

"Our city was destroyed in the blink of an eye simply because a fanatic rose to power and lost control," she stated.

The curiously omissive summary made Victor start, but he thought it best to not intrude.

"My demonstration was but a fraction of what they've harnessed through means well beyond your comprehension. You would do well to be concerned."

"Quite impressive," Jerico admitted, his hazel eyes continuing to adjust from the light show, "but I fail to see why we should take part in your war. We've made it this long just fine on our own."

"Do not underestimate the nature of the threat you face," she warned. The power of the Subverse — the source of such ability — is not limited to destruction of this kind."

Nevara glanced over to the German Shepherd closely guarding her. She raised a hand, then channeled aether into its limbs, forcing it to move.

Though clearly resisting her control, the hound could only quiver as it inched closer to the pyre.

The onlookers watched with equal horror, though Victor seemed to be the only one directing his gaze toward Nevara.

"Enough!" cried Jerico, her point made loud and clear.

"Now," she continued, allowing the dog to scurry from them, "imagine if a single being, without remorse or mercy, could do the same through all of time and space. Perhaps you might survive regardless, but certainly not by your own volition. Would such a condition be acceptable to you?"

"I must admit, you make a compelling argument," Jerico conceded. "Very well. You'll have all the fire and steel we can offer, just as long as we're clear who calls the shots."

Kurtis turned to his leader in surprise, though remained silent.

"As you wish," replied Nevara. "How shall we begin?"

Velroth surveyed his army with voracious pride. Though not abounding in sheer numbers, their brute strength and resilience, driven by peerless bellicosity, left few in the galaxy who could oppose them. With Xul's latest breakthrough, even greater heights could now be reached.

"Have the augmentations fully been distributed?" asked the Elarch.

"Yes, my lord," said Xul. "Fortunately, the prototype managed to suffice."

"Excellent. If they perform as promised, you just might have a chance at redemption."

"You honor me, Elarch."

Captain Uldred then stepped forward. "Shall we commence the attack, my lord?"

Velroth grinned. "Send a clear message to all who would challenge our supremacy."

The captain bowed, turning eagerly to mobilize for his departure.

"Perhaps it's better that this road was fraught with failure," Velroth spoke in rapture, "for I've had so much longer to prepare. With or without the underbreed, I will seize the power of the Subverse, even if I have to claw my way to reach it."

Xul flexed his metal digits in response. "Before your expectations can be met," he cautioned, "there is a notable concern that needs addressing first."

Velroth glared at him. "What might that be, now?"

"This technology remains untested at greater scale," the Architect explained, "due in part to insufficient bandwidth available. As the prototypes lack full autonomy, they rely upon a robust network for communication and auxiliary processing."

"Is that so?" The Elarch's mood had soured.

"Additionally, the synthiotes contain preliminary safeguards to avoid unduly damaging their host. Should the human threat prove greater than expected, I presume you would desire victory at any cost."

"And you would be correct."

"Well, as it stands," continued Xul, "these factors may be overridden, but not preemptively, I fear. During heightened use, a signal must be sent from here to enable further channeling."

"So, can this not be done?"

"Regrettably, a broadcast of that reach is beyond the scope of possibility."

"Unacceptable," replied the Elarch. "Surely, you can overcome such petty limitations?"

"Not with executive restrictions currently in place."

"I see." Velroth considered for a moment. "And were they to be lifted?"

"I would anticipate no issues, then, at all."

"Very well, but if I am to grant such access, I shall remain to supervise its use."

"Of course," the Architect acknowledged. "I would expect nothing less from you."

The warriors of Libertas entered Jerico's ramshackle quarters, keen to strategize for the crucial battle fast approaching.

Kurtis, however, departed in a huff, brushing past them without a single word.

"Everything all right?" Victor asked.

"He's a stubborn one," said Jerico, "but I'm sure he'll come around. Understandably, we've never faced a threat like you're describing, and some are quite discouraged."

"That's why we were hoping to iron out a plan."

Jerico leaned back in his chair, boots resting on the desk. "So, what do we know about the enemy?" he asked, habitually flicking an old-world lighter made of brass, getting down to business.

"They're strong, aggressive, and ruthless," replied Nevara. "More importantly, their technological superiority cannot be underestimated."

"We'll have to use guerrilla tactics, then," Jerico surmised.

"Which calls for lots of cover," Victor added. "The terrain seems plenty dense enough, but it couldn't hurt to have more portable solutions."

"Hmm, I know a recipe that'll come in handy," Jerico considered. "There should be a bit of saltpeter in reserve, and we can boil down some tree sap . . . Yes, that'll work just fine. And while we're on the subject, I might have another way to utilize the land."

"Do tell."

"There's a dam up the river that supplies our water. Blowing it could slow them down a bit, but we'd only get one shot."

"Is that wise?" asked Ross. "I'm not sure how well you'd do without it."

"We built it once before," said Jerico, "so we'll get it done again, assuming anyone survives. I'd say that living through this day is priority for now."

"Wouldn't that also pose some risk to us?"

"Not if we time it right. There should be enough Semtex left to do the job remotely, but don't expect anything of biblical proportions."

"We'll take any advantage we can get," said Victor. "One of our greatest tools is the environment."

"Speaking of which," Carrie noted, "shouldn't we be worried about the Blight?"

"It could certainly complicate matters, depending on the weather," Jerico admitted. "The storms are unpredictable, and you wouldn't wanna be caught in one. In that unfortunate event, get your ass to shelter."

"You mean there's no protection?"

"Sorry, but that's the truth of how it is."

"We can't just run and hide forever," Victor stated, "so we'll also need some more offensive options."

"In terms of munitions, the years haven't been kind to our stockpile," Jerico confessed, "but we're far from being entirely depleted."

"Then, I guess we'll need a bit of cunning."

"Have anything in mind?"

Victor's gaze rested pointedly on the lighter.

Jerico picked up the cue, replying with a grin. "Now, there's an idea," he granted, "though I'm sorry to say we're a little thin on resources in that capacity."

"That shouldn't be a problem," Ross assured. "I think we know a trick to help."

"Well, then, I look forward to seeing what you folks can do."

"We also need to be mindful of their objective," Nevara stressed more somberly.

"You mean our complete destruction?"

"It's not that simple," she clarified. "What they're really after is our DNA."

"They don't have easier ways to get it?"

"Not under the precise conditions for their plan to work. In that regard, they will seek to capture as many alive as possible."

"You say they destroyed your entire city just for losing control," Jerico pointed out. "Aren't those methods a bit conflicting?"

"Their leadership doesn't quite see eye to eye, owed in part to disagreements in philosophy, but I have an inclination as to which will soon prevail."

"You seem to know a lot about their operations," said Jerico suspiciously. "Also, forgive my candor, but I'd say you're not all human by the looks of it, so how exactly do you factor into this?"

Nevara glared at him. "My past is long and inconsequential to the matter at hand. Simply know that I've been fighting them for longer than you could imagine. Naturally, I've made it my business to learn everything I can, and you would be well advised to heed my counsel."

The omission of certain details made Victor throw another furtive glance, but he once again remained silent on the issue, trusting in her motives.

"Fair enough," said Jerico, "but as to your concern, I can assure you that we're not ones to go quietly."

"Be that as it may," Nevara cautioned, "we can't afford leaving anything to chance. The existential threat before us outweighs the value of any life."

"Are you suggesting a nuclear option, then?"

". . . I suppose I am," she answered, reflecting momentarily.

"Well, I'm afraid we don't have anything of that magnitude on hand. I'm also not sure where you'd find it; scavenging doesn't yield much these days."

Carrie made a puzzled face, remembering their trip. "What is there to scavenge here?"

"One of your cites fell not too far away. We've mostly picked it clean, though."

"Fell?" Victor noted. "You mean from the *sky*?"

"That's right," said Jerico, "though who remembers when?"

"How'd you survive the radiation leak?" asked Ross.

Jerico shook his head. "There wasn't any that I could tell."

"How can you be sure?"

"None of us are strangers here to what that stuff can do, so I think we would have noticed it by now. "

"So, the core must be intact," Carrie reasoned. "Something like that might qualify, given the power you would need to run a Haven."

"Can it be weaponized?" wondered Victor.

"Probably, but messing with sophisticated black-box tech is taking quite the risk."

"There might be some schematics in all the data that we pulled," Ross mentioned.

"Nevertheless," she warned.

"It may be our only option," Victor pondered. "Would you be willing at least to try?"

"Do you really have to ask?"

Ross nodded in agreement.

"If that's the route we're going," said Jerico, reluctantly onboard, "the ruins themselves should provide a decent stronghold. It wouldn't be my first choice, but it's also not the worst place to make our final stand."

"All right, then," concluded Victor.

"We should head off now and fortify," Jerico determined, moving from behind his desk. "I'll gather up supplies and men to bring."

The others turned to follow as he marched out of the room.

"Are you coming?" Victor asked Nevara, who lingered in the corner after growing rather pensive.

"I'm returning to Empyrea," she readily declared.

"Why?" he asked, Ross and Carrie stopping in surprise. "What could still be there?"

"That's what I intend to learn. As you said yourself, we'll need every advantage possible, and it's an avenue worth exploring."

"Fair enough," acknowledged Victor, "but it might not be that safe."

"Yeah. There could have been a reactor breach this time," Ross added. "That blast was pretty big."

"I can manage," said Nevara, dismissing their concerns.

"Well, if you're sure about it," conceded Victor, "let us know what you find — or if you get into any trouble."

She had already begun departure before he finished talking.

The remaining three exchanged uneasy looks behind her, none willing to press the matter further.

30

The return to his body left Lucas feeling nearly as imprisoned as before, forced deep into hiding while the Vanguard ever searched for him. One day, briefly able to indulge in rest, he chanced a sunset trip atop the roof of Victor's building, inviting Nevara to join remotely.

«*don't you think we're taking a rather unnecessary risk?*» *Nevara worried.*

"It should be a natural blind spot this time of day," Lucas reassured.

«*still, as the most wanted man in town, you should exercise greater caution.*»

"Perhaps, but I thought it was a risk worth taking," he affirmed.

«*may i ask why?*»

Lucas took a seat against the parapet. "We never shared a quiet moment — at least not in the real world. Who knows when all this could end, so why wait any longer?"

«*if that was your intention, i could have come in astral form.*»

"True, but some things need to be appreciated in a certain way." He stared out at the stunning view. "You said that you can see it, right?"

237

«as long as you maintain the channel.»

"So, none of this is working for you?"

«i didn't say that,» she responded. «i'm just not sure it's the best use of our energy. we need to remain focused on the mission.»

"I always am," he promised, "which is why I wanted a reminder of what it's for."

«did you really need one?»

"There's gloom and doom aplenty here, but it can't compare to what might be. I can only imagine how it looks from down below."

«it certainly is beautiful,» Nevara recollected.

"Even with the Blight?" asked Lucas.

«the scenery has changed somewhat, but it's majestic nonetheless.»

"I hope to see it together someday."

«that would be ideal,» she agreed.

"But do you think it's likely?"

«you know what lies ahead,» Nevara said more solemnly. «earning that horizon will be no easy task, but as greatly as the odds are stacked against us, i have never felt more confident in stopping him.»

"That didn't answer my question," Lucas noted. "I want to know the chances of an outcome where, after we somehow save the day and manage to survive, there's actually a life for us to live."

«is that what you've been worrying about?»

"You shouldn't be so surprised."

«i must admit,» she considered, «i wasn't entirely sure how you saw the nature of our relationship.»

"Understandable, I suppose. It's not like I had much experience in that department, and it hardly seemed appropriate to address."

«well, then?»

"After being so focused elsewhere in my life, I never thought I'd grow this close to someone else, but I guess with you, . . . it really can't be helped."

«i see,» Nevara pondered.

"Not that I expected you to feel the same," continued Lucas, "but after such a journey, I thought that maybe our time together would last beyond achieving hard-fought peace. Is that something you've given any thought?"

A momentary silence passed as he awaited her response.

«more than you could ever know,» she earnestly confessed.

Unable to repress the painful memory, Nevara watched it fade away as her vision filled with the sea of devastation before her. The desolate wreckage spanned a veritable island, stray bits of flotsam strewn well beyond the boundaries of the fallen city. Any search for survivors would have been pointless, even if she had the time to spare.

The years had left her numb to such depravity, but bearing witness to the latest of their countless horrors made her dread what such mentality could do, once all limitation had been cleared. It mattered not whose finger sat upon the trigger, for the power had corrupted all the same. Whether Velroth, Xul, or Lucas, a mind of such persuasion would never cease until defeated.

And so again the solemn duty fell to her, though in spite of every failure, she would succeed this day at any cost. Hopefully, the answer lay intact below, but finding it was sure to be a challenge, even with her strong affinity.

Soon enough, however, the signature became apparent — a fighting chance at last.

She then discerned among the broken edifices a nondescript apartment complex, sure this had to be the one, so Nevara landed on a nearby section of debris before quickly disembarking.

Outside, the cold winds added further trials, but neither they nor splashing ocean waves could shake her, for she knew what must be done.

Once more the trio journeyed through the forest, this time guided by their newfound allies. The dying flora set a rather somber tone, but at least it kept them grounded.

"So, you guys are the only survivors?" Victor wondered, hoping the reality wasn't quite so bleak.

"To tell you the truth," said Jerico, "I'm surprised we lasted this long, given what it took to get here."

"Things were actually worse before?" asked Ross.

"Depends on what you mean by that, but most who preferred the old ways didn't make it. Many who fled before the 'Great Ascension' weren't the trusting types, so they scattered far and wide, keeping mostly to themselves, back when that luxury existed."

"What changed?" asked Carrie.

"Nobody could have prepared for what the Blight would do," Jerico admitted. "Needless to say, it hit us hard, and the world shrank overnight."

"Having their lives uprooted can't have been easy," Ross lamented. "How did people cope?"

"About how you'd expect. First, it was a desperate free-for-all just to survive, then people quickly learned the strength in numbers, and marauders began seizing territory. Soon enough, larger tribes arose from them, creating order to some extent, but it then devolved into fighting over resources."

"That sounds about right," Carrie mulled.

"Over time, the Blight whittled us down to a handful of broken factions vying for control."

"How did that end?" asked Victor.

"Damn near wiped each other out," Jerico stated bluntly, "but for some, the Blight gave us perspective. Eventually, life of any kind became impossible with the way it was, and we knew that something had to change. Of course, not everyone was onboard. Some still thought they could cut it on their own, and others preferred an endless war to forfeiting their power. It was bloody chaos for a while, but the ones who recognized the need for cooperation managed to endure. Hence, we call ourselves the Remnants, because we're pretty much all that's left."

"Talk about perspective," Carrie pondered.

"Sorry that I don't have a more cheerful story to tell, but the fact we're still here after all of it must be worth something, right?"

"I would certainly say so," Ross agreed.

"But now that all the Havens are gone, I suppose the story gets even darker, huh? Someday, I'd like to hear your side of it."

"If we live to see tomorrow, it would be my pleasure," promised Victor, "though I'm honestly not sure how much of it you might believe."

"You'd be surprised. Folks around here are eager enough for something new. In any case, I present to you . . . the city of Paradiso."

Finally, their dreary, winding trek had reached its destination, and they beheld the unmistakable ruins of a decommissioned Haven. Gone were the majestic heights of skyscrapers and monuments to industry, for now it simply lay a crumbled mess.

"It's not quite as big as Empyrea," said Ross. "I guess they weren't all created equally."

"I'm not surprised they'd experiment with different population sizes," Carrie reasoned. "I'd imagine there were plenty of variables to iron out."

After entering through a narrow crevice, the explorers navigated a maze of battered buildings teeming with sickly overgrowth, an occasional ray of sunlight falling on them. Subtle as it was, the illumination afforded a grim view to what had been suffered long ago.

Though reduced to heaps of dusty bones, the disfigured residents offered a gruesome glimpse into the city's backstory, one seemingly fraught with more than civil strife.

"What the hell happened to these poor bastards?" Victor asked in horror.

"Well," speculated Carrie, crouching down to inspect one, "gamma rays from a nuclear meltdown would induce genetic damage, but I really couldn't say what might result from errant Subverse tech. Hopefully, we won't bump into any corium."

"I thought you said this place wasn't radioactive?" reminded Victor.

"We combed here plenty without issue," Jerico reiterated. "I definitely would have noticed our people turning into this."

"Besides," countered Ross, "I wouldn't expect mutations of this degree. Cancer, sure—" As the words left his mouth, he couldn't help but vividly recall a past he'd long repressed.

Carrie turned to see why he'd abruptly fallen silent, and the haunted look upon his face made it readily apparent.

"But," he continued, returning to the present, "these changes in the bone structure would have taken generations to appear, and I doubt that anyone from the city survived the crash." He scratched his head. "They could have been surface dwellers taking shelter or something."

"That's an idea," Victor granted, "though it's odd there wouldn't be any trace of clothing." He turned to Jerico. "Did you guys already salvage it?"

"They were like this when we found them, but that doesn't mean someone else didn't get here first."

"It could also have been vaporized," Carrie noted.

"I should mention that there aren't any hot spots in this area," added Jerico, "so they would have had to travel pretty far in this condition. I'm not too sure they would have made it."

"Have you ever seen the Blight do this before?" asked Victor.

"Not firsthand, so it seems they were more than likely natives."

"I guess we'll never know," said Ross.

Carrie scowled at the thought, continuing to ruminate over the bizarre discovery.

"Either way," concluded Victor, "we have to keep moving."

"You three should go on ahead," Jerico advised. "To make the best use of our time, I'll take my men and conduct a more thorough survey. I'm betting we can set up some decent fortifications."

"Sounds good," said Victor. "We'll meet up here before heading back."

Just like that, the dauntless groups went their separate ways, Libertas heading deeper into the labyrinth of darkness.

* * *

With nothing left to say, Ixio headed for the door, ready to stand between the Zephyrans and Xul, but a strong urge held him back. Though unable to entirely forgive her, he knew that she deserved more than such cold rejection, no matter the blame for what unfolded. By all accounts, this would be their last goodbye, so he might as well provide a modicum of consolation.

Before Nevara could rejoin her ranks, he called out, "Wait." As she turned expectantly, he removed the dyadic pendant from around his neck, holding it for her to take. "I think this can do more good for you. Just be sure it doesn't fall into his hands."

She hesitated, surprised by the offer. "If you intend to confront him, accepting this would be tantamount to crippling an arm. I can't be responsible for worsening your odds any further."

"I will protect my people with everything I have," Ixio assured her, "but I'm afraid that I can only buy them time. If I thought this gesture might inhibit me, I would not be so indulgent."

Still she seemed reluctant.

"If you are truly so concerned," he continued, "I shall not compound upon the guilt you bear." He separated the pendant into its two component halves: a triangle of purest white and another one of deepest black, both shimmering with a subtle iridescence. As a rather fitting compromise, Ixio then offered her the dark piece, keeping for himself the light. "This half suits you better, anyway." He smiled faintly, despite the holocaust outside.

Nevara took it graciously without further protest. "I will never forget you, Ixio," she promised. "If it takes an eternity, I will find a way to undo the damage I caused — I swear it to you."

Ixio nodded pensively. "Be it this life or the next," he responded, "I greatly hope our paths may cross again, my winter swan."

She left without saying another word, tears streaming silently down her face.

The outer conflict no less daunting, Ixio at least felt more at peace as he turned to face his destiny.

31

Following the subtle energy, Nevara doggedly traversed the smoldering interior, ignoring the skeletal remains fused in place along the way. Every one of them she failed unequivocally, but at least they might soon be avenged.

Drawn forth amid the ruination, she knew it had to be nearby. Would its power finally bestow the strength she needed, or was the whole endeavor yet another vain delusion? Either way, fate compelled her action, for certain doom awaited indecision.

From across the valley of accusive ashes, her eye then caught a shimmer from the sooty stone in question. She picked it from the rubble, reflecting how, though seemingly undamaged, the relic remained so tragically deficient.

If only she could see it whole again, but such fantasy had never come to pass, and now its darker twin lay seized by treachery, forced to serve his punitive desires.

Eons worth of history now rested in her hand, and despite the great expanses crossed, she still recalled the day its odyssey began . . .

* * *

Still reeling from the aftermath of their business on the surface, Nevara walked into Xul's laboratory to deliver a status update.

"The deluge has begun," she announced, finding him preoccupied as usual. "Evacuation and archival were completed without issue."

Xul seemingly ignored her, too enthralled by the stone upon his workbench. "What a curious bit of protomatter," he commented. "I've not seen any like this."

"Is that so?" said Nevara. "I thought it all functioned more or less the same."

"Such was the operating theory," Xul acknowledged, "perhaps because we had yet to find it in the hands of any other."

"What's different about this one?"

"Based on a cursory analysis, it would appear to retain a mirror image of the former bearer's consciousness."

Nevara's heart awakened in her chest, urging the need to quickly conceal her emotions. "How is that possible?" she calmly wondered.

"Through some entanglement, I would surmise. Drawing biologically from the Subverse is a most demanding task — of body, mind, and spirit. It should not be unexpected that an object through which such energy flows might imprint upon that signature."

"Curious indeed."

"And across all the lesser samples we recovered," Xul continued, "none seem to exhibit this phenomenon."

"How remarkable."

"Though not entirely surprising, considering how forcibly its owner had exerted himself. I would imagine that prolonged contact also played a role. In any case, it is likely that he was unaware of this occurrence."

Nevara had to ask, "Does this mean that his soul is bound to it?"

"A naive interpretation," scoffed the Architect. "Residual traces of awareness, memories, and personality exist as fleeting data beyond the material structures of the brain. Here, they just so happen to have been copied to a local storage medium. For all intents and purposes, you could say his entire being is preserved within this trinket."

"Unbelievable," was all that she could utter.

"Nearly so," said Xul, "but the evidence is plain to see."

"I'm sure it will have tremendous research value," she speculated.

"Of that, I have no doubt."

Sensing that her undue enthusiasm might betray some deeper motivations, Nevara thought it best to take her leave. "I look forward to hearing what developments arise," she said as she departed.

"If only we had the rest of it," Xul mentioned, stopping Nevara in her tracks.

"The rest of it?" she inquired nervously.

Xul raised the pendant to illustrate his point. "Based on the design, would you not agree that it seems rather . . . incomplete."

Moving closer, she offered her own inspection, careful not to be too hasty or dismissive in appraisal — and trying to ignore the counterpart against her pounding chest. "A valid hypothesis," Nevara cautiously conceded. "It could have easily come apart during your encounter," she suggested, but the Architect seemed unconvinced.

"We were more than thorough in our salvage efforts," Xul responded flatly. "Besides, I'm sure I would have noticed."

"Then, perhaps it was destroyed?"

"Unlikely, given this one managed to survive."

248

"I suppose that's true," she granted, her voice barely keeping steady as her mind raced for an explanation. The silence was unbearable, but what was she to say?

"Unfortunate," Xul concluded, "but with inundation under way, I suppose we must make do with what we have. After all, we're far from empty-handed, and partial as it is, this piece will certainly prove to be, as you put it, of 'tremendous research value'."

Nevara exhaled in relief, but her eyes lay fixed upon the stone. With Xul turning his attention to a holoscope's projection, she entertained a myriad of implications thought to be impossible. For all the damage she had caused, perhaps this meant a chance to set things right. Envisioning a brighter future for the first time in her life, she once more turned to leave.

From out the corner of his eye, Xul watched her buoyant gait, and across his pale face emerged an air of satisfaction.

After smuggling the gem to Earth in astral form and guiding its course through history, she never expected to hold it once more in her hand.

When last she placed it in the care of Marlowe Ikewell, she truly believed that he would help to end her labors. Alas, it was not he who sired the fated child, and though he would later come to raise the boy, perhaps the damage had long been done by then. If only Lucas learned the truth when he was younger, but it hardly seemed to matter now.

Staring at the ancient relic, she couldn't help remembering her failures. In her blind persistence, she had become every much as guilty for all of those atrocities — if not more so, for he was but a puppet she engendered, time and time again. Was it foolish to believe that she could ever bring him back?

The man she knew was gone forever; she could see that plainly now. But what good were such elegiac musings? Only action could redeem her folly, and only one solution stood at hand.

She concentrated aether in her steeled grip, and though the artifact had proven its endurance, even protomatter was not quite indestructible. As her crushing force intensified, the shimmering did, too. Fueled by singular intent, Nevara grit her teeth in fury, burying all the memories she once held dear. Ultimately, nothing but a powder thus remained.

She then withdrew the empty syringe of catalyst from her previous initiative, thrusting it into her arm to collect a barrel full of blood. After opening the plunger, she added carefully the dust, mixing her solution well. In response, a bioluminescent aura began to form, giving hope for such a wild plan. With only one step left, she drove the needle back into her arm, injecting the auspicious brew.

As it flowed throughout her body, a surge of energy ensued. Driven by her Anakhari lineage, the strain became so great that it dropped her to the ground. This time, though, she managed not to faint, holding firm to her unshakeable resolve. Fighting just to stand, Nevara rose one trembling foot after the other.

Once the sensation had abated, she sought to test her newfound strength, so she blasted out a nearby wall to clear her path ahead. Impressed so much by what was gained, she unleashed several flurries more of greater power and aggression, sweeping away all around her.

Satisfied with this rehearsal, Nevara headed for her ship, marching confidently onward, finally with the means to win.

* * *

Carrie focused on the inoperable door, endeavoring to drive it by aetheric force alone. To everyone's surprise, it jolted partly open, granting just enough for them to reach the core.

One by one, they ventured through, unprepared for what might lie ahead.

Once inside, Ross's channeled ball of light revealed a gruesome discovery similar to before. "More of them?" He looked around in shock. "If this room's been sealed since the power went offline, then Jerico was right: they're from the city, after all."

"Their NOVA PODs," Victor wondered. "Do you think they might still be functional?"

"The batteries would long be dead," said Carrie, stooping to examine the nearest remains, "but the storage is quite robust, at least in our models. They should have been fairly well protected from the elements in here, and since I did manage to energize the door, . . ."

Ross joined her to remove the POD, still firmly embedded in the skull despite a lengthy fracture.

"Well, here we go." She took a deep breath, holding the neural device between her hands, then repeated her technique.

After a few seconds, the unit activated with a glow, and Victor hurried over at the sign of tentative success.

"Nice," Ross declared. "Can you play back any video?"

Shifting the POD to one hand, Carrie pulled out her laptop to investigate. After wirelessly pairing them, she skimmed the file system for useful data.

Victor glanced back from the bodies to the heavy door, still pondering the implications.

Eventually finding something of interest, Carrie transferred the most recent livestream over to her computer. "Here we go," she said, and the others focused on the monitor, hoping to finally solve the mystery. The answer shown, however, was not what any had expected.

From the man's erratic perspective, they witnessed a scene of total carnage, those around him contorting before his eyes as they chased each other down. The footage ended moments after the man fell to his knees, furiously pounding his head against the ground.

Victor, Ross, and Carrie stared at their own horrified reflections in the black screen.

"What the hell happened here?" Ross was the first to speak.

"If the Havens were his testing grounds for evolution," Carrie theorized, "maybe Xul got tired of letting nature take its course."

"He was willing to gamble millions of lives just to accelerate his timeline, and this was the result," Victor summarized.

"We really are just petri dishes to him," said Ross. "He truly has no conscience."

"Nothing will ever stop this level of obsession," Carrie stated. "There's nowhere we'd ever be able to run or hide as long as he sees that potential in us."

"And now," Victor added, "we've given him the evidence to prove humanity is ripe for harvesting. All our genomancy — we've just been putting on an exhibition. Now he knows beyond all doubt the wait is over, so he'll be coming at us with everything he's got."

The trio sat in darkness for a few more silent moments, the air laden with despair.

"In that case," said Carrie solemnly, "we'd better get to work on that reactor."

They continued through the darkness shortly before reaching their destination. A subtle whirring noise gave hope that some part may be intact.

Carrie immediately got to work assessing the damage, Ross holding his light aloft as she removed the protective housing.

Victor lingered back, still mulling the grim revelation.

After a few minutes of tinkering, Carrie gave an update. "By my estimation, it appears functional enough to do the job," she announced.

"So, we're in business?" concluded Victor.

"Not quite," she clarified. "I hate to say it, but this machine is incredibly stable."

"Isn't that good?"

"Not if you want it to obliterate us," Carrie noted. "To trigger a detonation, we would have to hit the core with a decent surge of energy."

"You mean like from a giant laser?" suggested Ross.

"Technically, I think it was a particle beam," she speculated, "but yeah, if you go the conventional route."

"Is there an unconventional one?" asked Victor.

"Well, this is all Subverse tech, so I'm guessing it would be more susceptible to overload from aether, once I remove the safeguards."

"Nevara should be able to handle that pretty easily," he gathered. "Speaking of which, did she reach out to either of you?"

The others shook their heads.

"I tried checking in a few times, but no luck," said Ross.

"Hmm, maybe she's just been busy."

"Even so, wouldn't we still be able to sense her?" Carrie pointed out.

"Yeah," acknowledged Victor, still a bit concerned. "Hopefully, nothing's happened to her. In any case, we should head back and let the others know what we found."

32

After rejoining Jerico and his men, apprising them of the dark discovery, the group headed glumly back to camp. Despite the progress made in carrying out their plan, the outlook never seemed so bleak.

"So, that's the kind of fate awaiting us?" Jerico surmised. "It sure makes death an easy choice, if it comes to that."

"What happened wasn't by design," said Victor. "If they attain complete control, I think we'd have it vastly worse."

"Well, I'm feeling a little better about our chances, now that we've prepared a suitable reception. I'll send over another crew to bring the rest . . . of . . . the . . ."

Arriving back at home, Jerico found a much-depleted population. "Where the hell is everybody?" he called, looking around for answers.

"Kurtis took them," one of the inhabitants reported. "He said that the 'sky people' could go kill each other and that anyone who wanted to live should follow him."

"Son of a bitch!" yelled Jerico. "Any idea where they went?"

The man shook his head.

"That doesn't help our chances," lamented Carrie.

"No kidding," Jerico replied, "but it doesn't change the plan. If half of what you said is true, there's no escaping this. We're committed, one way or another."

"I appreciate your dedication," said Victor earnestly.

"It's all our asses on the line, my friend. I only wish that *he* would realize it. Goddamnit, Kurtis."

Still cursing the faithless coward, Jerico marched away to ascertain what resources were left.

Meanwhile, the others went searching for Nevara, soon finding her conspicuously isolated as she waited, once more deep in thought.

"Hey there," Victor greeted, catching her attention. "We got worried when we couldn't reach you. Run into any trouble?"

"I must have been distracted."

"That's understandable. Any luck on your end?"

"No," she lied. "Everything was destroyed beyond recovery. What about you?"

The others exchanged uneasy glances.

"Well, we did find the reactor fully intact," Ross answered optimistically.

"And?"

"There are a few technical kinks to work out," said Carrie, "but I think we're in business."

Nevara momentarily reflected. "Anything else?"

After an awkward hesitation, Victor broke the news to her. "We found evidence to suggest that Paradiso was a testing ground for some kind of radical bioagent, possibly a failed attempt at accelerating evolution. Knowing Xul, though, maybe he was just curious what would happen. Either way, the results were . . . disturbing, to say the least."

"Horrifying," said Ross.

Carrie nodded in agreement.

"I see," Nevara stated, more or less unfazed.

"You don't seem that surprised," Victor noted, concerned by her overt indifference.

"I'm not," she readily admitted. "While I can't say that I *knew*, it sounds perfectly in line with everything I would expect of him. He no doubt suspected that I would have opposed such measures, so I would have only been informed if the experiment succeeded."

"A Haven suddenly collapses in revolt, and you never bothered investigating why?" said Victor skeptically.

"Paradiso was hardly the first," she retorted with a glare. "Occasionally, Xul may have been directly to blame, but more often than not, it just followed the predictable course of human nature. I suppose I can't entirely fault him for attempting a correction every now and then."

Her candid words left the others rather stunned.

"You sound like you're defending him," said Victor.

Again she returned a sullen glare. "If you have nothing more to report, I'm going to survey the area," she snapped before departing.

From atop a distant overlook, concealed Vanguard troopers closely watched the surface dwellers and their guests.

"They're currently mobilizing for something," one officer reported through his POD. "From what we gather, though, there are limited combat resources, so any resistance would be undoubtedly short lived. How should we proceed, sir?"

"..."

257

"Affirmative. We still have eyes on them — except for the half-blood. She just left the base, but she can't have gone far."

"..."

"Understood," he said. "Transmitting coordinates now, sir."

Another officer then joined him. "Well, that was the easy part," conveyed his partner. "I still don't think we're ready for the next—"

A thunderous shock wave threw the men right off their feet, catching the entire squad.

"Fall back!"

But before they could recover, sharp ripples in the air tore through them one by one, sending blood and limbs flying everywhere.

Moments later, once the massacre subsided, all but one lay motionless on the ground. With his legs now severed, the remaining officer could only drag himself away in desperation.

Nevara stalked him with a purposeful gait, waiting until he finally abandoned his retreat.

Having now caught up to him, she wasted no time in beginning her interrogation. "Who sent you?" she demanded. "How did you find us?"

The man stared at her defiantly.

In response, Nevara sent a piercing surge of aether through his body. "Tell me!" she ordered.

Despite the agonizing pain, he maintained a stubborn reticence.

Nevara tried again with more intensity, ignoring his continued outcry.

It proved too great a strain to bear, however, and the officer was well deceased by the time she finally relented.

Victor, Ross, and Carrie then emerged from nearby brush, panting heavily as they discovered the grisly scene that had arisen.

"Oh shit," said Victor, the others at a loss for words. "What—"

"They know," Nevara cut him off. "Our location is no longer secure."

"Did they say what they were after?"

"They didn't do much talking," Nevara coldly answered, "but it's obvious enough. We don't have long before they launch a final attack to finish what remains."

"We'd better tell the Remnants," Ross advised. "They'll need to finalize their preparations."

"Nobody here has ever faced the Anakhari," Nevara warned. "These people won't stand a chance in their current shape, especially with half their numbers gone."

"Well, what do you propose?" asked Victor.

"We don't have time for them to undergo normal training, but we might be able to accelerate the process."

"How so?" asked Carrie.

"We still have the biomods," Nevara noted. "That alone should alter their DNA enough to utilize the Subverse. Additionally, we could bypass the normal adjustment period by channeling our energy directly through them."

"Is that safe?" wondered Ross.

"No less than sending them unprepared into battle to face a certain death."

Victor wasn't reassured. "You saw what happened once the Curtain was disabled," he reminded. "This sounds like it could be a whole lot worse."

"And what would you propose?" Nevara snapped. "Let them meet the same fate as Empyrea?"

"There has to be some other way. Even if they make it through this alive, there's no telling what kind of damage it could do to them long term. We can't afford to be so reckless."

"It will be justified in the end," she insisted. "We can make them better than they ever were, and whether they appreciate it or not, it will be for the greater good."

Victor eyed her with concern. "That sounds like something your father would say," he pointed out.

"I am *nothing* like him!" Nevara shouted. "He lives only to enslave and to exploit for his own ambitions. I have devoted my entire life to opposing everything he represents. We are finally in a position to deal him a serious defeat — to be rid of his oppression once and for all — and I will not fail now because you have no resolve."

As she turned to storm away, the others had to share disheartened glances.

"I'm sorry, Nevara," Victor called out to her, "but we have to put a stop to this."

"Is that so?" she wondered, frozen in her path. "And what gives you the right?"

Having just dispatched his army, Velroth followed Xul, and they arrived at the command center, where he would ensure extermination.

The spacious room was metal walled and lit by dim fluorescence. Spanning brighter all around were manned surveillance monitors, and in the center spun a floating hologram, which currently depicted the Ark's nigh lunar destination.

Outside the broad, frontal window, the swirling storm raged on as ever, though now with more symbolic value.

The royal guards watched Xul retrieve a pair of biometric authenticators. The first he gave, a hollow monocle, Velroth placed upon his eye. Soon it activated with an emerald glow. He then equipped a fitted glove, which also recognized his signature.

Proceeding to a mainframe terminal, Xul initiated the executive protocol. In concert with his long-embedded microchip, the Elarch's gadgets wirelessly granted access, displaying his vital signs across a nearby monitor.

Xul's operators ran their diagnostics, confirming as expected: for the first time in modern history, all constraints had been rescinded.

"Well?" asked Velroth. "Is it done?"

"Yes," the Architect replied, notably enthused. "Now that the final barrier has been removed, you have nothing left to do but allow the future to unfold."

"We already lost Lucas; we're not losing you!" Victor shouted as the confrontation escalated.

"Is that what you think of me?" asked Nevara with a glower. "You couldn't possibly know the horrors of this world as I do, let alone the forces behind them, but why should I ever have expected human minds to understand? Only now is the solution clear to me: the true power of the Subverse lies not in its ability to create . . . but to erase, and I must be the one to make that choice."

"Do you hear yourself?! Your lifelong mission was to stop them from controlling it — to free this world at last. Now you're just as obsessed as your fa—"

"I was a fool!" cried Nevara. "And too afraid to face the truth. If you cannot see the same, then stand aside, or pay the price."

The other three did not back down.

"In the name of everything you stood for," Victor painfully declared, "we have to end this now."

Her expression hardened further. "Then, be done with it already."

A trinity of ripples lashed across the air, but Nevara easily returned them, increasing their lethality.

The symphonic aftermath made quite an impact, distracting well enough so she could reposition.

An explosion from her palm launched Carrie into Ross, interrupting both of their attacks and rolling them across the ground.

Glowing spikes were shot at Victor, who dodged as many as he could before needing to deflect.

As he prepared some paltry counter, she closed the distance with a single blurry stride.

Reflected in her eyes now was a pulsing scarlet blade, and she raised it high to strike. Before she could reach his chest, however, something wrapped around her wrist, then snapped it back behind her head.

Turning angrily to look, she found Carrie pulling on the manifested cord.

Nevara summoned in her free hand a second blade, but it too was quickly bound, as Ross had flanked her other side.

Victor seized the opportunity, buckling her knees with a sudden gust of aether.

With his hands upon her temples, he channeled as much sedating energy as his spirit would allow.

"Come back to us, Nevara," he pleaded, but his efforts only amplified her overwhelming wrath.

"Let . . . me . . . GO!" she shouted with a punctuating blast, knocking everyone away.

The force was great enough that none could pose a threat, but maniacal fixation displaced any trace of guilt. Free now to pursue the necessary action, she turned and walked away, confident that nothing else would stop her, either.

33

Beaten and forlorn, the Libertas remainders tended to their wounds in silence, despondent at the prospects now ahead. They mourned the loss not only of their guiding light but of one they'd come to call a friend, gone from them even faster than the last.

Time was not afforded, though, for lamentation or recovery, as the somber stillness shattered with a sound both dreadful and familiar. From the sky above, the whirring of a heavy craft presaged its imminent descent upon them.

Too broken to defend themselves, the trio simply waited as the cruiser landed, then watched the high commander exit with a retinue of troops.

He strode toward them as his guards encircled, grinning smugly despite the consequences of their previous encounter. "I never had a chance to thank you for the makeover." He gestured toward his own disfigurement. "It really is quite liberating."

"You always were an ugly bastard," retorted Victor. "It's just more honest now."

Draconis chuckled in amusement, not particularly bothered.

"I'm surprised to see you still alive," Carrie added. "Wasn't there a city to repress?"

"I've yet to recoup what you had stolen. Surely, you didn't expect me to forget?"

"The samples are gone," Ross informed him. "You'll have to face your master empty-handed."

"Hardly," Draconis noted, overall unfazed. "I wouldn't underestimate the value of your kind. No doubt there will be immeasurable rewards."

"Glad that we could help," said Carrie.

"In more ways than you realize. If not for having to pursue your ship out of the city, . . . Well, I suppose I should be thanking you."

Victor glared at him. "So, how does it feel — knowing that even you're expendable?"

The commander's grin then faltered slightly. "Prepare for immediate departure," he barked to those around him, "and nobody take your eyes off them."

Alicen watched the monitors with growing unease, dreading the fast approach of the Anakhari's daunting Ark. A ship that size was nearly inconceivable, so anyone would have their doubts if made to stand against it. Her dedication, while far from wavering, sat ready to be soundly tested.

Hoping to ease her sharp anxiety, she turned to Lucas for reassurance. "As fortified as our position may well be," she prefaced, "we don't exactly know what they have on board. Are you sure that we can fight them with our current means?"

"Hard to say," admitted Lucas, providing little comfort. Sensing her trepidation, he turned to give his full attention. "Fortunately, we won't have to."

She furrowed her brow in confusion.

"If I can exploit a back-access channel I happened upon," he explained, "I should be able to force open a door straight to high command. With their army mustered halfway across the System, they've left themselves quite vulnerable, to say the least."

Alicen breathed a sigh of momentary relief. "I was hoping that our aspirations didn't end here," she confessed with a smile.

"Certainly not. This is but a stepping stone on the path to our new empire."

The revelation caught her off guard, completely shifting focus from the present situation. "I'm not sure what you intend to rule," she countered, "given the last of civilization was just destroyed."

"*Human* civilization, perhaps," Lucas clarified, "but I have something a bit more ambitious in mind."

She could think of only one other implication. "You don't mean . . . ?"

"Oh, but I do," he confirmed. "With the Elarch himself now drawn into our midst, the time is ripe for a proper coup."

Her eyes widened. "That is indeed ambitious."

"And once we deal with Xul," continued Lucas, "the interstellar gateway will deliver us right to their home world, where our true destiny awaits."

Alicen found the notion quite enticing, albeit undeniably fantastic. "Even if we could overcome all militant resistance," she considered, "would they really be so quick to serve?"

"Our powers alone suffice to prove us worthy, but once combined with their technology, we'll be nothing short of gods to them. Yes, I'm sure they'll be more than eager to submit — and achieve at last what Velroth could only covet."

He spoke with confidence that made his vision seem not only possible but practically a guarantee, and she would be right beside him through it all. "To think this reign of ours begins today," she noted.

Grinning amusedly, Lucas turned toward the telltale hologram. "My dear Alicen," he said, calm yet brimming with conviction, "it already has."

At the edge of the world, snow fell thickly across the dark and barren tundra. Upon it sat a lonely ship, the only sign of life apparent.

Far from prying eyes and deep beneath the ice, a remote facility lay deathly still, thanks to its new visitor, for through the halls Nevara marched, with no one left to stop her now.

Once inside the skeleton-crewed control room, her goal was just ahead.

She purged the place with relative ease, leaving but one man of little consequence. Against the wall he panted heavily, crumpled in a rather pathetic heap.

"High Judicar," she spoke, scanning carefully around, "you made it out alive. I can't say I'm surprised though, when from a sinking ship, rats are first to flee."

He offered no reply, staring wide-eyed in alarm.

"I do find it amusing that you would try your luck by coming here. What was it you had thought to gain? Perhaps forgiveness," she derided, "even after such unmitigated failure?"

"Please," he begged, "I'll join you in your fight. I'll do anything you say. Just give me one more chance."

She glared without compassion, her mind already set. "If you honestly expect a pardon, be glad you never made your way to Xul."

Nevara conjured forth a spear of scarlet, then drove it through his head, finishing the job.

Able now to take her time, she searched him for a certain item.

Found inside his pocket was the protomatter keycard, which promptly joined her arsenal. Unfit for self-injection thanks to various impurities, it would have to serve some other use, which remained to be determined.

Reaching next an admin terminal, she utilized her still-unnoticed backdoor in their system.

Soon, everything was ready, so she climbed upon the metal dais beneath a spanning arch.

34

Safe within his floating fortress, high atop the senary planet, Velroth paced with restless worry. How long had it been since his leadership was tested on the battlefield, rather than asserted from a throne or war room?

Xul stood firmly at his post, following the situation closely.

"The Curtain has been off too long," the Elarch said at last. "If not quelled soon enough, this rebellion threatens more than just your research."

"Perhaps, my lord, but mere potential is nothing without proper execution," Xul calmly reassured. "Any fleeting power they might have gained will surely not be realized."

"How can you speak so confidently when they've surprised us both before?" Velroth snapped.

"That's precisely why I studied them so well," countered Xul, "so trust me when I say they'll be no threat."

"Even vermin have their claws, and my presence would be better served elsewhere," the Elarch ranted, bounded by his fail-safes — an irony not lost on Xul.

"Allow me to reiterate," stressed the Architect amusedly, "that such encumbering constraints were by your own decree."

Velroth rounded on him angrily. "I am well aware," he barked, "and I stand by that decision, lest your unchecked curiosity would soundly doom us all. I was not the one who, once again, bet our future on their kind, continuing despite such hopeless odds. You seemingly learned nothing from the past."

Xul bowed his head reflectively, deciding not to argue.

"Besides," Velroth added, now slightly more composed, "I'm sure that Captain Uldred can lead the charge alone."

"Indeed, he can," said Xul. "Rest assured your legion will prevail, for even with the Curtain gone, my synthiotes are quite effective."

"That had better be an understatement, as far as your future is concerned."

"They will function as designed," Xul promised. "Of that there is no doubt."

From one of many labs inside the lunar outpost, Lucas used a holoscope to analyze his blood.

"I trust the signs are good?" asked Alicen, noting his expression.

"See it for yourself," he offered, switching to a three-dimensional projection.

Though not so scientifically inclined, she recognized the double-helix hologram. Even in a resting state, it pulsed with brimming energy, and the magnitude could only grow toward the Revelation's apogee. With widened, hungry eyes, Alicen watched the evidence laid bare, enraptured by the possibilities.

"I would say the future is looking very bright indeed," he commented.

Emerging from a most ambitious fantasy, she turned her gaze to him. "And together, we shall build the world anew."

"Why just one?" replied Lucas with a grin. "We will be as gods, after all: limitless, unbound."

Every word he spoke invigorated her unquenchable desire. Drawing closer to him, she felt her breathing deepen, and it became impossible to suppress the ardor in her chest.

"Security breach!" An urgent cry broke suddenly through her POD. "We're under heavy attack, and we can't—"

"Say again," Alicen responded. "Where did they enter? How many are there? . . . Come in!"

Nervously, she glanced at Lucas, then the two promptly headed for the control room with their guards.

A few seconds later, and another officer reported, "The defenses aren't holding, and we're being overrun!"

"Stand your ground," Alicen ordered before turning to Lucas. "How the hell did they get through already?"

"They might be more resourceful than anticipated," he admitted.

"So, what do we do now?"

Lucas carefully considered. "We can't afford to lose the reactor. As long as the Curtain stays deactivated, we'll continue growing stronger throughout the Revelation. It should also be the safest place in the station right now, so that'll buy us time to figure out our next move."

Along with his lieutenant and a few remaining followers, Lucas made his way back over to the power core, outrunning the fast-advancing firefight.

Once more at the entrance, he quickly typed the same credentials as before . . . but found himself denied. "Damn it! They locked us out."

"Is there any way to bypass it?" she wondered.

"If you can hold them off, I might be able to with genomancy."

"I'll do my best," Alicen assured, "but we won't last long out in the open."

Lucas nodded. "Just remember what lies beyond this door for us."

Somewhat reassured, the Elarch shifted focus to his next point of concern. "We need to address a secondary matter," he considered.

Turning courteously around, Xul kept his attention elsewhere.

"There are presumably survivors on the surface," continued Velroth. "Even being so primitive, they may still pose a threat."

"Do you, then, suggest another flood?" the Architect inferred.

"I doubt there's time for that."

"Far too wasteful, anyhow," Xul noted. "A steady signal of the body's mortal frequency would suffice to rupture every cell."

"That sounds most compelling," said the Elarch. "I trust we have such means?"

"Of course. Just leave everything to me."

Moments later, one of Xul's assistants entered through the door, wheeling in a heavy cart. Upon it sat two sealed boxes, exactly as instructed.

With everything in place, Xul swept across his forearm screen, entering a priming sequence. He then glanced out the window, waiting for the reconfigured settings. A final activation and . . .

"What is happening to me?!" Velroth cried, as his skin began to churn.

His guards responded hastily, but the same befell them, too.

No one else dared interfere, keeping to their monitors.

"Your body is rejecting the synthiotes," Xul replied. "Or, perhaps more accurately, they are rejecting you."

The Elarch seethed again — and not just from his rage. "You . . . arrant . . . fool!" he growled, falling to his knees as the Architect observed.

"I did warn you that it was untested," Xul reminded, "but I'm pleased to say they do perform exactly as expected."

Velroth stared in shock, unable to comprehend.

Xul approached him steadily, eager to explain. "Your position is wasted on one of such limited imagination. All this time, you could never envision what lay right within our grasp, blind by petty fears and insecurities to the potential witnessed long ago. Where you would further our *dependence* on the Subverse, I intend to govern it. Once this Revelation culminates, the fate of life will be secured. Avenging my dear brother's death is, admittedly, a welcome bonus."

Indulging in a bout of rare brutality, Xul tore off the Elarch's crown, whose clinging set of bloody wires revealed it as more than mere adornment. He scrutinized the diadem with mild curiosity, recalling the distant era when he first constructed it.

On the brink of reverie, Xul crushed its frame in his robotic hand to free the protomatter socketed within. After tossing aside the useless metal, he beheld his prize triumphantly, then opened a compartment on his arm, which housed the gem quite well.

Before Velroth could utter a final curse, viscous pewter goo seeped forth from every pore throughout his body. He soon collapsed, ultimately reduced to a melting heap of viscera and ceremonial attire.

From the resulting puddle, Xul carefully withdrew, in addition to the biometric authenticators, a subdermal ID chip.

Next, he brought them over to the ready cart, from which he then procured a pair of matching jars. At last, the time had come to use his homegrown hand and eye. Despite corporeal autonomy, they undulated with uncanny motion, thanks to cybernetic housing that kept them both alive.

Thus, having every piece collected, the Architect assembled them, first embedding Velroth's chip into the replicated hand. He then resolved the vacancies inside the monocle and glove, glancing at a monitor to ensure his clones were recognized. Fortunately, the brief disruption had not reversed the active protocol, so all was working properly.

Xul proceeded straight away to issue a directive. "Captain Uldred," he communicated through his metal arm, "I must countermand your current mission." He changed the floating hologram to show its parent planet. "You will redirect your course to Earth and await my next instructions."

Aboard the Moon-bound vessel of his battle-hungry warriors, the unexpected message caused more than some confusion.

"The Elarch made his wishes clear," responded Uldred. "If his orders have been changed—"

"Velroth's reign is over," Xul imparted, raising the mangled crown. "Should you require further proof, you need only say the word."

The captain weighed his options carefully, but after brief consideration, he knew the wiser course by far: accept the Architect's authority. "That won't be necessary . . . Elarch; I shall reroute us there at once."

"I'm very pleased to hear it. Also, when you reach your destination, it is vital that you capture them alive. Deliver me without delay as many as you can. Since we've lost the bloodlines and their specimens, prioritize the sole remaining heir."

Restrained beside his friends with the handoff under way, Victor sat by helplessly and watched, beset by coastal winds.

The high commander marched toward expectant Anakhari, so in order to distract himself, Victor stared across the bleak horizon.

"I trust he will be pleased?" Draconis dared to hope.

"You have no conceivable idea," Xul's deputy relayed.

"Then, I am also happy to inform you that, by great fortune, we managed to retrieve the precious cargo."

He motioned for an officer to bring the platinum case, and Victor turned, exchanging glances of confusion with his fellow captives.

"I only ask for the distinguished honor of presenting it in person," requested the commander, full of self-importance.

"Your services are needed here," the delegate replied, "for there remains a mess to clean."

"With all respect," Draconis pressed, "I should like to ensure that my duties have been executed fully. Should the contents prove damaged or defective—"

"I am more than qualified to judge that for myself, and if you so insist, we can inspect the samples here. Rest assured that your efforts warrant accolades to come, but as for now, the Architect cannot be bothered — by you or anyone."

Though deflated in response, the commander soon regained composure. "Very well," he begrudgingly accepted. "If it must be so, then please accept this gift on his behalf."

As the deputy approached to seize the case, a cold lust in his hollow eyes, Draconis popped the latches, fixing his gaze toward the Beacon in the sky. Defiantly, he threw the package open wide, and a fireball erupted, engulfing those around him.

Before Xul's henchmen could recover, the Vanguard promptly gunned them down.

Victor turned instinctively to grab the nearest guard, disarming him so as to lead his friends away. Before they could get far, however, the officers encircled them.

"Stand down," a voice instructed hoarsely.

Surprised to hear the commander speak again, Victor watched him stagger toward the cliff's tall edge before collapsing on a flattened boulder.

After looking at the officers, who made no motion to impede, Victor cautiously approached the man, unsure what to think.

"That was meant for Xul, wasn't it?" he guessed, still a little wary.

"A long shot, to be sure, but no one else was getting close enough."

Victor shook his head, struggling to comprehend. "Is this you choosing the 'path of duty', then?" he echoed the commander's words, delivered what felt like ages ago. "Why now? Why at your moment of triumph?"

"This day was never mine to win," Draconis grumbled. "When I saw that flash across the sky, it showed me where I really stood: years of loyalty for naught . . . and my honor well betrayed."

"Then, this was really just about your honor?"

The commander fired back a sidelong sneer. "I'm not asking your forgiveness, nor seeking any pity." He gazed across the untamed sea. "But there you have your answer."

Victor looked around uncomfortably. "So, what happens now?" he asked.

Draconis deeply sighed. "Now?" he grunted, strenuously rising to his feet. "Now I take my leave."

"After all that, you're just throwing in the towel?"

"This isn't my fight anymore, if it ever truly was. Either way, my role is finished now."

Victor noted the extensive injuries across his body. "We can heal you," he argued, only to receive a slighted grimace.

"How generous of you." Draconis winced. "Ever a man of virtue, even at the gates of Armageddon. Mercy will be your downfall if you aren't careful."

"It's not 'mercy' to admit that we could use your help," Victor angrily affirmed. "Swallow your damn pride and try to have perspective. As long as you draw breath, you have a duty to uphold — to your men and to the people — or have you forgotten that, *Commander*? The enemy is at our door, and the time is now or never. Xul must be stopped for good!"

The words lingered with a haunting resonance, punctuated by the restless ocean.

"A task left to better men than I," replied Draconis, resolute as ever. He turned purposefully to Victor, tossing something from his pocket. "Be better," he pleaded, stepping from the precipice to meet his fate upon the crashing waves and jagged rocks below.

Victor made it to the edge in time to spot the tattered corpse, and then the tide swept it away, with nothing left behind.

Ambivalently shocked, he found the Vanguard contingent mobilized around him, standing at attention.

"What are your orders, sir?" an officer inquired.

"*Mine*?"

"He left us to report to you."

Still in disbelief, Victor glanced down at what Draconis had imparted. Glowing in his hand was an iridescent sheen from the carefully protected keycard. Though rather useless now, it represented quite a weighty gesture.

He looked upon the men, helmets resting at their sides, and he distinctly recognized a few from days among the force. But regardless of their past, all that really mattered was the common cause ahead, so Victor gave a hearty nod, and off they went together.

35

Lucas opened the blast door just in time, their position overrun.

His remaining troops then fell to fire from right around the corner, so Alicen rushed across the hall to join him.

She was almost there, but to her shock, the door closed swiftly as she reached it.

Through the tiny observation window, Lucas calmly stared into her eyes, which had widened by the rank betrayal.

Before she could react, a bolt of scarlet struck her.

Unable to hear her final gasp, Lucas watched her body slide below his view, revealing her assassin drawing near.

Surprised not to find an army at the door, Lucas smiled faintly at Nevara's bitter scowl. The two were face to face again, albeit separated by a reinforced impediment.

She attempted to override the lock, but his sabotage left it firmly jammed.

"In the back?" said Lucas through the intercom. "There's not much honor in that."

"What do you know of honor?" replied Nevara coldly. "And let's not pretend she meant anything to you beyond a means to an end."

Lucas faintly chuckled. "You know me too well."

She glared at him unblinkingly. "If only I had sooner."

He suddenly adopted a far more serious demeanor. "I'm truly sorry it had to be this way, but nothing else would do."

Lucas bowed his head and turned toward the glowing azure nucleus. As he traversed the grated walkway, Nevara pounded fiercely on the door.

Recognizing the futility, she retreated several feet to unleash a violent stream of aether, accompanied by a deeply primal roar. Still it didn't budge.

Next she drew the keycard of the judicar, pressing it defiantly against the window, and there it sat in place.

Lucas paused, glancing out of curiosity, though he quickly grew alarmed at the reckless ploy.

He ran to intervene as Nevara backed away, raising her arm and taking careful aim.

Opening the door, he stopped her just in time, but as a dire consequence, the blast hit him instead.

Nevara charged, knocking Lucas back.

Both inside the reactor hall, their aether blades arose at once.

Injured and caught off guard, Lucas fought to stand his ground.

Unrelenting in her rampage, Nevara pushed him farther still.

A wild slash he barely dodged then cut the walkway's hanging beam.

Several more followed suit until their balance faltered, forcing both to halt.

They stared each other down, hesitant to move again.

"You don't have to do this," he implored.

"I DISAGREE!" she shouted, resuming her attack.

Victor led his newly expanded crew back to the heavy cruiser. "We don't have much time," he gathered. "They'll be hitting us with everything they've got, and we need to warn the Remnants."

"Yes, sir," replied the Vanguard officer, who made ready for departure.

"Are they gonna be prepared for this?" wondered Ross.

"Nobody is," Victor answered, "but we'll do the best we can."

Carrie had a sudden realization. "I should also point out," she noted, "that without Nevara, we no longer have a reliable way of overloading the protocore."

"Shit, you're right. Is that something we could do ourselves?"

"Well, she didn't seem to think we'd be able to move Empyrea. Even at full strength and focus, we might not have what it takes, and waiting until the heat of battle to find out seems like a hell of a risk, assuming anyone's in shape enough to try."

"That would be quite a gamble," Ross agreed. "Maybe we could try conventional explosives?"

"I doubt they'd be effective," Carrie guessed. "Besides, I don't think we'll have too much to spare."

Victor conceived a tentative solution with another possibility. "What if you could introduce a smaller, more sustained flow of aether?" he suggested. "Is there any chance that you could amplify it?"

"Hmm," she pondered. "I suppose I could set up a feedback loop of cascading resonance — snowball it, essentially — but the source would have to be perfectly consistent, and I'm pretty sure that *is* beyond our means."

"Maybe not," suggested Victor. In response to her confusion, he presented the protomatter keycard of the late commander. "This just might do the trick."

Unable to recover fast enough, Lucas quickly buckled under Nevara's repeated blows.

In desperation, he abandoned his aether blade for a crudely summoned shield, which blocked her heavy downstroke.

She hammered yet again, fueled by greater fury. Such was her unforgiving force that it snapped the pathway's last support, causing both to stagger forward.

With one hand free, Lucas barely caught the drooping edge, holding firmly as it creaked and swung.

Nevara, though, went tumbling over, but he grabbed her just in time.

Eying a narrow platform just below, he tossed her to avoid the fatal plunge. As he did, however, his grip gave way, leaving her to catch him in return.

"Why?" was all that she could utter, now clinging to his leg.

"I had to give this back." He smiled painfully, pulling down his collar to reveal a familiar inky pendant. "There's no doubt it suits you better, my winter swan."

How long ago had she last heard those words? Could this moment really be?

"Even when I thought I'd lost you," said Lucas with a grimace, "my feelings never changed."

Unable to let go, she had no choice but to pull him up to safety.

"Then, what was this all for?" she wondered as he lay across the grate.

"Same as always," he explained, handing her the stone, "even though our methods didn't quite align."

"They haven't in a while."

"True, but for once, that was intended."

Confusion filled her face, prompting Lucas to elaborate.

"You were so determined to save the world — to repay whatever debt you thought was owed — and every time, I had to watch as it destroyed you, knowing that the guilt would never let you stop."

"You remembered?" She stared in disbelief, moving to address his injuries.

Lucas nodded. "The memories came through dreams at first, but I realized they were something more. I witnessed every battle waged against them, back to the very first, when the war had just begun."

Tears welled in Nevara's eyes as she recalled them, too. "I thought you'd never be the same," she spoke, removing the bandage from his head, "or even recollect those days. Countlessly, I watched you die, always less than what you were. Grief became exhausting, and I feared your soul beyond return, so I swore we'd win this time . . . or be put to rest forever."

His weary face now healed, the Ixio she knew was finally made whole.

"When I saw those eyes again," she said, her hand resting on his cheek, "the hope had never felt so real, and then you went and broke my heart."

"I'm sorry for everything I had to do," said Lucas earnestly, "but I couldn't see another way."

"I understand that now. It seems my mind is clear at last."

Lucas pointedly withdrew a gadget from his pocket. "It's a good thing I held on to this," he noted with a smile. "It really does work, after all."

The sight of Carrie's biomod filled Nevara further with remorse, reminding her of how she treated those who championed her cause.

Sensing all the pain she bore, Lucas did his best to provide some reassurance. "The fight isn't over yet," he promised, "and we've still got more to give. However the saga ends, we'll see it through together, just as always planned."

"The hell you will!" a voice croaked angrily from above.

Braced against the railing and barely still alive, Alicen took careful aim, firing a single shot into Nevara's chest.

Lucas cried in anguished rage, glaring madly at the source. He caught the woman's vengeful sneer before she then collapsed, falling to the unseen depths below.

Frantically, he tried to set things right, but the wound was too severe.

Acknowledging the truth, Nevara grabbed his hand, holding it away. "Conserve your energy," she pleaded. "You'll need everything you have."

"I can't just let you die," he argued. "It can't just end like this."

"It doesn't have to," Nevara whimpered, offering back the relic.

Lucas watched it shimmer, overcome by sorrow. He placed his palm to hers, silently accepting.

"See this through for both of us," she stated. "You're the only one who can."

PART THREE

36

A menacing stillness lingered in the air as Earth's coalition braced for imminent invasion. Concealed by their natural surroundings, they stared toward the sky as Qel'therus entered orbit high above the atmosphere. Even without their full armada, the Anakhari flagship dominated the heavens with its presence, gargantuan enough to eradicate any threat encountered.

Before long, a raring swarm of transport shuttles descended through the smog, then landed on an open field just beyond the trees.

Aside from scores of unseen personnel within, several craft hauled heavy vehicles via concentric halos projected below their hulls.

"Tree crushers," Jerico inferred, peering with binoculars as the machines were dropped nearby. "They came prepared, I'd say."

"Given the size of that ship," Victor added, "I'm sure they've got something for all conceivable terrain. I wonder what they'd bring if they *didn't* want survivors."

The troops emerged without delay, organizing into a single row.

"Those bastards sure look mean," Jerico remarked. "She wasn't kidding about their size."

"Let's hope that she exaggerated other claims."

"Taking them down might call for everything we've got, but they'll bleed one way or another. Any idea what color it'll be?"

"We'll find out soon enough," Victor said intently.

"That's the spirit," Jerico affirmed, continuing reconnaissance. He scanned the ranks and found a notable among them imperiously marshaling the rest. "Check out that shiny devil with the scars. Must be quite a big shot."

Victor had no difficulty locating him.

Clad in darkened chrome amid a sea of onyx black, sharp horns curving above his jaundiced brow, the figure bore distinct preeminence — undoubtedly a veteran contender.

"Captain Uldred," reasoned Victor. "The Elarch must be watching from his ship." Glancing once more to the sky, he tried not to think about how ill equipped they were to tackle such a threat, for they had plenty to address beforehand on the ground.

"Hmm, I don't see a clean shot from here," Jerico determined. "Hell, I'm not even sure that armor-piercing rounds would get through what he's wearing."

"It's not worth the risk," Victor cautioned. "Even if we got lucky, it wouldn't deter them. In fact, without clear leadership, they'd probably lose any incentive to pull their punches."

"Perhaps, but you'd better not be counting on their mercy as a strategy."

"Not a chance in hell. I'm just making sure we consider every angle."

"Fair enough."

Facing the tree line, their battalion stood in tight formation, then began to march.

"Looks like this is it," Jerico observed, readying his rifle. "I'd say wait until you see the whites of their eyes, but they don't seem to have any."

"Then, how about the scales on their hide?" suggested Victor, the infantry approaching.

Jerico nodded firmly with a grin. "Sounds like a plan, my friend."

They held position, awaiting the proper moment as the wall of troops advanced.

Accompanying them were scout drones, which flew past the rumbling crushers.

Finally, their forces entered range, and Jerico gave the signal.

Erupting thus were guns and bows, setting off decisively the battle for humanity.

The Anakhari charged full speed ahead, blasting through the native bulwark.

Readily apparent was the disparity in firepower, so the defenders needed to withdraw, though not without sustaining many losses.

"Did we kill a single one?!" shouted Jerico, running deep into the woods.

"Just a few," answered Victor.

"Well, that's about to change." He turned to the rearguard archers. "Light 'em up!"

They all drew their flaming arrows, taking careful aim along the demarcation, and once enough had crossed it, a volley was unleashed.

Upon ignition of the makeshift napalm, a wall of fire then erupted, throwing the enemy into sudden disarray.

Those engulfed fell to the ground, endeavoring to quell the sticky flames. On their backs were tanks of protomatter vapor, which overheated and caused deafening explosions.

Undeterred, they plowed their crushers through, quelling the inferno and allowing others to advance, among the first being Uldred.

"Son of a bitch!" cried Jerico in disbelief. "I thought it would buy us more than that." He turned once more to his men. "Lay us down some cover, then everyone fall back!"

They opened cans of saltpeter and sugar before tossing matches into them.

Clouds of smoke soon allowed retreat, but the resistance fighters had to face an increasingly dire outlook, part of which meant dodging splintered wood and plasma.

Though the casualties proved impossible to count, it became clear enough which side was winning, for despite a fierce determination, bolts and bullets did little to overcome the gap in their technology of warfare.

"The trees won't last us long!" shouted Jerico. "We have to stop those tanks!"

Victor nodded, proceeding to relay an order to his officers.

With relentless throngs of Anakhari nearing, the Vanguard cruiser soared into view, suppressing them with heavy air support.

The enemy then hid behind their war machines, but a stream of missiles flew into them, taking most out of commission.

"Keep up the pressure," Jerico directed. "Show them what they'll get from us."

He drove his men to repel the invaders, striking down a few in quick succession as they routed.

A crack had now appeared in their morale, giving the first real hope for victory.

Before much progress could be made, though, a rippling streak tore through the atmosphere, blasting the cruiser with a kinetic mass that sent it crashing to the ground.

Emboldened once more, the enemy soon countered even more aggressively, prompting another hasty fallback.

"What the hell was that?!" shouted Jerico, searching wildly around.

"It came from there," said Victor, pointing to the watchful Ark above them. "They must have cannons for orbital bombardment."

"A railgun, if I had to guess," Carrie added. "With that kind of precision, they won't have to worry as much about collateral damage."

"That's gonna hurt us," Jerico confessed. "If they break through our fortifications, we'll be overwhelmed in no time."

"So, what can we do about it?" asked Ross.

Victor's look of deep concern didn't inspire confidence. "We'll just have to finish them off before then," he concluded.

"That's it?"

"We really don't have many options down here. Let's keep moving and try to find an opening."

They quickly fled to safety, but Carrie stayed behind, staring at the mothership.

Her gaze then turned and focused on the Anakhari ferrymen, who brought human corpses to their shuttles.

What good was simply hoping for the best, especially with a viable solution? If she would die soon one way or the other, then why not make a real contribution?

With her mind therefore resolved, Carrie separated from the others, heading toward the point of enemy deployment.

Carefully, she sneaked around advancing forces, making use of trees as cover. They very nearly spotted her, but the battle drew their interest.

Needing to crawl the final stretch almost flat against the ground, she made it to their landing site, apparently undetected.

After waiting anxiously for the area to clear, she scurried to the nearest ship and up its open cargo door.

Inside lay piled bodies, which sickened her at first, although she couldn't help but recognize their usefulness.

"What the hell are you doing?!" a whisper angrily called up to her.

Carrie turned abruptly, not expecting to be scolded by a voice she knew so well. "Ross? Why did— You need to get out of here before you're seen," she warned, surprised that he had followed her, albeit undeniably relieved to see him one last time.

"Me? What about you?" he snapped.

"Those cannons threaten any chance we have," she replied. "I have to do something."

"What exactly is your plan?" he asked, frantically checking to ensure they hadn't been discovered.

"For once, I don't know," Carrie admitted, "and as much as it scares me, I have to believe I'll be able to figure something out."

"In that case, I'm coming with you," Ross argued, pressing onward up the ramp.

Once at the top, though, his movement stopped when Carrie gave an unexpected kiss.

As he stood frozen in astonishment, she seized the opportunity to push him from the ship.

With a tear now streaming down her cheek, she mouthed, "I'm sorry," before the hatch then closed between them.

Processing many strong emotions, Ross tried desperately to get back in, but the shuttle soon departed, presumably at full capacity.

Distraught and scrambling out of sight, he was left alone while far from any help.

Emerging beyond the gateway's veil, Lucas beheld a setting unforeseen. Instead of walls and sleek devices, before him stood a barren sea of sand. Farther out were mountains, over which the glaring sun beat down. 'Bizarre' could ill describe the ambiance, for a desert hardly seemed congruous.

Without controls beside the platform, retreat would prove impossible, even if he had been so inclined. Stranded now by all accounts, the only passage lay ahead.

Treading onward carefully, rifle at the ready, he braced himself against the eerie calm. Not a trace of life appeared, but the desolation made him warier than ever. Perhaps his arrival in this place was by design . . . but that of someone else. As he walked with heightened senses, the feeling of unease increased.

Without warning, a robotic trio burst into the air, at last presenting what the biome hid. The sentries glided overhead, fast surrounding him.

Only downing one before they volleyed lasers — disarming him precisely — Lucas dived out of the way and raised a globe of aether.

Once more encircled and barely able to withstand, he recognized the need for offense.

Deflected bolts threw puffs of cloudiness, which gave him inspiration.

Drawing forth more energy, he spread it through the ground beyond his fading shield, then began to swirl a vortex. A wall of dirt arose to obfuscate himself, affording time to reposition.

Charging out of cover, he paced each careful step, readying a well-timed swing of his fresh aetheric blade.

The second sentry couldn't see the sudden strike of indigo, so it quickly lay defeated, leaving only one remaining.

Losing his diversionary duster, Lucas turned toward the final target. A fair distance away, he once more charged ahead.

As the haze continued fading, the third bot noticed Lucas, but it didn't try to shoot him, perhaps needing to recalibrate its sensors.

The weapon port glowed ominously red, but his blade was out of reach.

Sliding narrowly beneath its aim, he channeled forth a spear of light, piercing the hull before it fired. No follow-up was needed, fortunately, as it fell to join its siblings.

Leaping to his feet, Lucas panted and assessed the situation.

With one drone sputtering about, the threats were all but neutralized. That would not last, however, for tremors then emerged.

He look around to find the source, identifying yet another obstacle.

Stomping down the nearest mountain came a quadruped colossus, far more imposing than its kin. Despite boasting impressive size and weight, it maneuvered like a serpent, slithering with limbs that were connected to a dome.

Lucas had nowhere to run, so he could only stand his ground, knowing that his true goal still awaited.

37

Anakhari trampled through the woodland ruthlessly, exhibiting the means by which they once attained galactic rule. Opposition to their incursion was among the fiercest in recent memory, but their empire had weathered all, crushing flesh and spirit without fail. This time would be no different, and the humans found their fortune greatly waning.

"We're losing ground faster than I expected," Jerico worried. "At this rate, they'll wipe us out before we even make it to the ruins."

"You may be right about that," Victor agreed. "Time to unleash the floodwaters?"

"Might as well."

Jerico pulled out his radio to give the order, only to find static across all channels.

"Shit, they must be blocking our comms. We can't signal the boys up the river."

"That also means we won't be able to warn everyone in time," Victor warned.

"I know," Jerico acknowledged. "It's a hell of a bind, but if we don't do something now to turn things around, it's hardly gonna matter."

"Either way, the call is yours," said Victor, deferring to his elder.

Jerico reflected solemnly. "To the bitter end," he reaffirmed. "What say we go together?"

Without delay, the two intrepid leaders hastened up the steady stream, spurred by the distant sounds of converging combat.

Eventually, the rustic reservoir came into view.

"Impressive work," Victor complimented.

"We did what we could," panted Jerico. "Shame to see it go, but with your fancy tricks, we'll be able to rebuild it even better."

As they approached, a pair of Remnant sentinels emerged from cover.

"Already?" one of them asked. "Is it that bad?"

"It could certainly be going better," Jerico admitted. "They're using radio jammers, so we'll have to set the timers."

They hurried to the center of the narrow dam, and Jerico reached over the side to access the demolition charges.

"This'll be a tight window," he warned, "so make sure you run—"

A bolt of plasma struck him in the back.

Victor and the others ducked for cover, spotting a small detachment of Anakhari troops along the river. Heading them was Captain Uldred, who marched with steadfast deadliness.

"They must have followed us," reasoned Victor, pulling Jerico to safety as his men retaliated. "Those damn drones are watching every move we make."

"Stop wasting your time on me," insisted the injured lion.

"I'm not gonna leave you here to die!"

"You're the one they're after," Jerico reminded. "No need to get us both killed."

Victor shook his head, struggling to move faster as one of the Remnants fell nearby. "I don't care," he argued. "We're all in this together. We need your leadership."

Jerico tightened his grip on Victor's arm. "I think you'll do just fine," he reassured, forcing a painful smile and withdrawing something from his breast pocket. "Now, drive these bastards off our land . . . or die trying!" he ordered, pressing the antique lighter into Victor's hand.

Woefully honored, Victor gave a begrudging nod before scrambling back to shore. Jerico once more reached into his coat — the side pocket this time.

Only moments later, the captain directed his attendants to seize the fallen man, no doubt for prompt evacuation.

They moved forward to comply, but upon arriving at their target, Jerico brandished an unpinned grenade, defiantly tossing it toward the charges. Before anyone could react, a forceful detonation blew apart the structure.

Far enough away to be spared from real harm, Uldred suffered only minor shrapnel damage, though what truly seemed to bother him was the deprivation of a catch. The human caught his angry stare across the raging current, and the captain swiftly turned, undeterred, to issue further orders.

Victor took another glance at the lighter so simple yet profound, then secured it well before heading back to fight. Though unsure of his merit in answering the call, he rushed along the tide, matching its momentum with his spirit.

* * *

Carrie had some time to think along her trip through space, and lying among the dead proved conducive to a bit of introspection. Now she was forced to wonder how many other victims had resulted from her work, never before having to stare a cold one in the face. Was this to be expected, striving all those years to do her best while constrained by the direction of another? Well, the chance had come to own her labor, and regardless of the outcome, none would be able to say it wasn't hers.

Arriving shortly at the mammoth Ark, their shuttle waited for the hangar's maw to open, and once authorization had been granted, they then were swallowed whole.

Carrie slowed her breathing while they docked, sure to be as motionless as possible.

Soon thereafter, the cargo door descended, and several workers boarded. Without delay, they began to transport research specimens onto a floating dolly, but none perceived the stowaway.

Deathly still, Carrie found herself en route to some place deep within the vessel. Eyes completely shut, she could only guess at the distance traveled. Though charting a mental map allowed the prospect of escape, it served mostly just to ease her nerves.

A door slid open minutes later, and the temperature sharply dropped, forcing Carrie to mind her breathing even more, lest it betray a mark of life. She held frozen as they moved her to the floor, then waited for their footsteps to recede.

Alone for now, she sprang to hurriedly examine the locker where they'd stored her. Dumped inside were rows of bodies, yet vacancy remained quite ample.

Thus aboard and well determined, Carrie thought of what to do. Her unique position offered much potential, so it couldn't go to waste.

The bridge would have controls for weaponry, but assault was not her forte, assuming she could make it there unseen. With cameras almost certainly in use, wandering around seemed rather foolish. Staying here, however, was not an option either, so Carrie walked over to the panel by the door.

Unfortunately, she hadn't risked a glance at the means of operation, though it probably wouldn't matter without the proper code. She could wait, of course, for someone to return, but that would likely get her caught, and the odds were bad enough already. Even if she had her tools, this tech would not permit a speedy comprehension, since she didn't speak a word of Anakhari.

With only one thing left to try, she hovered her hand beside the panel, then calmly closed her eyes. There were, after all, universal principles of electrical design, and Carrie knew them well.

Following the circuitry, she found what appeared to be an actuator, then, taking a wild yet educated shot, channeled a tiny burst of aether.

As a satisfying payoff, the door slid promptly open, and Carrie peeked into the hallway, which was fortunately empty. Relying on automation meant fewer to run afoul of, but that was no excuse to drop her guard.

Stepping gingerly ahead, Carrie wondered where to go, then a familiar sound emerged. Down one end of the corridor, she heard the whirring of a protocore. What luck to have been tossed right near the engine room. Surely, opportunity awaited there.

Once inside, again bypassing security, Carrie scrambled to uncover a point of vulnerability. In spite of the dire situation, she was undeniably impressed by the technology to sabotage.

She struggled to find an interface to access, but the various monitors above displayed their plotted course: none other than the lunar installation, presumably their foremost destination after resolving the surface conflict.

Inspecting the intricate machinery, she ascertained mechanics present also in the Havens, and therein lay a possible solution.

Though triggering a meltdown here was well out of the question, if she could disable navigation and provide a little push, the former might not be required.

Such a bold approach, however, would need a decent surge of energy. Did she even have that much to give? Indeed, there was no better time to learn.

One by one, Carrie severed the conduits running from the engines to the protocore, ensuring that no further power flowed, save for what she generated.

Soon, the job was done, and she stood before the rearmost junction, pausing to appreciate the journey to this moment.

Her final challenge, while not the most cerebral, might at last afford atonement for all the misery she'd caused.

With no scarcity of willpower, Carrie reached into the Subverse, drawing deep through every cell. Gone were limits known of body, mind, and spirit, as she dismissed all need for preservation.

Verging on collapse, she unleashed her aether down the pipeline, and a violent lurch confirmed success, knocking her to the ground.

There she lay, fully spent, though finally at peace. Flashing lights and sirens overwhelmed her senses, then all faded welcomely to black.

Much to Lucas's dismay, his arsenal fared worse against the new behemoth.

Impenetrable armor paired with quick and deadly blows, leaving Lucas desperate for a weakness to exploit. Just when he might have found one, the mech responded with a vengeance, adapting to counteract him.

Despite the grueling challenge posed, he sensed a level of restraint. Was it doing more than trying to kill him? Or was there another goal entirely?

Nonetheless, with every sweeping strike, a pattern thus emerged, which was ripe for gaining leverage.

Lucas closely timed its cadence, and once the time was right, he dropped against the ground.

Energy flowed around him through the sand, concentrating in a circle. His movements had to be precise, for a brief miscalculation would result in sure impalement.

The hulking juggernaut soon raised a mighty leg, pausing as if relishing the moment, then brought it smashing down.

Lucas rolled aside, then pulled the conjured snare, catching the limb successfully.

He ran toward the body, trailing his chord behind him while adding to its length.

Under the frame and out the other side, he was targeted again, exactly as predicted.

With an effort made to thwart him, the tactic grew more difficult, but no matter how it wrestled, Lucas wove a convoluted web.

Every booming stride flung dust around them both, impairing visibility, but with extrasensory perception, navigation still was possible.

Soon, he had it sufficiently entangled, so after tying off the loose end of his lasso, Lucas emerged in view, ready to finalize his trap.

Staring at the automaton, he awaited its next attack, relying rather heavily on the manifested rope.

The mechanized monstrosity, unable to maneuver any longer, stumbled clumsily and fell.

Seizing the advantage, Lucas climbed its bowed appendage, clinging adamantly as it tried to shake him.

Once atop and struggling to balance, he raised his arms above it, condensing aether into the likeness of a boulder. Either task would prove strenuous alone.

Eventually, the force became too great, bucking Lucas from his perch. In doing so, however, the robot met with prompt misfortune, as a hefty weight then crushed its chassis.

Erupting sparks and fire, the goliath lost its bearings, and Lucas braced for impact.

With a seismic thud, it lay defeated, confirmed by the fading red light of its many sensors.

Lucas rose to his feet, still reeling from the aftershock. How far away was what he sought?

Surveying the outlandish mess, he welcomed any insight, but there seemed to be more questions now. Were these machines for mere security? If so, what did they protect? Surely, there must be more of them, perhaps a standing army. Could they be, in fact—

Before the ensuing calm could linger, the earth itself then turned on him, springing metal spikes to form a pop-up cage.

Based on their boxy layout, they were likely in a grid throughout. Why then, he wondered, had it taken so long to trigger them? The sentries would have won quite easily if he'd been stuck in place.

Lucas had no time to ponder further, for the ground collapsed beneath him.

38

Down a column of blinding sand, Lucas fell into a treetop canopy, continued painfully through several branches, then landed awkwardly upon a lush green surface. The humid whiff of greenery left him even more disoriented.

Not much the worse for wear, he stood and stared up toward the ceiling. Though dense leaves mostly blocked his view, he caught glimpses of the arid zone above before it closed.

Such environmental contrast proved more jarring than the manner of arrival.

"What the hell is this place?" he uttered, finding himself in what appeared to be a jungle flourishing and grand.

"A taste of what is possible," answered a familiar voice unseen.

Lucas quickly scanned the area, unable to locate its origin.

"Every detail before you represents a fraction of the power to be harnessed," the Architect continued. "Imagine all that could be achieved with full control of the Subverse."

"By you?" asked Lucas, carefully on guard.

"Naturally," was the response he got.

Lucas crouched and swept his hand across the grass. Deceptive though technology could be, as borne out by countless NOVA phantasms, he felt a connection that told him it was real, regardless of how it had arisen.

Hidden Xul remained.

"For someone with a deadline, you sure drag out the overture," said Lucas.

"Why miss a chance to study you in action? Or test those genomancy skills? We both need you performing at your best."

"So, the Mechagens must have already brought you the crown," Lucas gathered. "I doubt Velroth would allow this otherwise. Quite resourceful to find another use for them."

"I couldn't let good engineering go to waste," the Architect confessed. "Besides, a final showdown for the ages calls for the proper venue. Do you like it? After all, I modeled this world after your own. Granted, it has been many years since yours resembled anything of the kind, so I wouldn't expect you to recognize it. Then again, . . . perhaps you would."

Still guessing at Xul's whereabouts, Lucas had no choice but to indulge him. "What is that supposed to mean?"

"You needn't maintain the pretense any longer," Xul replied. "Your memories must have returned by now, at least to some degree. If only as dreams or fleeting visions, such eventful lives would well resurface. They are far too ingrained in what you call a soul to be so easily forgotten."

"And you were always there."

"Guiding you to the very spot on which you stand," confirmed the Architect.

"How fitting, I suppose, that we should end this now together."

"I couldn't agree more."

A net erupted from the ground, hoisting Lucas high, but with a crudely summoned blade, he speedily cut through it.

After falling once again, he did his best to rise, but the effort was disrupted by a striking metal arm.

Lucas raised his head, staring into eyes that, despite their icy blackness, bore a fervency he'd never seen before.

Xul was primed for battle, his robes replaced now with an exosuit to complement the dark prosthetic. "You have no idea how patiently I've waited, Ixio."

"Allow me, then, to disappoint," echoed Lucas with a glare.

From behind his back, he unleashed a forceful ball of energy, but the Architect responded with a brush, deflecting it into a nearby tree.

"The same old moves won't work this time," said Xul. "I've made an upgrade here and there since last we fought."

Lucas fired a volley of lesser blasts, which Xul suspended in the air before him with his outstretched metal claws.

Redirecting the attacks, he sent Lucas diving fast for cover.

Forced to recover and rethink his tactics, Lucas noticed a particular variety of flora distinguished from the rest, not by height or girth, but because of the succulent red orbs hanging from its branches.

So many memories came rushing through his mind, the simple sight imparting further gravity to their battle for the universe.

With newfound vigor, Lucas drew intently from the deepest wells of inspiration to steel his resolve. This day or never, with minds awake and shackles broken, truth and freedom would reign at last.

Slammed against the floor by a jarring acceleration, Ross jumped quickly to his feet. Though still a little woozy, the blaring alarms throughout the Ark now spurred him faster onward.

Staggering along, he concluded that it could only have been Carrie's doing. Somehow, even without much of a head start, she had already managed to sabotage the floating fortress.

Down the halls now flashing red, he sprinted to the engine room, where his guess was validated by her body on the ground.

A frantic vitals check, however, allowed him to identify the faintest hint of life. Though without a breath or heartbeat, her body retained some tethering to consciousness.

Even so, her condition called for healing well beyond what Ross knew possible — certainly more than seen in any hospital — but he forced himself to stay calm, nonetheless.

Deep in focus, he placed a hand over her heart, mapping the thoracic cavity with his inner eye to assess the damage. He did the same for her head, relieved to find the brain intact.

Next was to repair the worst-off tissues, requiring a manner both meticulous yet urgent, given the situation.

Soon, Ross could no longer sense any cardiac damage, so only one step then remained. Unsure of the parity with a medical-grade defibrillator, he hoped against all odds that pure intentionality would suffice. He therefore concentrated aether in his hand before guiding it straight into her heart.

With a convulsive gasp, Carrie awoke, surprising both of them intensely.

In response, neither knew quite what to say, but their expressions told enough.

"You didn't have to come," she croaked.

"And you didn't have to die as penance," Ross countered. "There's plenty of redemption left for us both in this life."

Her eyes reflected a genuine desire to believe it.

"Come on, we've gotta go," he pressed, helping her to rise. "Can you walk?"

"Barely," she replied, legs quivering under weight. "You really ought to leave me here."

"Shut up and live," Ross affectionately ordered, hoisting her upon his shoulder. "Martyrdom doesn't suit you — not when there's a job to do."

Carrie was encouraged by his candor. "Then, you'd better hand me my gun," she said.

"That's more like it," he asserted, happily obliging.

Without further delay, he hurried from the room, glancing at the collision warning flashing from the primary display.

This time, though, their path wasn't nearly so smooth, as they were forced to deal with stray technicians rushing to investigate the disturbance. Fortunately, Carrie held strength enough to raise her arm and return blaster fire alongside Ross, keeping them moving briskly forward.

Fighting their way back to the hangar bay, they found a hasty evacuation in progress by some of the more skittish crew members. With shuttles departing one after another, Ross and Carrie scrambled for a ride, security personnel in close pursuit.

Near the edge of the hangar, they finally hopped aboard an open cargo ramp, persuading the pilot to enable their escape.

"Aren't you curious?" Carrie wondered, Ross laying her down against the hull. "You didn't ask whether I succeeded in what I came to do."

"I don't have to," he replied, keeping his gun trained on the pilot. "Once you made it clear your mind was set, I already knew the outcome."

She smiled, clearly flattered. "I'm glad you learned to trust my work."

As they sailed from the Ark, he watched its immutable trajectory. "I must say, you really found a way to make an impact."

"Two birds, one stone," she noted.

"That's my girl," said Ross, causing her to glow with pride.

Endeavoring to overcome their fluvial impediment, Captain Uldred mobilized his shuttles, but most were otherwise engaged. Lacking sufficient space to transport everyone across, they started hauling timber to barricade the water.

Though their losses no doubt mounted, the number gave them little pause. It was therefore difficult for Victor to believe his efforts had been fruitful, especially coming at so high a cost. Jerico's noble sacrifice deserved to count for more, and he would have to now ensure it.

Without significant delay, the Anakhari were advancing once again, plodding stoutly toward the shore. Despite being so exposed, they prevented any window to exploit, chipping away at cover with a salvo and offering no quarter to their prey.

Having assumed command once back among his ranks, where none had time for mourning, Victor found the need to withdraw them deeper still.

Fleeing while the onslaught raged behind him, he stopped abruptly at an outcry of distress. Instead of putting first his own life, Victor turned at once to help the wounded fighter.

The officer expressed his gratitude for the bold and selfless aid, but then a shock wave rippled through the air, throwing both men dazedly off their feet.

A shuttle hovered just in view, and its gunner jumped from the open cargo hatch, excitedly heading toward them.

Still too shaken to stand and run, Victor frantically sought to arm himself with anything at hand, grabbing within reach a fallen bow and its three remaining arrows. Totally unskilled with such a weapon, he clumsily pulled back on it and fired, missing by a hefty margin.

The gleeful gray assailant responded with a jeer.

Victor nocked another arrow and then somehow struck his target, but the sturdy chestplate negated any luck.

Further mockery ensued, now closer than before.

Perhaps there was a more effective way, so with only one shot left, Victor focused his mind and channeled aether down into the broadhead. The resulting flow grew quite unstable, especially against the tension of the string.

Once released, the luminous arrow sliced along the air with a glimmering trail, piercing through at last and collapsing the grunt mere feet away.

Tossing the bow aside, Victor rose to join the others, but turning around revealed an even bigger problem.

Blocking his path was none other than the captain, crushing the throat of the man whom Victor tried to save.

Before he could react, Uldred knocked him to the ground again with a firm kick to the chest.

A series of raucous cheers erupted from the masses en route across the river.

Fast approaching, the captain drew what appeared to be restraints, not unlike those carried by the Vanguard.

Unwilling to concede, Victor desperately threw dirt in Uldred's eyes, sending him recoiling in annoyance to create an opportunity.

A quick strike to his knee then caused the brute to buckle, proving that their kind could not be called invulnerable.

Encouraged by his limited success, Victor followed with a boot right to the face, hoping to dislodge the tubes connected to his backpack. Unfortunately, they didn't even budge. Already had his impetus been stalled.

Enraged, Uldred lunged ahead, though the human managed narrowly to dodge him.

Clearly disadvantaged, Victor had to get away before the others joined their captain. He therefore stumbled onward, soon breaking line of sight with the enemy's position.

Not about to yield, Uldred raced behind in feverish pursuit.

Victor's forces had already taken flight, so he was on his own. Faltering, therefore, would likely mean his end, leaving a disorganized resistance and giving Xul a rather useful test subject.

Before much distance could be made, Uldred closed the gap, and their combat thus resumed.

Employing stones and branches, Victor fought as best he could, but the single-minded threat was not so easy to shake off. Less encumbered and more nimble, he still avoided capture through the denser vegetation, yet such evasive measures could not endure for long. Although committed to avoiding it, he had to also entertain a more unsavory solution.

39

Among the trees and sprawling undergrowth, Xul continued stalking Lucas, tracking him with sensors long ago installed. Each one kept their distance, skirmishing when possible.

With his opponent having such a clear advantage, Lucas found it difficult to land a single blow. Everything he tried seemed well anticipated. For now, he could only skulk about, waiting for an opening.

Neither one expected an alert to break the silence. "We've lost control of the Ark, my lord!" spoke the admiral through Xul's prosthetic limb. "Intruders got aboard and sabotaged the engines. Navigation's also down, so we cannot change our course. At this rate, we'll collide before repairs are done."

"Is that so?" responded Xul impassively. "And you are certain of this outcome?"

"Unfortunately, yes. Many have already fled, but we can still evacuate a number of the samples. I'm afraid there's not much time for more. Please advise on how we should proceed."

"Stand by," Xul ordered, promptly entering a series of commands into the panel on his forearm.

High above the tertiary planet, a satellite reacted, repositioning itself at once to acquire the newly designated target. Momentarily thereafter, it was tightly locked and tracking. Then, as fast as light could travel, the void of space illuminated from a blazing ray of scarlet, and the call was terminated with no explanation given.

"You really have no decency," said Lucas.

"And who are *you* to judge?" Xul questioned, proceeding with a lecture. "Unending cycles of rise and fall," he continued grandly, "predictably repeating the same mistakes ad infinitum. That is the nature of your kind. It never mattered what accounts endured the ages; after but a single generation, all firsthand knowledge faded into legend."

"Rewriting history didn't help."

"The trials of wars, the true cost of peace — these experiences, along with whatever lessons you might have learned, always died with those who had borne witness. How could such a civilization ever hope to secure lasting prosperity for itself, much less be granted the raw power of creation?"

Amid the self-indulgent screed, Lucas chanced a sneak attack, which Xul blocked yet again.

"The Zephyrans were doing fine till you showed up," Lucas mentioned, hastily retreating.

"They were also rather young, but their destiny was not so hard to fathom. Age, alas, can be no guarantee of wisdom, for even among my own kind — those who 'conquered death' — I found nothing but regression and fear of the unknown, all buried underneath a banal thirst for conflict. Along with his natural expiration, any respectable ideals of the Elarch had simply evanesced."

Lucas tried another move, but Xul would not abide, for he was quite determined to avoid being interrupted.

"It would seem, then, that my perspective is unique, so who better to navigate the pitfalls previously suffered, striving toward perfect harmony for life of every form? He who fully comprehends the mysteries of the cosmos, from subtle to sublime, deserves more than any to claim the title of its architect. Could you really argue that the fate of all existence would lie better in the hands of someone else?"

Striking with a conjured blade, Lucas bounded from the branch he'd climbed to, but Xul caught him in midair, then threw him soundly back across the ground.

"You just don't learn," Xul chided, "but at least you proved my point."

"I wouldn't be so sure," Lucas countered, taking careful aim.

By the time Xul realized his target, there was not much he could do, so he quickly braced for impact.

Lucas fired aether at the protomatter keycard, precisely dropped below the Architect.

The following explosion slammed him hard against a tree, only sparing Xul because he'd fast produced a shield made of light.

The damage didn't stop, however, as the cratered earth now rapidly expanded, swallowing everything nearby.

Unable to escape the growing maw, Lucas found himself descending even further.

Ross and Carrie both sat anxiously aboard their shuttle, en route back to land.

Their pilot had been cooperative thus far, but the tension hadn't eased, making it difficult for Ross to split his focus and still attend to Carrie.

"With all the craziness today," he noted, breaking the heavy silence, "I never had a chance to give this back to you." He handed Carrie her silken ribbon, pointing his gun toward the cockpit. "Sorry I didn't have a chance to get the blood out."

"I suppose it's more appropriate, after what we've been through," she replied, accepting the gesture nonetheless.

Ross nodded with unease, clearly wanting to say more. "It hurt me to think I'd have nothing else to remember you," he confessed.

"*Nothing?*" she asked him playfully. "Am I really that forgettable?"

"I don't think anyone who survives all this could possibly forget it, and you've done more than enough to leave your mark."

"It's not over yet," Carrie warned.

"True, but I'm feeling optimistic, especially after what you just pulled. Besides, I meant what I said before: you wear it well."

"If you insist," she conceded, indulging him with a smile before tying it in her hair.

Unable to long enjoy their tender moment, they soon were interrupted by a familiar flash of light across the sky. Confusing, though, was the target of the blazing scarlet ray.

"What the hell?!" Ross exclaimed, gaping at the Ark's destruction. "Did we do that?"

"It must have been an executive decision," Carrie reasoned. "I guess the station is worth more to them than . . ."

Her voice continued fading as she leaned against the wall.

"How are you holding up?" asked Ross, turning his attention fully to her.

"It might be too early to tell, since I don't really know the damage caused by aetherburn."

"Well, once we win down there, I promise I'll do everything I can—"

A sudden blow knocked Ross right off his feet, disarming him before he fell. The pilot had exploited their distraction and seized his opportunity, leaving the ship on autopilot to deal with the hijackers.

Before he could do more, however, Carrie halted his advance, managing to draw her blaster and shoot him in the head.

He stumbled back into the dashboard before slumping to the floor.

Their cruiser plunged abruptly from the sky, accompanied by a rather loud alarm.

Recovering from his oversight, Ross hurried to examine the controls, which no longer seemed as operable, by him or anyone.

"I don't think we'll be able to land this thing," he readily concluded.

"Then, what do you propose?"

Ross looked frantically around for emergency equipment, finding none in sight.

Struck by a wild possibility, he began examining the various materials of his clothing.

Carrie watched intently, curiosity replacing panic.

Unsatisfied by his own too stiff or porous garments, he turned toward the ribbon in her hair.

She couldn't help but blush as he reached over to untie it. "Did you change your mind already?"

"Trust me," Ross assured, conjuring a thin sheet across the floor, the ribbon held in one hand as a template.

It didn't take long for her to realize his plan. "I think you're gonna need 20 feet at least," she calculated.

"Right," he said, finishing the job in seconds.

They walked out across the lowered cargo door, the howling wind stinging their skin.

With a fistful of cloth wrapped tightly in each hand, they secured their arms around each other, standing face to face. Eyes wide, Carrie nodded, and off they jumped together.

Plummeting as one, they held the makeshift parachute billowing wildly overhead, and neither could avoid a glance at the rapidly approaching earth.

They began to spin, adding to the already profound lightheadedness as their arms strained desperately to catch the air.

Sensing her waning strength, Ross fastened his legs around Carrie's waist.

Consciousness fading, on the precipice of collapse, a jolting snap finally tempered their descent.

Moments later, their ears were hit by the shuttle's ringing crash, nearly drowned out by so much rushing wind.

"Hold it!" shouted Ross.

The strain intensified, but his grip remained firm. Hers, however, faltered enough for the sheet to unravel steadily.

Soon, they fell below the barren trees, slamming onto solid ground — or as much as could be said for a pit of slimy sand.

"Come on, we've gotta move!" urged Ross, shaking Carrie awake.

Still tightly holding on to her, he angled his body forward and, with great determination, clambered to escape the quagmire.

Once fully extricated, he was able to appreciate their luck, glancing at the wreckage of what had been their ship.

"I can't believe that worked," Carrie uttered faintly.

"We can't lose now," Ross panted, "not after surviving that."

Unable to escape from or defeat his quite formidable opponent, Victor grew increasingly exhausted, desperate for a solution as the army neared full marching speed.

Staring down the captain, he feared the only options were a needless death or capture, and no one could be seen around to help him. Much to his relief, however, he suddenly became aware of a promising new gambit, so he broke from their encounter, rushing straight into a nearby thicket.

Both surprised and insulted by the sudden departure, Uldred quickly pursued, slashing through the brush with a fiery whip of energy.

Rampaging along unimpeded, he soon found his quarry panting on the ground, trapped within a narrow glade.

Though slightly disappointed over the short-lived chase, the captain wasn't one to overindulge with duty on the line, so the outcome would have to suffice. With a growl of satisfaction, Uldred swaggered forth to claim his prize.

Victor glanced up silently with a bitter look of defeat. With no recourse left to save him, he conjured a small blade, raising it to his neck.

Once more, the captain lunged, grabbing at Victor's arm. His target remained stationary this time, but Uldred passed right through him, landing with a muddy splash.

Adding to his great confusion, the soil hampered all attempts to stand, swallowing him inch by inch.

"Now!" Victor shouted, and from behind a tree emerged Ross and Carrie.

Together, they sawed the heavy bark with a glowing cord of aether, the solid end around her wrist as he continued channeling.

Uldred fought with might and main, only sinking deeper.

A creaking knell foretold his doom as he furiously struggled.

Moments later, the towering hardwood fell, crushing him under tons of heft.

The Libertas trio rejoined before it to admire their crafty teamwork.

"Good timing," Victor told the disheveled pair. "You two okay?" he asked as Ross raised Carrie back upon his shoulder.

"I've seen better days," she noted, "but I think the price was worth it."

"What do you mean?"

In response, Carrie gestured to the sky. "Haven't you noticed?"

Victor followed her pointed gaze, then became aware of the capital ship's removal. "Nicely done," he stated. "That should give us a fighting chance, for sure. First, though, we'll need to regroup. Let's get the hell out of here while we can."

The three took a hidden path from the enclosure, running desperately toward their allies.

Loud stampeding followed freshly after, the Anakhari having fully crossed the river. No longer governed by their captain's discipline, they would ensure the certainty of death. Though preferable to Xul succeeding in the grander scheme, there was far from solace to be found, given the vicious reputation that preceded them.

Even as their battleground constricted, however, the core strategy remained the same: no surrender, no matter what.

40

Through the dark descent of havoc broke a sudden bitter cold, jolting Lucas even more. Fortunately, it meant a somewhat softer landing on a bed of snow below, but that was the only favor he could see, for he now found himself surrounded by a blizzard, blinded on all sides.

Still trapped in yet another one of Xul's bizarre contrivances, Lucas had at least obtained a point against the Architect. Finally in a position of advantage, he wasted no time in applying it.

Leaping over toppled trunks and flattened foliage, he quickly found his target, sweeping down upon him with a conjured blade of aether.

Vulnerable at last, Xul was forced to match in kind, the cybernetic damage taking quite a toll on him. "You really are a pest," he snarled, briefly having lost his cavalier demeanor.

"You never thought your lab rats might one day bite you back?"

"I find it so amusing," the Architect opined, "that you blame us for the authorship of mankind's wretched plight."

"It's not exactly hard," retorted Lucas, attacking him again.

"Then, it might interest you to learn," said Xul, calming the winds a bit, "just how little of your 'civilized' existence resembled anything like peace."

"Would I, now?" asked Lucas.

"Of course, you might denounce it simply as our influence — a notion not entirely untrue — but in all my machinations, a few strategic assets could often set the tide, and the collective unconscious would ebb and flow as needed."

"A tide that you set all the same," Lucas countered.

"Outright force on our part was more the exception than the rule. Fortunately, the system had a way of self-correcting, thanks to certain tendencies of yours."

"But you were perfectly willing to accept the casualties," Lucas noted, "setting us against each other whenever you were threatened."

"That's awfully judgmental. You think your hands are clean?"

"I'm not the one who just destroyed a city."

"Not in this lifetime, perhaps," Xul granted, "but I was referencing your far more distant exploits."

Lucas betrayed surprise at the accusation.

"Did you really think that her subversion went unnoticed?" Xul mocked in response. "The day your artifact had vanished from my lab, every suspicion was confirmed."

"So, you just let it all unfold?"

"Time and time again, I watched as you emerged, never quite yourself. My disappointment might have outstripped even hers, for you once represented a long-sought-after archetype. With every iteration, though, you only seemed to lessen."

"But not the damage that I caused — the damage you allowed."

"Am I to weep for such a trivial expense, given what's at stake? How many tears have your kind shed for livestock slaughtered for your own survival?"

"This was never about survival," argued Lucas. "Your mad lust for power is all that ever drove you."

"Such a narrow mindset could not have brought you here, so please do not insult us both. The Subverse holds allure for all those with ambition, and control of it is logically inevitable. Why, then, should I leave that to the whims of any other, when I alone possess the wisdom and the vision called for?"

They traded further strikes, neither backing down.

"In any case," continued Xul, "I never said we were blameless for your misery, but you can't deny your affinity for breeding it. Whatever role I played in designing your collective hell would have mattered little, had your kind not done so well maintaining it themselves."

"But you always were 'the Architect'," asserted Lucas. "Always at the helm."

"You don't give yourself due credit," Xul remarked, "as the two of you helped immensely in my mission. For every action undertaken, you ensured a measured reaction, always toward a single end. Why ever would I have intervened?"

"You really weren't concerned what I might do along the way?"

"Any power you perceived was mere illusion. After all, the most promising results arise when subjects aren't aware of the experiment. Your walls might have been imperceptible to you, but they were always there. Every loss was calculated and acceptable."

"Even the lunar outpost?" Lucas wondered.

"Of course," the Architect replied.

"Then, why protect it so aggressively? Why destroy your ship — kill so many of your own?"

"You seem to misconstrue my motive," Xul informed him. "Such a delicate endeavor does not need further variance, especially at this crowning moment. Simply put, the Ark had served its purpose."

"So, you don't care at all about the Curtain?"

"This facility, I'm pleased to say, is now more than capable of unattenuated broadcast, so it hardly matters whether you disabled a redundant amplifier."

"Perhaps," acknowledged Lucas, "but what if I mirrored the frequency instead, neutralizing your signal altogether?"

"A clever boy indeed," Xul echoed, "but it would be unwise to overestimate the impact of such a minor contribution."

Now it was Lucas's turn to grin. "Who said that's the only thing I gave them?"

The terrestrial engagement had shortly recommenced, resulting in a savage stalemate as the battle raged. Deeper in the forest, cover proved more plentiful, but no amount, it seemed, could withstand the Anakhari.

Yet even with such firepower and augmented genomancy, they had to give their all to put the mongrels in their place. Without air superiority, every soldier played a role to shift the tide, and every shot was made to count. As predicted, their bloodlust only heightened, each fallen comrade distilling more the glory to be won. Many now ignored the call for preservation of more specimens, save for capturing the highly valued three.

Those of Libertas were undeterred, however, fighting valiantly on the battlefront beside their allies.

Such was the ferocity that none had noticed the darkening of the copper sky, which became a sinister shade of red.

As roaring winds tore through the woods, heavy particulates in the air swirled about, reducing visibility to but a few feet.

"They control the weather, too?" Ross yelled in confusion.

"I don't think anyone's in control of this," Carrie guessed.

"Blightout," one of the Remnants answered. "It's only getting worse from here."

"We can't fight in these conditions," Victor noted. "Fall back to Paradiso!" he promptly ordered. "We make our final stand."

Unable to see much of their surroundings, they sprinted awkwardly through the perilous terrain, ducking to avoid stray blaster fire. Fortunately, their protective goggles, alongside Vanguard helmets, afforded a slight but notable advantage in weathering the storm.

Unfortunately, it did little to prepare them for the ravenous mob of blightfiends that appeared, growling menacingly amid the chaos.

Once more, their only option was to run, which meant having to ignore the screams of those waylaid.

Although the beasts did not discriminate among potential meals, they posed far less a challenge for the other side, who swiftly overcame them with minor inconvenience.

The trio's luck, however, had finally run dry, as a snarling pack encircled and prevented any passage.

Such a disappointing ending to their struggle, but there at least was morbid consolation in depriving the Anakhari of that honor.

Weapons raised and triggers at the ready, they glanced at one another, resolute in the acceptance of their fate.

The first repulsive creature charged, but a flurry of small-arms fire and arrows struck it down from somewhere out of sight.

Contributing in kind, they soon were able to neutralize the animals without another loss.

Through the haze emerged a shaggy face, keen to set things right.

"Kurtis," Victor said with mixed emotions. "It took you long enough."

"I owed Jerico as much," the deserter humbly stated. "Think he'll manage to forgive me?"

Victor's expression of sorrow revealed the solemn truth. "I'm sorry," he replied.

Kurtis lowered his head in genuine remorse. "Then, let's give him a proper send-off," he resolved.

Bolstered now by reinforcements, the survivors made their way to shelter, earning precious moments for preparation before the ravagers arrived.

Victor kept a lookout at the entrance, waiting until he saw the last man through.

Bringing up the rear was Kurtis, who exuded true commitment as he shepherded his people.

Without a word to say, Victor briefly stopped him, offering the brass memento of their departed friend.

Though visibly affected, the Remnant shook his head. "You already proved yourself more worthy. Just promise you won't lose it, or there's gonna be hell to pay."

Victor nodded earnestly, and together they went inside, then secured the entrance with a barrier of rubble.

"Set the traps!" he shouted, manifesting an extra layer of protection.

No sooner had he finished than a volley struck the outside.

Hoping it would hold until they readied all defenses, Victor withdrew into their bastion, careful to avoid the tripwires and proximity mines now armed.

Scrambling to utilize every resource, he conjured camouflaging film across the chasms that separated many broken pathways.

Finally, they regrouped within the plaza, once a masterwork of architecture.

The Vanguard defectors, reintegrated Remnants, and Libertas crusaders all made for cover wherever they could find it: around corners, behind fallen pillars, and perched atop narrow platforms of debris.

With everyone as ready as could be, attention mostly turned to Victor, compelling him to offer words of reassurance.

"This is it — our final hour," he began firmly. "After years of hiding in the shadows, pitting us against each other, the enemy now stares us in the face, but for the first time in history, we stand united against *them*. However few of us remain, we fight as the last defiance against the greatest force of tyranny the world has ever known. Even if we must give our lives here today, they will never claim our birthright, be it the blood in our veins, or the liberty that drives us. Remember who we are. Burn this day into their memories, and with humanity's dying breath, remind them of the cost for those who would play God."

A crash then rang throughout their stronghold, signaling the breach had come. Soon, a flood of angry shouts drew near, and with tense anticipation, the defenders held position as the traps were duly sprung.

Adapting rather quickly, the Anakhari stormed ahead, and their clamoring crescendoed until they all came charging into sight.

Victor gave the signal, and a firefight erupted once again. Although the total forces numbered fewer than before, such a claustrophobic setting robbed any hope for much reprieve, encouraging only more barbarity.

Shotguns thundered from the Remnants while the Vanguard interspersed their flashbangs, but for so much noise created, the waves just kept on coming.

With ammo running low, they could sense the fast-approaching test of brawn, one sure to present an even greater tipping of the scales.

41

Xul's patience had worn considerably, their taxing duel still complemented by an equally exhausting tirade.

"Do you even comprehend what you so stubbornly resist?" he angrily inquired. "Entropy is the bane of all creation, exempting nothing from its constant degradation. Why perpetuate a curse that can be ended? Have you not suffered it enough throughout your many incarnations? Well, in case you have forgotten, here's a fresh reminder."

Xul used the lull in battle to input a command on his forearm console. Immediately, the shrouding winds then halted, revealing a more expansive landscape beyond the snowy plane.

Lucas gaped at the darkly familiar hellscape, no longer sure of what was real.

"Perhaps she never told you," Xul continued, "but the likeness of your prison was inspired by my home, Solmar — at least what it now resembles, thanks to a dying sun. Such is the outcome of inaction, the universe allowed to take its natural course. Can you not see that I am the only solution?"

"Forging yourself a key doesn't entitle you to what it opens," responded Lucas, "assuming you could even wield what's inside. Don't you find it odd that no amount of time or cutting-edge technology could give your kind the genofactor?"

"What are you suggesting?"

"Do you really think the secret lies in flesh and blood alone? Just a few lines of genetic data? For all your cunning, Architect, you never entertained the obvious conclusion."

"And what might that be?" Xul grew louder and more aggressive at the condescending tone.

"It *is* your nature," Lucas answered, "but not where you've been looking. It's what drove the Zephyrans to die instead of serve you. It's why humanity will always persevere. And it's why you cannot ever know the true creative power of the Subverse."

"I know it best of all," growled Xul, "and I will make you understand, one way or another."

They clashed again with more intensity, abandoning precautions that would only slow them down.

"Surely, you must feel it?" said Xul. "The harder you push, the more unstable your consciousness becomes, not to mention the very fabric of existence. Even if you had a chance at stopping me, is it worth losing all that you possess?!"

Lucas remained silently defiant, exchanging further blows.

"Regardless of what you might accomplish here today, your legacy can only be of infamy, if anyone remembers you at all. Like so many others, your deeds will fade into obscurity, buried and forgotten by the empty sands of time. What is there to gain? Why fight the march of progress?"

The human simply stood there, enraging Xul substantially.

"Even in your lesser forms, you wanted something more, always reaching for that higher life. Here, at last, your salvation lies. Why delay your long-awaited bounty? Seize it while you can, and leave this filth behind. If you continue burning through your soul, there will be nothing of you left — nothing but assured perdition. Would you really pay that price for them?!"

"No," Lucas firmly stated, "but I'd pay any price for *her*."

The Architect responded with a sneer.

"Honestly, I have no urge to be the savior of this world, but she gave everything for its redemption, so I think it only fair to match the wager. That's my real motivation for this, and that's what you could never understand."

Xul was briefly paralyzed by utter disbelief. "Such a waste," he spat, full of palpable contempt. "I once considered you a visionary, like myself. For a time, I imagined that we might even rule together, but now I know that you were never so deserving."

"I guess it can't be helped."

"That goes for your entire race, too insufferably clouded by emotion to recognize perpetual decay. With the Subverse brought to heel, I will be sure to eradicate all trace of such debilitating sentiment."

"That 'sentiment'," Lucas countered, "is what got me here to meet your challenge, and it's the very thing that guarantees your failure."

Xul snorted back indignantly. "Soon, I will force you to renounce those words," he growled. "And what a pleasure it will be."

* * *

Mayhem abounded throughout the ruined city. The shifting of dilapidated structures revealed scattered rays of light, which conveyed a wickedness above as cataclysmic as below. Gone was any semblance of unified formations, proceeding forth instead a free-for-all of carnage. Were those involved more similar in kind, it might have been impossible to know combatants by the scant illumination, but their differences in makeup left no room for being mistaken.

Victor darted through the melee, assisting wherever he was able, but felling a single of their numbers proved arduous a task for even several men.

Spears, axes, and machetes all swung wildly, the occasional projectile fired only when a likely kill presented, but those were few and far between.

Running rampant as expected, the Anakhari posed as much a danger to themselves with unchecked use of aether. Defensive applications were not even attempted, for that would spoil such great fun.

Suddenly, an explosive roar stopped Victor in his tracks, along with many others.

He turned and saw the tenacious captain, somehow still alive but clearly worse for wear, as damage marred his flesh and armor, with one horn broken off.

Heaving with unbridled rage, Uldred centered on the man responsible.

"So, you bleed red, after all," Victor noted of his injuries.

Whether he could understand those words or not, the berserker charged ahead, then seized his target rightly.

Slammed into a pile of debris, Victor stumbled to regain his footing.

Bearing down with scorching madness, the captain was positioned for revenge.

Unexpectedly, however, he yelled in pain and spun around, for Kurtis drove a knife into his back.

After knocking him aside, Uldred reeled to remove the long protruding dagger.

Acting on the brief diversion, Victor threw all caution to the wind and tackled his assailant.

The two went crashing through the weakened floor, tumbling down abyssal depths and into isolation.

Landing moments later in a pitch-black space, Victor ignited an emergency flare, but all he found was the captain awaiting his chance to strike.

Victor dodged but narrowly, then tossed aside their only source of light, hoping to make himself less visible.

The darkness helped in his avoidance of the more ferocious blows, but those he managed to land himself were of little consequence. Without much room to maneuver, the tiring exchange barred any more elaborate techniques, forcing Victor to rely solely on his martial training. Under the conditions of their new arena, a decisive outcome would have to follow.

The captain soon resorted to more lethal methods, growing irritated by the hit-and-run approach. Again he summoned his whip of aether, dwarfing all else with its fiery glow.

He then lowered with a flourish before sweeping it around himself.

Victor jumped aside but in so doing lost his balance, falling backward to the ground.

Before he could recover, the burly captain pinned him where he lay, clenching his throat with exultant gusto.

As Victor struggled to breathe, his eye caught a steady leak from the broken conduit running to Uldred's mask.

Against the dwindling flame, that vapor shimmered quite distinctively, so, recognizing opportunity, Victor wrapped his hand around the vent.

The frenzied captain didn't pay it much attention — not until the protomatter started burning from inside, throughout every cell of his body down to the very DNA.

His eyes then widened, but as he tried to back away, Victor grabbed the horn above his brow, holding him in place.

Unable to withdraw, Uldred amplified his grasp, but Victor wouldn't yield.

Lucent cracks emerged across the scaly hide, and Victor's face grew deeper blue.

Locked in a deathly stare, each gave every bit of strength within, be it numinous or physical.

By a slender margin, the human proved victorious, for the mighty brute collapsed.

Gasping now for air, Victor strained against the crushing corpse, expending all he could to move it. Certainly, such was not the time for rest.

Once he freed himself, Victor gave a cautious look toward his foe, ensuring he was truly slain this time.

Admittedly, the dim light flickered while his brain was low on oxygen, but upon closer inspection, a subtle crawling became noticeable just beneath the skin. A quirk of their biology, perhaps? Too bad the doctor wasn't here. Regardless, there was no other sign of life detectable, leaving Victor satisfied.

Thus, with his remaining energy, he began the dogged climb, determined to rejoin the action.

* * *

With equally unwavering persistence, the two archrivals danced among the wasteland shadows, neither giving in.

"Of all you did to get here," said the Architect, "I confess that you surprised me with your willingness to kill her."

Startled by the statement, Lucas briefly dropped his guard.

"Again you thought I wouldn't know? Her bioreadings told me everything, and these past few hours were especially intriguing."

"It doesn't bother you in the least?" asked Lucas, genuinely curious.

"While I had invested greatly in her," Xul acknowledged, "I could not afford to grow attached. I'm sure you understand."

"And you really think you're qualified to father all creation?" Lucas wondered with disgust.

"You still view me as a monster? You believe that I delighted in the course of action called for?"

"Should I be thanking you instead?"

"Such unpleasantness requires fortitude, which is precisely why I'm qualified," Xul argued.

"What a laughable excuse."

Xul attacked in quick succession, clearly affronted by the judgment from his lesser. "Although it matters little now," he mused, "I can't help but note your differences in style. She might have lacked your power, but her skill was quite impressive."

"You knew about that, too?"

"Of course, but acting upon it would have hardly been worthwhile — not when she would lead me back to you."

Lucas didn't comment, awed by Xul's omniscience.

"She spent so long reserved, hiding her abilities for fear of what I'd learn, and now that she finally saw fit to unlock her true potential, she had to throw it all away. Shame you couldn't reason with her; the combination of raw intensity and honed technique would have made you two unstoppable."

Lucas grinned emphatically. "I couldn't agree more." Raising his left hand, he unleashed a dark miasma out before him.

Enveloped by the noxious cloud and caught off guard, his gloating adversary couldn't dodge in time, for Lucas followed with a clinching strike, delivered by a vibrant violet lance.

Once the vapor dissipated, Xul focused on his punctured chest, then brought his gaze across the spear and to its holder, whose eyes reflected now a matching hue.

Lucas didn't blink, sure to leave no doubt.

"Impossible," said the Architect in shock. "Her Anakhari genome is incompatible with yours."

"Perhaps, but that's not the only side of her, in case you need reminding."

"So, you imprinted half her consciousness?" concluded Xul, falling to his knees.

"Not exactly," Lucas clarified. "She's very much intact, thanks to a certain anchor." He revealed the pendant around his neck.

"You fully hybridized . . . with a soul binding?!"

"Did the possibility not occur to you?"

No reply was given, for Xul collapsed to the ground, where motionless he lay.

"Was it as good for you?" Lucas asked aloud.

«you have no idea,» Nevara answered in his mind.

«i just wish you didn't have to take so long.»

"I had to wait for an opening. Besides, didn't you enjoy the sermon?"

«most of it i'd heard already, but it was nice to learn what he really thought of me.»

"That's probably all the closure you could have hoped for." Lucas glanced around the seemingly endless panorama. "Now, any idea which way to go?"

42

After a dizzying race through the gigantic station, guided by Nevara, Lucas arrived at the center of command. Though no doubt vital to the operation, it sat in eerie quiet, curiously empty.

"What the hell is all this?" he noted of the dark pools across the floor.

«i don't know, but i'd try to avoid it,» Nevara cautioned.

Lucas ran over to the consoles. "I hope we're not too late," he said, searching for any point of access.

«well, they haven't reported in yet. that has to count for something.»

"After Xul destroyed the Ark, it's also possible they went rogue."

«unlikely. no matter how self-serving he can be, captain uldred is loyal to the end.»

"Shit! The system's on complete lockdown," discovered Lucas.

«his death may have triggered it automatically.»

"So, the backdoor won't do us any good. He really didn't want anything ruining his grand finale."

«without a passage through, they're on their own.»

"We'd have to wait for the Revelation to peak, and even that might not be enough. Who knows if the conditions will be anything like before?"

«we can't afford to wait that long.»

Lucas frantically paced the room. "If we can't open a door," he speculated, "maybe we can just tear down the walls."

«i'm not sure what you mean by that.»

"Amplifying the Subverse field could make the barrier between our worlds porous enough to cross. It might not be exactly the same as last time, but the threshold could be lower for coming the other way."

«if it were that simple, wouldn't xul have done it already?»

"Not if he had to wait for all the pieces to fall in place. Still, that doesn't mean there wouldn't be a plan for eventual acceleration, considering how much he's tried to jump the gun before."

«fair enough, but any tools for that would be well hidden.»

Passing by the lengthy window above the central console, Lucas turned abruptly, his gaze fixing out in empty space. "Maybe not," he hinted. "It's a huge antenna, after all."

«of course!» she readily comprehended. «but without access to the mainframe, we have no way of setting the proper frequency.»

"Unless there's a more direct approach," Lucas reasoned. "Any suggestions in that regard?"

«perhaps it could be retuned with a strong harmonic resonance.»

"Seems plausible enough, but what could generate that kind of—" With a sudden realization, Lucas reached for the pendant around his neck.

«yes, that should do it,» agreed Nevara.

"And what would happen to you?" he asked with apprehension.

«i can't say for sure, as it depends on the strength of the imprinting — on which source more dominantly tethers to my consciousness.»

He relaxed his grip. "Then, there has to be another way."

«we're out of options, and if we do nothing, humanity will fall, with or without xul. if this is what everything has led to, then it's a sacrifice i can fully accept.»

"I don't know if *I* can," Lucas confessed to her. "How many times do I have to lose you?"

«at least we can make that choice together, since i can't maintain a spatial presence by myself.»

After sacrificing so much else already, Lucas begrudgingly conceded, now at the moment to prove that it had all been justified. "How would we even get it up there?"

«if you can provide the energy, i can carry it.»

Lucas took a few more seconds to reply. "You'll have everything I can muster," he promised. "Where's the nearest airlock?" He looked around for an exit.

«that won't be necessary, as i should be able to shift its phase affinity long enough to get outside. once i'm in position, i'll need a final burst to spark the fireworks.»

"All right, then," decided Lucas.

He sat down, crossed his legs, and closed his eyes, holding the dark stone out in front of him.

Beckoning the energy to flow, he could sense with his inner eye a hand forming to grab it, then came the arm, the torso, and the rest of her.

344

Fully embodied, she reclaimed her half of the legendary relic.

After nullifying its physicality — a task not unfamiliar — Nevara sailed with alacrity across the citrine sky, and high above the surface, the planetary bands came slowly into view.

«can you see them now?» she asked him.

"They really are quite something," he confirmed.

Beyond the gaseous atmosphere, a sobering backdrop of darkness accentuated her glowing target, and soon she was upon it.

«now!» she signaled.

Lucas fueled the surge into her pendant, driving concentrated aether with every ounce of spirit. The protomatter shimmered like it never had before, brilliantly reaching its capacity.

The resulting explosion of cosmic proportions dwarfed any such imaginable through conventional means, cascading fast throughout the marvelously constructed rings.

Finally at peace, Nevara closed her astral eyes, enveloped by the grandeur of the blinding light.

Back in the fray, Victor stumbled through the ruins, wearily observing how drastically the tides had shifted since his brief departure. Ammo had run dry, and many had fallen, few standing tall. After all they had done to come this far, he struggled to accept the truth before him.

Without strength enough to contribute nor the willingness to bear their screams, Victor turned, resolute, toward the ravaged city's core. If it was to be his final act as leader of their resistance, he would at least ensure an end to so much suffering.

Victor wondered how many might support his verdict, or would they prefer instead to fight until their last, regardless of the pain and risk it posed? Jerico never shared the entire plan among the Remnants, fearing it would dampen their spirits unnecessarily. Had he been right to do so? Were certain details better kept from burdening the masses, or did that kind of secrecy equate them to The Order?

Along the way, he looked for any signs the battle may be won, but there was only pure despair throughout.

Deeper inward, past a sea of lifeless bodies, he happened upon his two compatriots.

Slumped against the corner in a quiet room, bloodied and panting heavily, Ross held Carrie in his lap, doing his best to heal her.

With a somber glance, Victor conveyed his bleak intention.

Understanding fully, Ross then bowed his head in resignation, though he did not give up on Carrie.

Onward Victor pressed, navigating darkness to the heart of Paradiso.

After soon arriving, he stood alone to make the call, far from those who might yet stop him. Here, there was nothing to distract from his objective.

Keycard thus in hand with grim determination, he exposed the detonation mechanism and moved into position, desperately hoping for a fated intervention.

Wise enough to doubt such folly, he brought the trigger closer.

Only inches now away, the card began to vibrate with its resonant response.

Closing his eyes, Victor made the final plunge, and a flash of light pierced through his vision.

Confused at not being dead, he found his wrist held back in place.

"The day is not yet lost," a voice then reassured him. "Your friends continue fighting for you — *all* of them."

Victor marveled at the strange new figure, who bore a likeness he had seen before. "Lucas and Nevara?" he guessed with dawning comprehension.

"Yes, and only by their tireless dedication can we aid you in this hour."

So many staggering thoughts and feelings came flooding into Victor's awareness. "And who exactly are you?" he asked, nearly overwhelmed.

"Long ago, we called ourselves the Zephyrans, but many names have since been used for what we then became."

Victor didn't know how to respond, so he continued to blankly stare.

"There will be time for answers later, but for now, trust only that we share a common foe, and on this day, without dispute, we pledge to rid them fully from this world."

"Then, let's get to it," Victor eagerly endorsed, still reeling from the change in circumstance.

Shaking from exertion, Lucas forced himself to stand. Though he couldn't see the aftermath of what they'd wrought, a certain inner voice conveyed the signal of success.

"Are you still there?" he asked, trying to sense Nevara's consciousness.

«more or less,» she answered, providing him relief.

"I guess I'm a pretty decent anchor, then."

«that you are, my dear, but did it work?»

He nodded. "The Stellarans apparently made it through to Earth. For once, everything worked out just as we had hoped."

"Wonderful news," croaked a raspy voice from behind. "You really managed to find them . . . after all this time."

Lucas turned in surprise to find the Architect standing at the threshold, somehow less impaired than when they'd left him.

"Technically, they found me," Lucas clarified, guarding himself again. "I only granted passage."

"How amusing," noted Xul, "though I'm sure you're being too modest. I can't imagine they would have bothered coming all this way without just cause. You must have offered quite the inspiration."

They stared each other down.

"I told you I had more to give," Lucas echoed in defiance.

"Indeed, you did," said Xul, a manic luster in his eyes, "and I couldn't be more grateful."

Lucas lost his momentary boldness, anticipating something else in store.

"You brought back to me the ones who got away, confirming what I always knew. Despite the Elarch's refusal to believe it, they had to still exist somewhere, in some form, and here they are at last. Dare I say, they may prove to be finer specimens than you."

"Your experiment is over," Lucas proudly stated. "Without the rings, you can't enter the Subverse."

"Don't be so sure," Xul countered with a flexion of his claws. "You've never experienced the Revelation as I have."

Striding closer into view, he made clear the full extent of damage sustained through their encounter.

"How are you alive?" Lucas wondered, no longer able to perceive the wounds amid Xul's broken armor.

"Amazing, aren't they?" Xul acknowledged of the synthiotes. "Designed to uniquely repair my tissue — at least what of it remains."

"Yet another clever way of cheating death."

"You didn't think I would let it end so easily?" mocked the Architect.

"Well, now that we're both out of cards to play," said Lucas, hands reflectively in his pockets, "I suppose this will be the final round."

Xul's eyes creased in jubilation. "Then, let it be one for the ages."

43

Hurrying back to where he'd left the other two of Libertas, Victor caught the alarming sight of several bodies freshly lying in the hall.

After dashing into the room, he found Ross alone and barely still alive.

"Shit!" yelled Victor, rushing over to his friend. "What the hell happened? Where's Carrie?"

"Uldred," the doctor answered faintly.

"Impossible. I made sure he was dead this time."

"He looked it," Ross acknowledged. "The way he moved . . . Something was . . . controlling him."

"It has to be Xul," concluded Victor. "Who else would micromanage death?"

Ross grabbed his arm intently. "Get her back," he implored, fading to unconsciousness. "You can't do anything for me."

"He's right," said the mysterious new arrival, who waited by the door. "I will attend to his injuries, but you must prevent the girl from reaching Xul."

Victor took one last look at Ross before entering pursuit, quickly grabbing the revolver off a fallen Remnant.

Why hadn't Victor made the connection sooner. Obviously, Xul would be after Carrie most of all, given her precious pedigree. Without the elites or their genetic samples, she was the final vestige of his cultivated bloodline.

But where could he be taking her? With the Ark removed from service, there would only be a single path to reach his lab: the outpost in Antarctica. Even for a zombie, though, the blightout posed a hazard, so he would have to head somewhere to call a shuttle.

Driven largely by a tactical acuity, Victor did his best to track their winding course. Fast ascending, he found encouragement in the growing sound of nature's fury, and soon appeared an outlet to the surface. His intuition payed off well.

Outside, the storm continued to rage, giving no sign of abating. Victor spotted Uldred a short distance away, Carrie slung over his shoulder and the knife still in his back. He stood unfazed amid the whirlwind, awaiting evacuation by a small ship carefully descending from above.

Sensing Victor's presence in spite of the conditions, he promptly turned around, revealing the appearance of a strangely walking corpse. Robotically, the undead captain placed Carrie on the ground, then lumbered his way forward.

Victor drew his weapon and shot between the eyes — to no effect, however, for the beast continued marching. He fired twice more just the same, but nothing came of it.

As the shuttle swerved in response to the battering cyclone, Victor noticed the underside of the freight projector directly overhead. Perhaps, like everything else, it ran on Subverse tech.

Without another move to try, he channeled what remaining aether he could muster through the gun and into his final bullet. Taking careful aim, he fired yet again.

A luminous ball of energy rode the skyward projectile straight into his target, jolting it awake with a faint white glow.

Pulsating halos began discharging downward, the captain standing just within them, and even at diminished capacity, the field proved strong enough to lift him off his feet. Unable to resist, Uldred continued rising into the apex of the blightout.

Though discerning just a bleary outline, Victor watched the flesh being shredded from his body.

Seconds later, a pewter skeleton emerged, shifting rather oddly of its own volition, and soon it too was blown away. Even by the cunning of the Architect, there was no recovery from that.

The pulsing halos, no longer tracking the captain, began locking onto segments of debris, rocking the shuttle until the growing turbulence caused it to veer erratically out of sight.

With Carrie in his arms, Victor hastened back inside.

"Ross," she noted. "Is he safe?"

"He's in good hands," Victor promised. "Turns out we've got some extra help."

"Who knew?" she muttered before passing out.

Back in the command center, the epic denouement reached its endgame, each unrelenting titan fraught with tense determination. Their movements grew more labored. Attacks were more deliberate. Neither ready to concede, they slowly circled, panting heavily with blades both at the ready.

"Even now, you still fail to comprehend the truth," berated Xul. "The natural order is throttled by inherent limitations, and only through me can there exist a bedrock of harmony and stability. How blind can you be to continue marching down this path to oblivion?"

Lucas glared, his legs trembling with fatigue. "You sure talk like you've got it all figured out — even when the Stellarans prove there's mysteries you can't possibly fathom — but it seems you'd rather dominate a drop of water than explore the ocean. You claim to be a scientist, yet so eagerly embrace the death of novelty. The way I see it, you're nothing but a fraud, and you've already lost."

Xul had entertained enough. He charged, handily disarming Lucas with a furious blow before grabbing him by the throat.

Utterly exhausted, Lucas gagged while staring into dark eyes mad with zeal.

Both knew everything had led to this, and neither failed to appreciate the moment.

Glancing down, Lucas noted the narrow trail of unprotected flesh behind the hardened exosuit. In one swift motion, he drew the ancient dagger from behind his back and plunged it deep into the rift, forcing the Architect to drop him with a wince.

"Ah, *that* blade," Xul remarked. "I wondered what became of it. Admirable trick, but it failed to kill me before, and I doubt it would fare much better now. Pity that you never learned your lesson," he surmised, pulling the blade out of his chest.

Upon so doing, however, a look of deep unease then filled his face, followed by a grievous lurch toward a nearby console for support.

In response, Lucas withdrew from his pocket a small device. "I wouldn't be so sure about that," he countered.

"You . . . rewired them?" Xul shook his head in disbelief.

"No, but one could say I rewired *you*," said Lucas, increasing the confusion. "She really is quite clever," he noted of the biomod's inventor. "This little gadget here suppresses Anakhari DNA, seemingly enough that your bots no longer recognize you. It's too bad you had to be so stingy in their programming."

Unable to endure, Xul fell to his knees at last. "Think you've won?" he snarled, delivering a final stroke across his forearm interface. "You should know better by now."

"What did you do?" demanded Lucas, quickly losing confidence.

"The harvest has begun," Xul growled with satisfaction. "Soon, there will be nothing left of them — nothing but raw data. Even if humanity survives, you can never be rid of me. Or did you think your minds were yours? You were engineered to serve, so at least you'll die knowing your purpose was fulfilled."

With renewed assurance, Victor promptly led a final charge against the Anakhari menace.

Rallying whatever survivors could be found, he started with his friend, who became abundantly relieved at seeing Carrie rescued.

"What are the odds?" wondered Ross. "Somebody was looking out for us, after all."

"Apparently, they weren't the only ones," Victor hinted. "It seems we might have misjudged an old associate."

"I'll be damned. So, he never left the team."

"I can't say anything for sure, but I'd love to find out later. For now, though, we've got business here to finish."

And so they did, for with a glorious resurgence, Libertas, Vanguard, Remnants, and Stellarans readily overwhelmed their mutual tormentors, turning the tide handsomely in their favor.

Together, they watched in amazement as their newfound allies effortlessly fired aether at the enemy, deflected their attacks, and cut them down with great precision, sending their numbers quickly routing.

Soon, they cheered a joyous cry of victory, embracing as brothers and sisters, united by a most-hard-fought survival.

Back within the plaza, which somehow lay more ruined, Victor nodded silently to Kurtis, then approached the Stellaran from before. "We owe you everything," he noted. "To think it's really over."

"Not entirely," the figure warned, "as there is yet a matter to address."

"Right. I suppose we have to counter Xul more directly, but at least we dealt him a serious blow for now."

"Perhaps, but I promised we would rid those demons from this world, and their plague has not been fully purged."

"There might be stragglers on the loose," Victor granted, "but we'll get them all eventually."

"You misunderstand my meaning," clarified the entity. "I refer to a more insidious corruption: that which lies within your very core."

Victor's mood then plummeted upon the dark disclosure. "You can't be serious," he said, recoiling.

"Interwoven deep inside you, they lurk where light cannot so easily expose them, forever able to arise."

"That's not a guarantee."

"But can you justly say that such a notion is impossible?"

"We barely escaped extinction from them! Why would we embrace their nature?!"

"In time, your efforts will be forgotten, and the sins of the past shall repeat as always."

"They don't have to," insisted Victor. "Look how far we've come. We deserve a chance to prove ourselves without them."

The higher being remained unswayed, despite the earnest plea. "Yours is not the only world endangered by their kind. Though you have demonstrated admirable prowess, there is simply too much risk in allowing man to live."

Before Victor could continue, they were both distracted by a chilling alteration of the Anakhari corpses around them.

Lucas watched in horror at the melting of Xul's body, which turned into a viscous pool of sludge combined with cybernetic pieces on the floor.

Before he could process the rather gruesome scene, it became even more unsettling, as a cloud of dark particulates arose from all the other puddles.

"What now?" asked Lucas, gaping in confusion.

«whatever you do, don't let it touch you.»

As the room began to fill, he spun around to find the nano-dust blocking their only exits. "I'm not sure how to manage that."

«the lever on the wall — activate the emergency vent!»

Lucas hurried over, staying low to avoid the fast-approaching veil.

After a spat of helpless waiting, the fog began receding just before it reached him.

"This always was his plan," said Lucas, finally understanding. "He never had to win the battle, just push them hard enough. As long as both sides reached their limits, he'd have all the data he could ask for. That was his design."

«we have to stop it somehow.»

"Do you really think he would have left a way?" asked Lucas, combing through the Architect's remains.

«if he did, there's only one place it would be.»

His eyes fell upon the mechanical appendage. "Of course," he granted, moving to obtain it.

Not surprisingly, however, the display proved unresponsive, and further examination yielded no solution.

«well, it was worth a try, at least.»

"There has to be some way to turn it on."

«i fear it may be biometrically encrypted. even with a power source, it only responds to his blood, and there doesn't seem to be any of it left.»

Realizing the obvious alternative, Lucas replied, "That's not entirely true."

«i don't follow.»

"You are his daughter, after all."

«but i would — we would — have to manifest it. you know i can't control it.»

"Yes, you can. I'm right here with you, and I won't let you lose yourself again. Together, we can keep it contained."

«and if i can't, it will infect you for nothing. i've waited so long to get you back.»

"You've overcome too much to not complete your journey. Xul made you in his image to exploit, but he never expected you to become strong enough to surpass it. For me, it was an easy choice; I had no other life to live. My only option was to forge a destiny for myself, but you chose to defy the agenda set before you, risking everything for truth and justice. Prove now, once and for all, what really defines you by embracing everything you are — everything I love."

«in spite of all i put you through?»

"No, *because* of it. Ever since the start, you gave me purpose, always pushing me to reach my highest self. It's only fitting I return the favor."

«then, please forgive me for what i'm about to do.»

"Just do your best." Lucas closed his eyes and relaxed as best he could. "Ready whenever you are."

Nevara focused on her essence hitherto repressed, weaving it selectively into his DNA.

Though not at first arousing bodily sensation, the changes were perceptible through energy awareness.

"So, this is what it feels like," Lucas commented. "I have a new appreciation for your burden."

«don't get used to it, if you want to keep your sanity.»

"You don't have to worry about that," he assured, the process now more physically apparent as it crept along his hand.

Finally, the transformation was complete.

«i think you know the next step,» she stated gravely. «i'm truly sorry.»

"Right," acknowledged Lucas.

Gritting his teeth, he raised the fallen dagger, then unflinchingly proceeded to sever his forearm at the elbow.

Pressing through the pain, he attached the oversized prosthetic, which, to his relief, accepted his genetic signature.

«at least the ui is intuitive,» she noted of the glowing screen.

Perusing the system, he failed to uncover any hidden means for reversing the harvest. He did, however, acquire access to the Beacon, recognizing the coordinates of Paradiso set for targeting. His eyes lingered until Nevara interjected.

«are you really considering what i think you are?»

"Do you see any other way? Once the information is decoded, we have no idea where it might be sent. If it fell into the Anakhari's hands — or anyone's, for that matter — it could mean the end of all that is. Even without Xul's cunning, someone would figure out how to use it, and they'd likely tear apart reality in the process."

«we don't even know the full extent. there could be survivors.»

"But can we afford the risk?"

Neither wanted to answer.

«this really is our greatest failure, isn't it?»

Lucas took a moment to reflect. "Or perhaps the final test: sacrifice everything closest to us, all for the sake of the greater good."

«that sounds like xul's logic.»

"Except without the ego. That has to count for something, right?"

«still, we'd be deciding the fate of the universe.»

"Only to restore balance — to undo a profoundly unnatural perversion. If we wait any longer, we might not even have that option."

«. . . do it, then.»

Lucas primed the satellite, observing from afar through digital detachment as he became the undisputed arbiter of death. How detestable that such a resolution should be relegated to a button press.

Without any ground-view confirmation, he could only bow his head, bearing yet another hefty tragedy.

"I suppose there's one last job to do," he solemnly concluded.

44

As the Revelation crowned, Lucas made his way down to the core of the facility, where Xul had planned to enter and possess the Subverse.

Standing as a final safeguard was a panel by the door, designed for one particular clawed hand.

"At least we got that step out of the way," Lucas noted dryly, guiding the mechanized digits into their appropriate slots.

The door then opened to reveal a majestically shimmering wall of pearlescent light, purported gateway to the infinite unknown.

"Here at last," Lucas proclaimed, facing the abyss.

«it seems this would entail what they call a leap of faith.»

He paused to reflect. "But where exactly are we placing it?"

«even xul was never sure, yet for all his brutal pragmatism, he staked everything on this. i suppose that counts for something.»

"That isn't what concerns me," Lucas clarified. "If his theories are correct, we're dealing with something unimaginable. Is this really ours to wield?"

«recent circumstances have proven me unworthy of such power, so i defer to you.»

"You deserve another chance."

«i've already had so many, and look at what resulted. at the scale of this impact, there may not be tolerance for a blunder like the last time.»

"It wasn't your fault. The catalyst—"

«awakened only what i welcomed. i gambled lives, forsook my friends, never once considered that your heart had not been lost. i embraced a toxic force beyond control, ignoring the cost because i believed only in my utopia. we both did terrible deeds in the pursuit of that, but you never lost yourself along the way — not after you had wholly been reborn. in opposing all that xul embodied, i became his mirror image. only you understand both aspects of this power: creation and destruction.»

"Xul was just the first to get this far. Why wouldn't there be others? Any mind so desperate for control can only strive toward apotheosis. Who would ever go to these lengths purely for altruism?"

«quite the argument, but i still sense hesitation.»

"With absolute power to shape the world as we see fit, what mysteries could possibly remain to unfold? Would life itself have any purpose?"

«there would still be endless joy to discover.»

"But without conflict."

«would that really be so bad?»

"It would be unbalanced."

«all that drama might have spurred the two of us, but could you call it an ideal state for man?»

"I doubt that many would adopt the path we chose, let alone prefer it, but to remove every obstacle before them . . . Who am I to make that call?"

«you are the one standing on the precipice — the one who made it far enough to choose. you have borne suffering greater than any could ever experience, so you would understand its meaning best of all.»

"Too well, I fear, to the point I can't envision a world without it. Truth be told, I've long borrowed from your optimism."

«foolishly unwarranted as it was?»

"Maybe you always knew something you just couldn't put into words."

«you give me too much credit.»

"Yet here we are, finally able to set things right. Everyone we lost, everything we ever imagined, all the time spent dreaming of a better world . . . How could I turn back now?"

«this doesn't have to be the only way. the world may still recover on its own.»

"But to what extent? After eons of manipulation, there's no telling what kind of lasting damage has already been done. Passing up this opportunity could be just as irresponsible."

«maybe a fresh start wouldn't be so bad. wipe away everything, and the baseline can be restored.»

"A clean canvas," he considered.

«a blank infinity for us to write anew.»

"As liberating as that idea sounds, life's come too far to count for nothing. And for all we know, the outcome would be just the same or worse. We've earned every right to be proud of our scars. Are you really prepared to erase them?"

«you're right. time marches on, and any course ahead must preserve the past — all of it. clearly, there is no easy option, but the choice is yours to make.»

"It shouldn't be mine entirely."

«who else is there?»

"Why not both of us?"

«i already told you, i—»

"Can't make it alone, and neither can I. It's too much for any one mind, but maybe together, we can finally balance the scales . . . as two sides of the same coin."

«and so the pendulum would finally rest.»

"More like walking a tightrope, I'd say."

«would that even be possible?»

"We're pretty deep into uncharted waters. If there ever were a way, this would be it."

«yet you still hesitate?»

"If we are destined to become opposing forces, harmonizing to the end of time, we may never be together like this again."

«but our spirits would be forever intertwined.»

"Even if it means someday finding ourselves at odds?"

«i think that's practically a guarantee.»

"Is that a fate you could abide?"

«what else might we do? enjoy a sunset paradise for all eternity?»

"That doesn't sound so bad."

«i think you borrowed too much optimism.»

"Yeah, it doesn't suit me quite as well."

«besides, if conflict really is integral to man's existence, then i suppose we couldn't ask for a better proposition.»

"How perfectly imperfect."

«so it shall be.»

"Then, may we meet again on the other side, my winter swan."

«after you, my champion.»

He smiled wistfully, stepping across the threshold.
"Onward to destiny."
«the destiny we choose.»
"Always."

www.ingramcontent.com/pod-product-compliance
Lightning Source LLC
Chambersburg PA
CBHW032136270626
47172CB00008B/89